"Put Me Down," Veronica Insisted.

"I'm tired. I want to go to bed."

He scooped her up in his powerful arms and carried her to the edge of the lawn, near a row of hedges. Slade's mood tonight reminded her of the carefree Slade she had once known.

"Sounds like a terrific idea. Let's go to bed together—right here."

"Now I *know* you've taken leave of your senses," she retorted coldly.

"Why not here?" Slade insisted. "The hedge gives us privacy. Look around you. It's like a secluded Garden of Eden here, and I'm Adam. How about it—Eve?"

PATTI BECKMAN
has proven to be a prolific and creative author for Silhouette Books. She has written five Silhouette Romances thus far and one First Love. *Bitter Victory* is her first Special Edition.

Dear Reader:

During the last year, many of you have written to Silhouette telling us what you like best about Silhouette Romances and, more recently, about Silhouette Special Editions. You've also told us what else you'd like to read from Silhouette. With your comments and suggestions in mind, we've developed SILHOUETTE DESIRE.

SILHOUETTE DESIREs will be on sale this June, and each month we'll bring you four new DESIREs written by some of your favorite authors—Stephanie James, Diana Palmer, Rita Clay, Suzanne Stevens and many more.

SILHOUETTE DESIREs may not be for everyone, but they are for those readers who want a more sensual, provocative romance. The heroines are slightly older—women who are actively invloved in their careers and the world around them. If you want to experience all the excitement, passion and joy of falling in love, then SILHOUETTE DESIRE is for you.

I'd appreciate any thoughts you'd like to share with us on new SILHOUETTE DESIRE, and I invite you to write to us at the address below:

Karen Solem
Editor-in-Chief
Silhouette Books
P.O. Box 769
New York, N.Y. 10019

PATTI BECKMAN
Bitter Victory

Silhouette Special Edition
Published by Silhouette Books New York
America's Publisher of Contemporary Romance

SILHOUETTE BOOKS, a Simon & Schuster Division of
GULF & WESTERN CORPORATION
1230 Avenue of the Americas, New York, N.Y. 10020

Copyright © 1982 by Patti Beckman

Distributed by Pocket Books

ISBN: 0-671-53513-7

First Silhouette Books printing April, 1982

10 9 8 7 6 5 4 3 2 1

SILHOUETTE, SILHOUETTE SPECIAL EDITION
and colophon are trademarks of Simon & Schuster.

America's Publisher of Contemporary Romance.

Printed in the U.S.A.

Bitter Victory

Chapter One

$\mathcal{V}$eronica Huntington tossed the newspaper onto the top of her refinished desk. It was no concern of hers, she thought bitterly, that Slade was running for one of the highest offices in the state. He had always been ambitious. Too ambitious, Veronica remembered with a pang. Still, she thought, a man like Slade had no business being a senator. He was too morally corrupt.

The photograph of the dashing, silver-haired man Veronica had fought so hard to forget smiled confidently at her from the front page of the paper. For a moment Veronica couldn't tear her gaze from the rugged features, the broad forehead, the strong chin, the depth of his intelligent brown eyes.

"No, I won't fall into that trap again!" she muttered aloud. "He may be devilishly good-looking with that shock of silver hair, but I know what a rat he really is!" With that, she flipped the newspaper over to conceal the picture. But still she felt agitated. Impulsively she gathered up the folded sheets, crumpled them savagely into a large wad, and tossed them into the trash can with a wry grin of satisfaction. She dusted her hands, nodded with approval, and turned her attention to the many tasks at hand.

Setting up a new office had been a challenge. The money she had saved from her job at the public-relations firm in Sydney, Australia, the last two years hadn't bought as much as she'd hoped. *Two years,* Veronica mused. It had taken her that long to get Slade Huntington out of her system. But she had finally learned to live again, and nothing else would ever hurt her as deeply, no matter how long she lived.

She had learned a valuable lesson from Slade. By withholding her feelings and never again allowing herself to care deeply and exclusively for someone, she would insulate herself from the devastating pain she had experienced at Slade's hands.

A rap at the door diverted Veronica's introspective thoughts to the reality of the present. She opened the office door to a small man dressed in paint-spattered coveralls.

"I'm Gus, the painter," he said with a shy smile. "You called about having your name put on the door?"

"Oh, yes." Veronica nodded. The smell of paint wafted up from a collection of various-colored jars nestled in a bucket in his hand. Down the hallway, a door opened, and a clack-clack of a typewriter in operation suddenly grew louder, only to become muffled when the door closed again. A woman in a crisp gray business suit passed by, her heels making clicking sounds on the terrazzo floor of the hallway.

Veronica pointed to the place on the mahogany office door where she wished her name to be painted.

"Now, I got lots of colors here," Gus offered, holding out the bucket for Veronica to see. "Women usually go for the more pastel shades, you know, like blues and greens. But the men, they like them bolder colors: black, navy, or dark brown. I even got a red if you want to call a lot of attention to your door."

"How about a nice, neutral shade?" Veronica ventured.

"If that's what you want," Gus muttered, his voice revealing disappointment. "I took one look at you in that red dress and I figured you to be the more daring type. 'She'll ask for red, for sure,' I said to myself. I'm pretty good at sizing people up, you know," he went on, warming to the subject. "You can tell a lot about a person from the colors they like, y'know?"

"Yes," said Veronica, suppressing a smile. Following that line of reasoning, she thought, she'd choose an icy blue for Slade Huntington, to represent his cold heart.

Finally she decided. "I like this one," she said, pointing to a bright yellow. "I plan to use a shade like that in my logo and on my letterheads, and it will show up well against the dark wood."

Gus smiled approval. "Well, now, I wasn't so far off, after all. Yellow. Why, that's almost as good as red, I tell you. Bright, sunny color. Fits you well, ma'am. Just like your smile. I knew I had you pegged right from the start."

"I guess you did at that, Gus." Veronica smiled. It was impossible not to be amused at the little fellow's philosophizing. Probably he was more interested in chatting with people than in painting signs on their doors. He was a welcome diversion, taking her mind off the morbid, brooding mood she'd slipped into over Slade this morning.

"Beggin' your pardon ma'am," Gus went on conversationally as he stirred his paint, "but you sound a bit foreign to me. Are you from England? You sound kinda like that."

"Australia," she said. "That is, I'm an American citizen, but I was born in Australia and never entirely lost the accent. Now, this is what I want on the sign," she explained, handing Gus a slip of paper on which were typed four words: Veronica McDonald, Public Relations.

She decided to use her maiden name in her business. She felt confident Slade had filed for divorce after she had run away from him. This state had a no-fault divorce law which made it relatively easy, and Slade, being a lawyer, would know how to handle such matters. But she did want a copy of the papers in her hands to reassure her that she was totally free of him forever. As soon as she was settled in her new office, she planned to check into the matter.

Veronica left Gus to his task and returned to her desk in the office. It would only be a matter of days until she would be open for business, she thought with a feeling of anticipation. It had taken four years of college and two years of apprenticeship to prepare herself. But now she was ready to strike out on her own. She felt confident of her ability.

She had rented the office unfurnished. She had refinished the desk herself after locating the solid, sturdy piece of furniture at an auction. She had picked up the swivel chair from a store that was going out of business and the steel file cabinets at a fire sale. The green potted plants and the decorator prints on the walls, which gave the office a homey look, had come from various garage sales. All in all, she had spent more time than money, and she was proud to have collected so much attractive office equipment with a modest expenditure of her limited capital. She had a special feeling of satisfaction that she was not using one cent of Slade's money. She was no doubt entitled to alimony, but she had no intention of asking for it.

At times the prospect of venturing into this business all alone with only her own resources frightened her a bit, but, on the other hand, she liked the feeling of knowing that for the first time in her life she was totally responsible for herself and only herself.

Veronica settled into her swivel chair behind the desk and turned to gaze through the large picture window. From this vantage point, she could see beyond the rooftops to the desert and the distant purple mountain range of this western state that she loved so much. The view through this window was what had sold her on this particular office. One look and she had known she was ready to sign the lease.

Only one thing marred the view—a billboard on a building across the street with a large picture of Slade Huntington and the bold letters: Slade Huntington for State Senate. He'll Make Our Government Honest Again.

The sign had gone up after she rented the office or she would have had second thoughts about signing the lease, in spite of the otherwise lovely view. But she consoled herself with the thought that the political race would be over in a few weeks and the sign would come down, and she planned to be here for a long time after that. In the meantime, she tried to ignore the sign.

She turned back to the desk and began the task of getting it in order as she fantasized about her first client. He would have seen her ad in the newspaper and would be a major account—a promotion of national proportions, perhaps a celebrity from the entertainment field or a manufacturer with a brilliant new product. It would entail network television spots, articles for slick magazines, interviews with VIPs, jet flights around the country.

Then she chuckled, coming back down to earth. In reality, her first client would probably be a local clothing-store merchant who wanted the promote a discount fire sale! She sighed, knowing it was going to take time to build the kind of reputation that would attract any major accounts. She'd better prepare herself for the long grind ahead. . . .

Her reverie was interrupted by voices outside her office door. She heard Gus's voice and the rumble of another masculine voice, indistinguishable, yet vaguely and disturbingly familiar.

The door opened.

A large, broad-shouldered man entered her office.

Veronica felt as if every biological process in her body came to a stunned halt.

She stared in disbelief at the shock of silver hair contrasting with a rugged, suntanned face, the broad shoulders, the arrogant smile. Her own breathing almost deafened her. Her linen dress felt tight and confining. Her fingers ran gingerly over the smooth desktop. It felt like ice. A strange smell assaulted her nostrils, and only dimly she realized it was the aroma of her own fear.

The sign across the street had come alive and walked into her office!

"Slade," she mouthed. The word was dry and raspy.

"Hello, Veronica," Slade Huntington said. He dropped a briefcase on her desk. His brown eyes raked through her. The pain took her breath away.

She'd thought the two years had softened her memory of him. But now, with shocking impact, she was reminded of what an imposing, powerful man he was. Contrasting with his silver mane were fierce, frowning slashes of dark eyebrows above those brown eyes with their strange depths of swirling golden flecks. His shoulders were massive. Yet he walked lightly for such a large man. "A jungle cat stalking its prey" was the description an overly zealous reporter had used in describing Slade in a courtroom. But, she thought, trite as it was, the description fit him.

In that moment, Veronica hated both herself and Slade Huntington. She hated herself for the emotions that tore through her—emotions she wished dead and forgotten. But a man who meant nothing to her could not affect her this way. With chilling shock, she knew that her hate for him was as strong—and as hurting—as ever.

She was furious at him for walking in on her like this with no forewarning. How cruel of him . . . and how completely in character!

"I saw your advertisement in the newspaper," Slade explained, sitting on the edge of the desk, towering over her. " 'Veronica McDonald, Public Relations.' I decided to become your first customer. I'm running for state senate, as you may know." He glanced through her large office window at the billboard picture of him, so prominently displayed, and he smiled. "We need a good public-relations expert for the campaign. Speech-writing, media hype, direct mail, that sort of thing—"

"Slade, you're a bloody no-hoper!" Veronica gasped, finding her strength at last and arising from her chair to put as much distance between herself and Slade as the small office allowed.

The corner of his mouth showed amusement. "A 'no-hoper.' Let me see; it's been a while since I've had to interpret that Aussie slang you revert to when you're aroused. If my memory serves me right, 'no-hoper' means a fool. Do you think I'm a fool, Veronica?"

"If not, you're daft—out of your mind!"

He raised an eyebrow. "On the contrary," he replied

with maddeningly cool composure. "What better person to promote my campaign? You know me personally better than anyone else," he said, his words heavy with an implication that brought hot blood to her cheeks.

With bitter fury, she knew that this unbelievable scene was completely in character for Slade Huntington. He thrived on the dramatic, on theatrics. That was the style that had made him one of the state's most brilliant young criminal-defense lawyers. When Slade Huntington strode into a courtroom, the jury knew they were going to be treated to a dramatic spectacle rivaling any TV play. He was up to his old tricks right now, she knew angrily, thriving on her consternation, loving the tension, the dismay written across her face. Surprise. Shock. His favorite courtroom tactics. Why not use them now?

"Slade, get out," Veronica ordered, her voice trembling with emotion. "This is a cruel joke. I don't like it one bit. You've had your fun. Now please go."

Her words were bouncing off him like raindrops dancing on a waxed surface. He was listening with an indulgent smile but not absorbing a thing she said. "You never were able to completely eradicate your Aussie accent, were you, even though your parents brought you to the States when you were still in grammar school? It's much stronger now, since you spent the last two years down under. I always thought it was appealing the way you don't quite pronounce your *h*'s at the beginning of words and the way you make the letter *a* sometimes sound like 'eye.' I've missed being called 'Slyde.'" He chuckled.

"Yes, well, I have a few other choice things I might call you which you *won't* like if you don't get out!"

He shook his head. He moved from the desk,

backing her into a corner. Veronica gazed into brown eyes that were glittering hard with determination. Her heart pounded. Slade wanted something and was hell-bent on getting it.

It had been a mistake to come back to the United States, Veronica realized with a sudden rush of panic. After two years, she'd been sure Slade would have divorced her, dismissed her from his life, and married Barbara Lange. But here he was in her office, and she knew him well enough to know that he had a definite purpose in coming here and had no intention of leaving her alone until that purpose had been realized.

He had said he wanted her to handle the public relations end of his campaign. That didn't make sense. "Knowing you as I do," she said through her teeth, "I would tell the voters what I think of you, and you'd end up with one vote—your own!"

"Not at all," he said calmly. "When you know the facts, you'll see that I should win this race. The incumbent, Kirk Malden, is a corrupt man, bought and paid for by organized crime and special interests that don't care a snap for the people of this state. I intend to restore some decency and honor to the state legislature."

"Honor? *You?*" she exploded. "I just hope the voters have a sense of humor."

She walked away from him, then turned to him. "You're out of your mind to expect me to work for you. There are a dozen competent, excellent people in my profession in this city. Why did you come to me?"

And even as she spoke the words they sent an icy shiver down her spine. There had to be some other reason Slade was here, and she wasn't sure she wanted to hear what it was.

"Why did I come to you?" Slade repeated. "Well, isn't it natural that I'd want my wife to be helping with my campaign?"

Again shock rendered her speechless. When she found her voice, she gasped, "Your *wife?* But surely you've taken care of the divorce long ago," she spluttered.

"No. And neither have you. That seems to say something about us, doesn't it?" he said with a smile, his voice suddenly low and soft. He moved close to her again. She could feel the heat of his body, matching the warmth that her pounding heart pumped through her arteries. He was gazing directly into her eyes, undermining her strength. He said huskily, "Veronica, I'm not sure if I can ever completely forgive you for running out on me the way you did. But I'm willing to try."

His arms moved around her. She felt her legs tremble, her knees go watery, as his thighs touched hers, burning through the fabric of their garments.

His powerful gaze plunged deeply into her distraught eyes. "Welcome home, my lusty little Aussie girl," he murmured. His fingers buried themselves in her thick hair. "I've often, late at night, pictured you with that chestnut mane of hair tumbling down around your bare shoulders, those bronze freckles across your stubby nose, and your stubborn chin. I've thought about the proud way you cock your head. I remember your exclamations of pleasure when we made love, and remember often seeing you in the shower, with the water slick and glistening on your leggy, rangy body. . . ."

His warm lips crushed down on hers. She was helpless in his powerful embrace. Veronica felt her hatred of Slade melt into tiny rivulets of decaying emotion and trickle away as a storm of bittersweet memories cascaded through her. The throbbing desire for him that had always flamed through her body at his touch blazed forth again in all its fury as if it had never been extinguished. Her traitorous body shrieked to be close to him, to feel her flesh melting against his, to be one with him.

"Take your clothes off for me now, Veronica," he whispered against her lips. "Let me see your lithe, supple body. We're still legally married. You have a couch in your office. We can lock the door. . . ."

She grasped for sanity.

It came in a cold dash of ugly memories. The scene would forever be scalded into her brain in agonizing detail. She could even remember the color of the wallpaper in the motel room. Most of all, she could remember the color of Barbara Lange's filmy negligee tossed carelessly across the bed where she had spent the night in Slade's arms. The color had been scarlet, like the letter for adultery in Hawthorne's story. The lipstick smear on his pillow had been scarlet, too. Their suitcases had nestled side by side near the bed.

Now she wrenched from his arms, scrubbing his kiss from her mouth with the back of her hand. "Get out," she said, shaking from head to foot. "Get out of my office, Slade. I am not going to work for your campaign. I don't pretend to understand why you haven't filed for divorce long ago. That's a little matter I'll take care of immediately. I am most certainly not going to handle your public relations."

"Sure you are," he said cheerfully. He strode to the desk and opened his briefcase.

Veronica looked at him warily. His confidence unnerved her. He never went into a courtroom unless his case was well prepared and he was confident of winning. What trick did he have up his sleeve? Was he bluffing? That was another one of his tactics. But chilling intuition told her that this was no bluff. He had come here knowing he was going to get what he wanted. She felt like a helpless victim watching a deadly trap close slowly around her.

"Now," Slade said in a businesslike voice. "Here are lists of registered voters that my volunteers have already checked for their addresses and party affiliations. This is the phone number of Jim Baxwell, publisher of the *Morning Sun*, the newspaper that's supporting me all out." He was spreading papers across her desk. "This is the itinerary I'll be taking in a speechmaking trip around the district, a list of campaign rallies, barbecues. Stuff like that. We thought we might go in pretty heavily for a direct mail campaign. That has worked well for other candidates. One of the things I'll need you to do is write some speeches for me. As I recall, you're extremely good at that sort of thing. I'll have to brief you on all the issues so you'll know the points I want to hit strongest in my speeches. I'll need a strong speech ready by Saturday."

"Saturday?" Veronica echoed. She felt numb, out of touch with reality. Surely, this was some kind of dream from which she'd soon awaken.

"Saturday," Slade said flatly. "This is a race, Veronica. It's a race for office, for time—for votes. I want you to set up press conferences in all the major cities in our district. I'm going to hold a political rally in each one, and I want you to handle the details. And here's a report on the impact of that new big dam and reservoir —how the two locations under consideration will affect the ecology and the economy of the state. That's one of the big issues of the campaign, you know. My opponent, Malden, is backed by the group that wants it located up at Three Oaks Canyon. That's going to be an ecological disaster. It should be built farther south, at the Crystal Falls site. I'll fill you in on all the ramifications of that issue later. Organized crime is another big issue. Malden is backing a move to weaken laws against gambling and prostitution and pornography. We have to hit him hard there. He's opening the doors for organized crime to move into the state. . . ."

"You're wasting your breath, Slade," Veronica protested. "You're trying to involve me in every aspect of your race. You don't want a public-relations person—you want a campaign manager."

"Oh, I have a campaign manager, and he is an excellent one, Jake Foreman. You probably have read about him. He's successfully managed a number of candidates on a state level and several on a congressional level. Jake and I have talked about you at length, and we're both in agreement that you'll definitely handle much of the public relations."

"I definitely will not, and that's final!"

"No, it is not final," he countered, fixing her with a stern look. "You're working for me now, and you'll do what I tell you. This is going to be a bitter race. It may become vicious before it's over. It's going to take all our energy. And, by the way, we don't have to worry about finances. There's some big money in the state behind me. I'll tell you more about that later, too."

"Can't you understand?" she said tearfully. "I don't want to hear all this. I don't want to work for you—"

"Sure you do," Slade said with a strange, veiled threat in his voice. "I've missed you these last two years. Now that you're back and I've found you again, I don't intend to let you get away."

There was a tense silence between them. Why was it so hard for an old love to die? Veronica wondered, feeling a dull ache in her heart. The old, poignant memories kept it alive, that's why . . . the memories of a summer night in his arms, the memory of marriage vows, the memory of a dream they had once shared . . . memories of countless little daily events they had experienced together . . . the passion that disturbed her even now . . .

The phone rang, jarring Veronica from the almost hypnotic trance she had slipped into.

Without taking her eyes off Slade's face, Veronica reached for the instrument. "Hello," she said automatically.

"Hello. Is that you, Veronica?" The voice came out of the past like a thunderbolt, slamming into her, striking sparks of anger and humiliation. She gave Slade a murderous look, then turned her back to him.

"Hello, Barbara," Veronica said icily. "I'm sure it's Slade you want." She struggled to keep her voice steady.

"Yes, I was told he could be reached at your number. So you're back . . ."

Veronica thrust the phone at Slade and stalked to the window to stare at the mountains through tear-filled eyes.

Just what was Slade Huntington up to? He had appeared in her office unannounced, offered her a job as his public-relations expert, kissed her, implied he still felt something for her. He had given her the impression that he wanted to resume some kind of relationship with her, more personal than business. He had not filed for divorce. Why? How could he possibly feel anything for her if he was still involved with Barbara Lange? Obviously he was. The write-ups in the newspaper about him said he now had his own law firm, and one story had mentioned that Barbara Lange was a member of the firm, still very much in his life. The old, bitter jealousy flared in Veronica, threatening to consume her.

"I told you I didn't want to be interrupted for anything except an emergency," Slade said impatiently into the phone. "Oh. That. Yes, well, I'll discuss that with you tonight . . ."

Tonight.

Over dinner?

When they were in bed, perhaps?

Veronica ground her nails into her fisted palms.

Slade replaced the phone. Veronica stood frigidly looking out the window, her back stiff, determined not to give Slade the satisfaction of seeing the tears in her eyes.

"I have to go now," Slade said to her back. "I'll leave these papers so you can familiarize yourself with the campaign. I'll call you in the morning."

Veronica drew a shuddering breath and turned to face Slade. "I am bloody well *not* going to work for you," she said with finality.

"I don't have time to argue with you now," Slade said forcefully. "Do as you're told and we'll discuss it later."

"Do as I'm told?" she gasped. "Who do you think you are, anyway? You can't order me around. This is a free country."

"You'll do as I say because I'm your husband," Slade said quietly.

"That," she retorted, "is a mere legal technicality, an oversight which I intend to rectify as quickly as I can get to the courthouse. By the way," she added cuttingly, "could you recommend a *good* lawyer?"

He shook his head patiently, as if dealing with a child. "No, you'll do nothing of the kind, Veronica.

What you are actually going to do is go and pack your things. Tomorrow I'm going to pick you up and take you home. And next week you're going to leave with me on the campaign trail as my wife."

"As your wife?" Veronica stared openmouthed at him. And then a light dawned in the confused fog that had surrounded this baffling situation. "So that's it!" she cried. "Now I begin to understand. At first I thought you'd gone completely insane. But you're very much sane, and very much the old ruthless Slade Huntington, thinking only of number one. You're campaigning for state senator, so it's important for the public to see you as a solid family man. A divorce would not be good for your public image. So, instead of divorcing me and marrying Barbara, which would mean your opponent could throw quite a bit of mud and family scandal about your marital problems, you're going to have your cake and eat it. A respectable wife to keep up your public image, while you carry on your affair with Barbara backstage."

He frowned at her. "So that's what's eating you. That old jealous streak again. Is that why you ran out on me?" He shook his head. "Jealousy can get to be a pathological problem, Veronica."

The sordid picture of the motel room flashed across Veronica's mind again—the rumpled bedclothes, the negligee, the lipstick smears on the pillow . . . their night of sordid passion still heavy in the air . . .

"What gall you have," she gasped. "The old double standard, eh? I'm supposed to be the understanding wife while you carry on with your law partner, and if I object, then it's my problem for being neurotically jealous! What kind of a twisted macho concept do you have of a wife's role?"

"I'm not going to stand here and try to talk any sense

into you. I've decided that you only understand one thing, Veronica, and that's force. Unfortunately, twentieth-century laws prevent tying you up to keep you home. But there's another kind of force, and I'll use it if necessary to keep you from running out on me for a second time. Now I'm involved in a hard, bitter fight, the hardest of my career. I need my wife by my side. And, like it or not, you're going to be at my side during the day and in my bed at night. I told you before, and I'll repeat it: I don't intend to let you get away again."

The chill that Veronica had felt that first moment when he walked into her office swept over her stronger then before. Slade Huntington was a man who knew how to use force to get what he wanted. The trap felt closer about her now.

"And what if I refuse?" she asked, trying to hold on to her courage.

He shook his head. "Don't Veronica. Don't push me. Don't make me have to do it."

"Do what?" she asked, trembling inside.

"Use the one weapon that I know you can't face. I don't want to do it, but I will if I have to. Don't make me."

"I—I don't know what you're talking about," she whispered, a dreadful realization growing inside her.

He nodded soberly. "Yes, you do, Veronica. You know quite well that you and I are the only people close to your sister Aileen who know about the secret she has kept from Brian. You know she didn't tell Brian when she married him, and she's never told him. . . ."

Veronica's face turned deathly pale. "You're utterly despicable," she choked. "I can't believe you'd do a thing like that."

"Believe it." He nodded, his eyes stone hard. "Yes,

believe it with all your heart, Veronica, and don't forget it for one moment. Everything is fair in love and war. A political campaign like this is war."

"As for love," she said, the words ashes in her mouth, "forget about that, right?"

He shrugged. "Get your things packed. Tomorrow night you'll spend in my home, in my bed."

"In your home, maybe," she said, slumping with defeat. But then her eyes scorned him. "In your bed, never. . . ."

Chapter Two

Slade left the office as tempestuously as he had strode in. Veronica sank into her chair, gripping the edge of her desk for support. Her head was swimming, her thought processes in shambles.

Today's encounter reminded her of the emotional storm Slade Huntington had caused in her life from the first time she had laid eyes on him. She remembered vividly the impact he had made on her heart that first day she'd seen his tall, broad-shouldered figure striding across the college campus. That was six years ago, but even then his hair was a striking sight, a kind of premature silver that ran in his family.

Veronica had been so mesmerized by his imposing appearance that she had blindly steered the bicycle she was riding straight into a tree. The next thing she knew, the silver-haired Adonis was helping disentangle her from the crumpled bicycle. He was grinning with amusement, she was red-faced with mortification.

"Are you injured, young lady?"

His resonant baritone was perfectly attuned to his six feet of brawn and muscle.

"No," she stammered. "Just humiliated. That was pretty stupid of me."

He frowned. "Your skirt is torn. Sure you weren't hurt?"

She glanced down and blushed again when she caught sight of her bare thigh gleaming through a six-inch rip in her skirt. Quickly she clasped the skirt together. "I'm okay," she insisted. "Just a bloody idiot to come a gutser that way."

He stared at her. "I beg your pardon?"

"Oh, excuse me. Sometimes when I'm upset, those old slang expressions slip out. 'Come a gutser'—to make a dumb mistake, to fall down."

He continued to gaze at her with a look of interest. "That's not an American expression. And you do have a bit of an accent. English? Canadian?"

"Australian."

He nodded. "That explains it."

"Well, I'm an American citizen," she said, "and have been since my family migrated here when I was in junior high. But I suppose a trace of the accent lingers, though I'm not aware of it . . ."

He smiled again, in a way that brought a strange trembling to her legs. "It's attractive. *You're* attractive."

She gulped, unconsciously reaching up to brush her tangled hair back from her forehead, then remembering the tear in her skirt and grabbing for that again, modesty winning out over vanity.

The instinctive moment did not get by him unnoticed. His eyes teased hers as he said, "An old-fashioned girl, too."

"What . . . what do you mean?"

"You've heard the old joke, haven't you? The difference between an old-fashioned and a modern girl? In a windstorm, the old-fashioned girl reaches for her skirt, the modern girl grabs for her hat."

Veronica shrugged, tilting her chin at a saucy angle. "I'm modern enough," she said challengingly.

"Are you, now?" He knelt to pick up her scattered books and handed them to her. "Are you modern enough to have lunch with a man to whom you have not been properly introduced?"

Her heart began pounding. "I might be."

"My name is Slade Huntington."

She smiled. "Hello, Slade. I'm Veronica McDonald."

They started down the campus lane, Slade pushing her bicycle, her books under his arm, while she walked beside him, clasping her torn skirt.

"You're limping," he said. "You did hurt your leg."

"It's nothing serious," she insisted, but she winced in spite of herself.

"Well, perhaps we should stop by the hospital and have a doctor take a look at it to be on the safe side."

"Oh, certainly not. It's just a little bruise. It'll be okay as soon as I'm in my room and take my weight off it for a bit."

"Where's your room?"

She pointed toward a nearby dormitory.

Slade insisted on seeing her safely to her room, an offer which she did not protest in view of the fact that she was already helplessly smitten by this large, imposing man whose gaze struck her with the force of laser beams and whose personality radiated out in electrical shock waves.

He locked her bicycle in the stand downstairs, then helped her to her room with a gentleness surprising in such an obviously physical, athletic type. She was both relieved and unnerved when they entered her dorm room and she saw her roommate was away. She wasn't sure if she could trust being alone with this devastating hunk of masculine sex appeal.

She should have realized from that starting moment

that the strongest thing she and Slade Huntington had going for them was powerful physical attraction. From the first moment their bodies were like magnets, drawn toward each other by an irresistible, invisible force. She hadn't known this man ten minutes, and feelings such as she had never experienced before in her life were coursing through her body in throbbing waves . . . feelings that sent a hot flush to her cheeks.

"Now, all modesty aside," he said sternly, "you'd better let me have a look at that bruise."

Her emotions ranged up and down the scale from shy embarrassment to hot excitement as he firmly sat her on the edge of the bed, knelt beside her, and gently moved her skirt up to examine her injured thigh.

"That's a nasty bruise," he said, frowning, "and there's a cut, too. See, it's bleeding. Do you have a first-aid kit around here?"

"In the bathroom," she said thickly, pointing.

He rummaged around in the medicine cabinet and returned presently with bandages and iodine.

"This is going to smart a bit," he warned.

She lay back on the pillow, gazing wide-eyed at him as he bent over her bare, injured thigh. She had a wild impulse to dig her fingers into his lush, wavy silver mane.

She bit her lip as the medicine stung. But a strange part of her welcomed the pain, which somehow added to the excitement that was pounding through her at his touch. She was in the grip of emotions totally foreign to her. It was as if she had suddenly slipped into the body of another woman—a woman who was feeling desires and passions as old as Eve . . . a woman more wanton and physical than Veronica McDonald had ever dreamed of being.

"Are you a premed student?" she asked.

"No. Whatever made you ask that?"

"You go about doctoring my leg like you know what you're doing."

"I was a high-school football coach for a few years. I patched up a lot of sprains and bruises during that time."

"Oh, that explains it—" She caught herself.

He looked at her and grinned at her confusion. "Explains why I'm older than most of the boys on campus?"

She blushed. "I wasn't thinking that."

"Of course you were. Well, it's true, I am a bit old to be going back to school, some ten years older than your contemporaries here on campus. I decided teaching wasn't my bag, after all, and I wanted to be a lawyer."

"So you're a law student!" she exclaimed.

"Yes. Do you have anything against law students?"

"Certainly not. Though I am glad you're not a premed."

"Now, what"—he laughed—"do you have against premeds?"

"Nothing sensible. Just prejudiced, I suppose. My sister married one. He turned out to be a rat. She got a job to help put him through med school. After he started practicing medicine, he had an affair with his nurse and kicked my poor sister out. And she with two small kids."

"Well, he does sound like a rat," Slade agreed. "Though I don't suppose all premeds are like that."

"Some of my best friends," she quipped, "are premeds. I just wouldn't want my sister to marry one."

He grinned. "How about that? A pert, freckle-faced Aussie girl with a sense of humor. I like that."

She blushed. "You didn't have to mention the freckles."

"Why not? They're cute. A definite asset. I like the way they're sprinkled across your snub nose. Tell me, do you have a few on your shoulders, too?"

"That's none of your business."

"I'll bet you have a bit of a temper, too, and a lot of stubborn pride."

"What on earth makes you say that?"

"The way you carry your head, erect, with your chin raised. The way your shoulders are squared when you walk."

"Oh, that. That comes from having a father who was a professional military man. He had my sister and me standing at attention before we could walk. I wouldn't dare stand any way but straight."

"It's attractive. I like a long-legged girl who knows how to stand straight and carry herself with a proud bearing." Then he said, "Veronica McDonald, you're a fine-looking, lusty Aussie gal that I'd like to get to know a lot better."

She met his eyes with a straight-on gaze that amazed her with her own boldness. "I think," she said, her voice husky with promise, "that can be arranged."

A slow smile moved across his face. His glittering gaze held her captive. She was fascinated by his brown eyes with their unusual swirling golden flecks. "Then," he said, "maybe we can continue this conversation over dinner. That is," he added with quick concern, "if you're up to a bit of walking."

"Let's try," she suggested.

She rose from the bed, acutely aware that his arm would touch her, giving her strong support. She limped about the room, leaning on him. She was scarcely aware of her injury, the discomfort forgotten in the quivering sensations that ran through her body at the close contact with this man who had walked so boldly into her life.

She excused herself long enough to run a comb through her hair and dab on a bit of eye shadow in the privacy of the bathroom. She gazed at her reflection, wishing she were more confident of her looks. "The trouble with you, girl," she told herself, "is that your cheekbones are a bit high and your mouth slightly too wide." Her teeth were all right, white and even. And, with a bit a mascara and eye shadow, her tawny eyes were large and attractive. Probably, she thought, her eyes and her mop of gleaming chestnut hair were her strong points. As for the sprinkling of freckles across her snub nose, well, she'd always been self-conscious about them, but Slade had said they were attractive. Was he just being kind? No, she didn't think so. He struck her as the type who said exactly what he thought, and the devil take you if you didn't like it.

On their first date, she had limped beside him to a small diner just off campus that college students frequented. They shared a meal of hamburgers and soft drinks, for which Slade apologized. "I wish I could afford to offer you steaks and champagne, but I'm afraid for the present I'm on a very tight budget."

She waved aside his apology, her sparkling eyes telling him that his presence had magically transformed the hamburgers into filet mignon, the soft drinks into imported wine.

In those first exciting moments of discovering each other there had been so much to talk about, so many things to learn about one another.

Slade told her about the financial struggle he was

going through to obtain his law degree. "Only one more year to go," he said ruefully, "and it looks like I'm going to have to drop out after this semester and get a job before I can finish."

"That's a rotten shame," she sympathized. "Can't you get a bit of a loan from your family?"

"Hardly." He frowned. "I come from a big family. It was a struggle for my father just to keep us fed. I've been on my own since I was fifteen. Luckily, I was good at sports. My high-school coach took me under his wing. I got an athletic scholarship that saw me through college the first time when I earned my teaching certificate. I started my career as a high-school athletic coach in a small town."

"I thought you looked like a football player," Veronica observed.

He nodded. "I was all-state in my high-school days and an all-American back in college. I'd considered going into pro football, but decided on coaching instead. I really liked working with the kids, but after a few years I became dissatisfied. I couldn't see much future in the direction I was going. That was when I became interested in a law career. I saved my money, and here I am back in college—at least for the time being." Then he smiled, his eyes making her warm all over. "How about you, little Aussie girl? How did you happen to wind up in America?"

"My parents migrated here when I was in junior high," she explained. "Dad retired from the military, wanted to try his hand at something new, decided all Americans were rich and successful, so he packed up the family and we came to the States. He did pretty well, too, for a while, until—" Her eyes clouded with a stab of remembered pain. "Well, he and my mom were killed in an auto accident. Then it was just my sis and me."

Slade frowned sympathetically. "Sounds like it was a rough time for you. I'm sorry."

She raised her chin. "We managed just fine. Aileen stepped in and took over raising me. I don't know what I would have done without her, though."

"Aileen would be your sister."

She nodded. She rummaged through her handbag and found her wallet, which contained a few family snapshots in plastic sleeves. "That's my sis, Aileen. And these are her children, Michael and Debbie."

"Cute kids. Aileen doesn't resemble you at all, though. I would hardly take you for sisters."

"No, she looks like my dad's side of the family." Veronica turned over the plastic sleeves, stopping at another snapshot, this one cracked and faded. It was the picture of a handsome young soldier with his arm around a pretty army nurse. "My mom and dad, when they first met, back during World War Two."

He studied the photograph. "Well, I can see where you get that thick bronze hair of yours and that cute sprinkling of freckles. You're a dead ringer for your mother."

"Yes, and Aileen is dark, like my father."

She gazed at the old snapshot, caught up in poignant memories. "When I was a little girl," she said slowly, "I loved for my mother to tell me the story of how they met. I must have heard it a hundred times. My dad was in a front-line hospital with a leg wound. The Japanese were bombing the area. The bombs were getting closer to the field hospital. A young nurse—my mom—crawled through the rubble and helped my father limp to a bomb shelter, and they huddled in the dark, their arms around each other for comfort, as the explosions shook dirt and rubble down around them. My dad told her, 'Hey after the war, I'm going to find you and marry you!' And he did!

"When I was little, I thought my parents were like glamorous storybook characters. My father was a war hero. He got several decorations for bravery. It wasn't until I was nearly grown and looked back that I realized the war years had been the high point of his life. He tried being a civilian for a while after the war, but it didn't work. He failed at several business ventures. So he went back into professional military service. Both Aileen and I were born on military bases."

"Any other relatives back in Australia?"

"My grandparents—Dad's folks. Still hale and hearty. We've been back to see them a few times. I lived with them a lot when I was growing up. Dad didn't want me shuffled around from school to school the way army children often are. So during school season I lived with my grandparents. I think you'd like them. They're real pioneer stock, hardy, fiercely independent people. They tackled a region of the harsh outback, built a ranch there, and made a success out of it. Something about you reminds me of them."

He chuckled. "I've seen some of Russell Drysdale's paintings of the people who live in the Australian outback. Do I look like an Australian cowboy?"

She lowered her eyes, embarrassed. "I didn't mean it that way. I—I just have the impression that you're a rugged individual who lives life on your own terms. That's the best way I can describe my grandparents."

He sobered, looking at her thoughtfully. "Well, maybe you're right, Veronica. I suppose that pretty well sizes me up."

She felt a quickening of her pulse as he spoke her first name. It somehow put them on closer terms.

"I suspect you rode horses quite a bit back on your grandparents' ranch," he ventured.

"As a matter of fact, I did. But what made you say that?"

"You have a healthy, outdoorsy look of a girl who grew up leading an active life around farm animals."

"Well, you're right about the horses. I loved them. And I was active outdoors. I guess that's why I have so much energy. I've never really ever been sick a day in my life."

"Just like I said before," he teased, "a fine-looking lusty Aussie gal."

She colored. "I suppose I'm to take that as a compliment?" she asked, measuring his gaze with her own look of independence.

"I certainly meant it that way."

His eyes were filled with a teasing, mocking expression that stirred a response of challenge in the gaze she returned. But they fell silent, looking into each other's eyes. Veronica felt herself grow weak as he plumbed the depths of her being with his relentless, probing gaze that searched and demanded to find her most intimate self. She drew a shuddering breath. Never had she felt so powerless in the grip of a man's look. He had the inner strength to hypnotize her. His gaze moved to her lips and her mouth suddenly quivered, knowing he wanted to taste it.

He said softly, "Ready to go?"

She nodded without a word, gathering up her purse in a daze.

Night had fallen over the campus. She walked slowly beside him. His arm was around her. They did not speak. Presently they came to a stone bench in a secluded nook under oak trees that hid the moon. He led her to the bench. She went willingly. They sat close, their knees touching. She could see only a blur of his face in the darkness, but the magnetic pull of their bodies supplied its own vibrant illumination.

He whispered her name once, softly; then their lips met in their first kiss. It was gentle, exploring, yet aquiver with a passion held in check for now. His arms drew her closer. Everywhere her body touched his, she felt her flesh burn.

Drawing back from him required every shred of willpower she could muster. "I'd—I'd better go in," she whispered shakily.

She could feel his gaze probing the darkness. She sensed the desire in him, almost palpable in its overwhelming intensity.

"Yes," he said huskily. "But I want to see you again very soon. Tomorrow night?"

Her scattered thoughts vaguely remembered something about a term paper that needed her attention, but she brushed that aside in this greater urgency to be with him. "Yes, all right. . . ."

They started to rise, but the hunger was too great in both of them, and their lips eagerly met again. Veronica finally tore her lips from his. "Whew," she breathed. "That had better be enough for now."

"All right," he said reluctantly. They walked slowly toward her dorm, their shoes crunching softly on the graveled walk. Veronica's emotions were in such a turmoil, she couldn't trust herself to speak.

It was Slade's voice that broke the steaming silence between them. His words had a rough edge, letting her know the extent of his physical arousal. "I would say we have an extremely strong mutual attraction going for us."

Veronica was grateful for the darkness that hid her burning cheeks. What she was feeling right now was downright disgraceful. How could a properly brought up young lady with a morally conservative background be guilty of the wanton feelings coursing through her body? She hadn't known this man four hours, and she'd necked shamelessly with him on a campus bench. Worse, her impulse had been to throw all restraint to the wind, sprawl right out there on the bench, and give herself up to total fulfillment in his arms.

Thank heaven and the moral guidelines that had been instilled in her in the private religious school her grandparents had sent her to during her formative years, she had kept hold of some shreds of sanity!

How long she could hold on to her chastity around this new man in her life was up for grabs. She knew that with a mixture of fright and excitement. She had read stories about women who experienced this overwhelming passion when the right man came along. Now it had happened to her, and with such devastating suddenness that she was left breathless.

She lay awake most of that first night, trying to put in perspective this unexpected turn of events that promised to turn her life upside down. When she thought about Slade, his voice, his eyes, his touch, her heart pounded and her body throbbed with surging waves of heat. She felt shaken and at a loss to know how to deal with this overpowering experience.

Her lips felt swollen from his kiss. Her breasts ached. Her fingers longed to entwine in his. She had known him less than twelve hours, and already she was desperately lonely for him.

Love at first sight?

That was sheer nonsense. Stuff for romantic stories and movies. She didn't believe in it. Her reasoning mind told her that love grew with the knowledge and respect of one for another. She barely knew the man.

What was it, then, this pounding emotion that kept her twisting and turning on her pillow, her mind feverish with thoughts of him? Pure physical attraction. That was the only rational explanation. An explosion of desire between a man and a woman whose biology had put their bodies on a crash course.

That was a frightening concept. What resources could she use to control the wild impulses this man could stir in her? Or did she want to control them? she asked herself frankly, her cheeks suddenly flushing in the darkness. Until now, she had never faced the problem of whether she should surrender to a man. She was old-fashioned enough to want to wait until she was properly married. Would she be strong enough to cling to her ideals? She knew she would despise herself if she slept with this man out of pure physical lust without even the consolation of knowing she loved him.

They were together almost constantly after their first meeting. They met on campus, in the library, in her room, in his. They talked, they touched, they planned. And as she really grew to know Slade Huntington, Veronica found that she was in love with him.

Their kisses drew her even closer to the moment of total surrender in his arms. He shared a room just off campus with another law student. One weekend, his roommate went home for a visit, leaving the place to Slade.

Slade and Veronica spent the evening there, sharing a meal of cheese and fruit and a small bottle of wine by candlelight. Music from Veronica's transistor radio added the romantic strains of Chopin from an FM station.

Later, Slade cradled her in his arms. She whispered his name blindly as his kisses sent a trail of fire from her lips to her throat. When he tenderly cupped her breast, she shuddered, clinging to him.

The last fragment of her resistance melted away. She knew that tonight she would surrender if he wanted her.

It was Slade who kept within the boundaries. He stroked her hair, looking soberly into her eyes. "I think I'd better tell you . . . I'm falling in love with you, Veronica."

Her eyes became liquid with tears of joy. "And I you. . . ."

They were silent for a long moment, treasuring the feelings they shared. Veronica thought, all of my life, I want to remember how I feel right now. This moment only comes once in a woman's life.

"It's serious with me, Veronica," Slade began again. "I don't want just an affair with you. I want it to be permanent. I want us to get married. Is that the way you feel?"

Her finger softly traced the line of his strong chin as she loved him with her gaze. "Yes," she whispered, her throat filled with emotion. "Yes, I do, my darling." She thought she would burst with happiness.

If she could have glimpsed the future, she would have fled the room that night as if it were the pit of hell. But only the present was known to her that night, and it was a present filled with the shimmering happiness of a young, trusting girl in the arms of her first love. That night she could have died for Slade.

The time was to come when she could have killed him.

They talked until dawn, making plans, trying to find a solution to the problems Slade faced in getting his law degree.

Veronica broke the news of their engagement to Aileen that same weekend, on Sunday afternoon. Aileen lived in a small apartment in town. Veronica played with her niece and nephew. After a while the children went to visit friends. Aileen made a pot of tea. They sat at the apartment's dinette table. Veronica's eyes were sparkling, her face aglow. "I have some exciting news."

Aileen gave her sister a close look. "I've been thinking you had something to tell me. You look like you're high on something. You haven't been taking some kind of pills, have you?"

Veronica grinned. "Nothing like that." She hesitated, overtaken by a mixture of shyness and joy. "I'm . . . well, I've met a wonderful man," she said all in a rush. "We're in love and we're going to be married."

Aileen was speechless for a long moment. Her eyes filled with tears. Then her hand found Veronica's in a tight squeeze. "My little sis. I'm so very glad for you." Then she looked concerned. "Who is this bloke? Is he all right?"

"More than all right. He's wonderful."

"Careful, girl. They all seem wonderful when you first fall for them."

The edge of bitterness in Aileen's voice was unmistakable. Veronica understood why it was there. After the rotten deal she'd gotten from the man she'd married, she had every right to be bitter.

"Slade really is a wonderful man," Veronica said quickly. "Slade Huntington is his name. He's a law student. He's older than most of the fellows I know on campus. He was a teacher and high-school coach for several years before he decided to get his law degree."

"How much older?"

"He's in his early thirties, about ten years older than I."

Aileen nodded. "Well, that part is okay. Maybe he's more settled. Has he been married?"

"No."

"Kind of odd, d'you think, a fellow getting to be that age and never married?"

"Why? Lots of fellows stay bachelors until they're ready to settle down in their thirties. He just never met the right girl before. Anyway, he wasn't sure about his life. He didn't want to go on with his coaching job. I guess he wanted to get his life headed in the right direction before he thought about marriage."

"Well, have you made plans? Are you getting married right away? Or after graduation?"

Veronica frowned. "We're trying to work all that out. It's something of a problem," she admitted. "Slade has another year to go on his law degree, but he's run out of funds. He'd have to drop out of school, get a job. If we got married under those circumstances, he might never finish school. We've talked about it, and it makes a lot more sense for me to drop out for a year and work so he can finish with his law degree. Then he'll put me through my final year."

Aileen's face paled. "I'm not sure that's wise. . . ."

Veronica analyzed the clouded expression in her sister's eyes. "You're thinking about what happened between you and William," she guessed.

Aileen nodded. "It was the same situation. He was having a dreadful struggle, trying to get through med school. Trusting, dumb me, I worked my fingers to the bone, seeing that man through school. I did it gladly, because I loved him. I thought he loved me. Then, when he got his practice going, I thought I could settle back and enjoy my home and family. I thought we'd grow old together, see our kids through school, get married. We'd have grandchildren—" Her voice broke.

Veronica's heart ached with sympathy for her sister. "I know how he hurt you, Aileen. And you sure have a right to feel bitter. But Slade isn't like that. You'll see when you meet him. He'd never do me that way."

Aileen gazed at her sister with a worried expression. "I hope you're right with all my heart, Veronica," she said hesitantly. "It's just so hard to judge a man, to know what he's really like, until you're married to him. I never dreamed William would treat me the way he did. He seemed so kind and considerate, so dedicated to helping people. He wasn't in practice for a year when he came home that night and calmly told me he was having an affair with Madeleine, his nurse, and he wanted a divorce. Now that I look back over it all, I doubt if he ever loved me. I was . . . *useful* to him. He needed my help to get through school. Women always have been suckers to feel that they're needed."

Aileen rose and paced the room. Bitterness and anger were making her otherwise lovely face look pinched. "I'm so afraid you're letting yourself in for the same situation. It's happened to lots of women, not just to me. A guy needs help finishing school or getting started in a profession or job. He latches on to some trusting woman to see him through the rough times, to be his slave, his meal ticket. Then, when he's established, she no longer seems so attractive to him. He finds someone younger, sexier, and kicks the old work-horse out."

She turned and sat beside Veronica again, clasping her hand. "You're my kid sister, Veronica. I feel responsible for you. That time in the hospital, after the accident, when Mom was conscious those few minutes before she passed away, she asked me to look after you. She knew she was dying. I promised her I'd protect you and see you got a good start in life. There was just enough from Dad's insurance to see you through college if you're thrifty. It would break my heart if you threw away your own college education and got hurt the way I was hurt. I'd feel I let you down somehow. . . ."

"Aileen," Veronica said, squeezing her sister's hands, "you're all worried over nothing. Honestly. I can understand how you feel, but Slade isn't like William at all. This is totally different. It's going to be all right, you'll see. And I'm not that much of a child anymore, for heaven's sake." She laughed. "I'm twenty, you know. I'm fully grown. And, if you want to know the truth, I'd better marry the guy, or I'm going to start sleeping with him anyway. It's gotten to that point."

Aileen sighed. "You're right, Veronica; you are grown and able to make a decision like this yourself. Just be careful, darling. It's so difficult to have good judgment when you're in love."

The time was to come when Veronica would remember her sister's words as if they'd been etched in bronze. *It's so difficult to have good judgment when you're in love.* She went into marriage with Slade blindly, with a trusting heart. And at first she was sure she had done the right thing. The nights in his arms were wild, uninhibited episodes of total fulfillment. They couldn't get enough of each other. Sometimes their lovemaking went on until nearly dawn, and Veronica went to work in a daze while Slade stumbled off to class.

Veronica dropped out of school when they married and found a secretarial job. With that salary plus the small amount of her father's insurance, Slade was able to stay in school. They lived in a one-room garage apartment and counted every penny. Later, Veronica was to look back and remember those as the happiest times of their marriage.

Slade studied feverishly and graduated from law school with top honors, easily passed his bar examination, and then went to work for a prestigious law firm.

Veronica was bursting with pride. It was obvious that Slade was going to be a brilliant trial lawyer. He had a flair for courtroom tactics. His imposing, broad-shouldered figure, his resonant baritone voice, and his magnetic personality exerted a powerful influence on a jury. His knowledge of the law was thorough and impeccable.

Veronica continued to work during the first year of Slade's law career, until his income had risen to the point that they could live comfortably. Then he insisted that Veronica return to school and complete her degree. At that point, she would have been content to forget any further schooling and remain a housewife. But Slade was firm. He said he was committed to seeing she completed her degree.

Afterward, Veronica wondered if that decision was the point when their marriage got into trouble. She was twenty-three when she returned to the classroom. She'd been away for two years. She had to throw all her energy into studying to keep up. Meanwhile, Slade was giving his all to building his law reputation. They saw little of each other that year. Veronica was busy with her schoolwork. Slade was dedicated to becoming an outstanding young criminal lawyer. He was engrossed in his career, often spending weeks out of town on important criminal cases.

It's just for this year, Veronica reassured herself, missing him dreadfully when they were apart. As soon as I graduate we'll be together all the time again.

During this time, Aileen went through a new crisis in her life. Veronica had been so wrapped up in her schoolwork that she hadn't seen her sister in several weeks. One Saturday morning, Aileen came by for a visit. Veronica was shocked.

Aileen looked haggard. Her dull eyes were darkly circled. She was nervously chain-smoking. "What is it, Aileen?" Veronica asked, frightened at her sister's appearance. "Are you ill?"

"I suppose you could say that." Aileen suddenly put her face in her hands and began sobbing.

Veronica quickly led her to a couch and sat beside her, trying to comfort her. Up to this point in their lives, Aileen had been the strong one. Veronica had gone to her with her problems since Aileen had taken the place of her parents. Suddenly their roles were reversed. Now it was Aileen who needed help.

"I'm so ashamed." Aileen choked. "I never dreamed I could let my life get into such a mess." She drew a shuddering breath, making an effort to gain control of her voice. "Ever since William tossed me and the kids out to marry his nurse, I've been seeing a lot of men, Veronica. I'm—I'm afraid your sister has let her morals go to the dogs." She bit her lip, her eyes averted. "I'm pregnant, Veronica," she blurted out.

Veronica was speechless. Aileen was the last person

on earth she could have expected to get into this kind of predicament. Aileen had been the straitlaced member of the family. She had married young. She raised her children with a firm hand. Her character had been the rock of the family, Veronica had always thought.

But, looking back, she remembered the change that came over Aileen when her marriage broke up. She'd become bitter and rebellious. She'd quit going to church. Veronica knew she'd started dating a lot of different men. It had been a phase she was going through, Veronica had thought, a form of defense and escape to run away from her broken heart and sense of failure.

Veronica remembered all the times she had cried on her sister's shoulder and needed comforting and help. Now she could return a bit of her older sister's kindness. She put her arm around Aileen. "Chin up, sis. We've been through some tough ones together and came up swimming. We'll do it again, together, now. Just hang on a bit."

Aileen gazed at her with a helpless expression. "It's not so much about myself I care. But what will it do to my kids, Veronica? And that beast, William. If he finds out I'm having a child out of wedlock, he might use it somehow to take Michael and Debbie away from me."

"I'm going to talk to Slade," Veronica said determinedly. "He'd know how to handle anything legal William might attempt."

Slade came to their rescue like a hero. Veronica fell all the more hopelessly in love with him for the kindness and concern he showed Aileen. The idea that he might one day turn into every bit as much a rat as William and go so far as to use Aileen's tragedy for his own selfish purposes was as foreign as the most distant galaxy from Veronica's mind.

"Abortion is out of the question," Aileen had said firmly. "I'm not going to add that to my conscious."

"You don't have to," Slade assured her gently. "I can arrange for you to discreetly have your child in an institution for unwed mothers in another city. Then we can handle the adoption procedure. Unless you want to keep the child."

Aileen shook her head. "It would be better the other way. I'm in no condition to take on raising another child by myself." Tears trickled down her cheeks. "I only want to be sure that whoever gets my baby will be good people," she said chokingly.

Slade had been a kind brother-in-law during this crisis in Aileen's life. And after Aileen's trauma of having her baby boy and giving it up for adoption, Slade had joined Veronica in trying to get Aileen's life back on an even footing. It was Slade who introduced Aileen to Brian Davis, a fellow attorney who had gone into politics. Brian was running for the state legislature. Romance had quickly blossomed between Aileen and Brian. A few weeks after they met, they were quietly married. Slade and Veronica had stood up with them at the altar.

Aileen did not tell Brian about the illegitimate child she had mothered. She was frightened that a man with political ambitions wouldn't dare have a wife who had been involved in anything scandalous or sordid. She had sworn Veronica and Slade to secrecy about the matter. Slade had assured her that there was no way any of Brian's political enemies could ever find out about the child she'd had out of wedlock. Veronica hadn't felt it was wise for Aileen to marry Brian without telling him the truth about her past, but she'd finally agreed to Aileen's request.

From that point on, Aileen's life had gotten back on

a happy course with her new husband. But Veronica's marriage was coming under more pressure as Slade's ambitious law career made increasing demands on him.

"I'm worried about you," Aileen told Veronica one day. "You and Slade are never together. He's forever off on some courtroom trial. You're buried in your schoolwork."

"I don't like it, either," Veronica assured her, "but it's only temporary. I'll graduate this spring, and then I'm chucking the schoolbooks out the window."

Aileen nodded. "That's good. I don't want you to go through the mess I went through in my first marriage. William was like Slade, totally immersed in his medicine practice. Because of his profession, he was spending more of his time with doctors and nurses than with me. One of his nurses, especially. I've noticed," she added, looking at Veronica closely, "that one of the junior law partners in his firm who works closely with him on some of these cases is a woman."

Barbara Lange.

Veronica winced. Aileen had touched a sore spot. Veronica was very much aware of the attractive female lawyer on Slade's staff. Barbara was a law-school graduate who had gone to work for the law firm shortly after Slade accepted a partnership there. She was a dark-haired beauty with a brilliant mind and a sexy body. Veronica's peace of mind was not helped by the fact that she'd seen Barbara give Slade that special look of a woman interested in a man. At a party given by the local bar association, Barbara had told Veronica, "That's quite a man you're married to." The raven-haired woman had glanced across the room to where Slade was standing. Veronica saw the pupils in her eyes distend with an intensity that made Veronica furious. Then Barbara's gaze had swung back to

Veronica, and with cool insolence she'd said, "If you ever get tired of him, please let me know. I'm dying to sleep with him on a regular basis."

Shock had taken Veronica's breath away. Then she understood that a blatant frontal attack was Barbara's style. She was a calculating woman who knew what she wanted and could be ruthless in getting it.

The two women measured one another with icy stares. It was plain enough that from that moment they would be competing for the same man. Stiff-lipped, Veronica had retorted, "I'm certainly not tired of Slade, nor he of me. He's my husband and I'll thank you to keep that in mind."

"You sound very sure of yourself."

"I am."

A corner of Barbara's lips moved in a taunting smirk. "Don't be. When Slade and I are on an out-of-town court trial, we stay at the same motel. It's a short distance from my room to his." With that, she walked away.

Veronica spent several sleepless nights worrying about that parting shot. Aileen wasn't the only person to warn her about Barbara Lange. Slade was a gregarious man who had surrounded them with a wide circle of friends. Several of the wives among their friends made veiled remarks that Veronica knew were intended as warnings. Sensing a predatory female on the prowl after a friend's husband, they felt a mutual concern to alert Veronica about the threat to her marriage.

Veronica wasn't sophisticated enough or experienced enough to know exactly how to go about handling the threat. She loved Slade so much, had put him on such a pedestal, that she couldn't conceive of his betraying her. On the other hand, she couldn't lightly dismiss the threat of Barbara Lange. The woman made no bones about her desire for Slade. And she was extremely attractive, ambitious, and skillful at using her sex appeal to get what and where she wanted. Beside her, Veronica felt naive, unsure of herself. She thought she was definitely not as glamorous as Barbara. Surely a man as virile as Slade would be aware of the sensuality of his female law partner.

Veronica counted on the end of the school year to bring Slade and herself closer together again. She was frightened by the gulf that had grown between them. Slade was totally preoccupied by his law career. They no longer shared the moments of close communication that were so important. She couldn't bring herself to tell Slade of her feelings of insecurity about Barbara Lange, afraid she would sound like a jealous, nagging wife and drive him further away from her. But she bolstered her sinking morale by telling herself that once her schoolwork was behind her, she would become closer to Slade again; she would go with him on his out-of-town cases; they would rediscover the closeness of their early months of marriage.

Ironically, it was the very week she completed her final exams that she got the anonymous phone call that brought her life crashing down in ruins.

That week, Slade had gone to a nearby city to defend a client in a highly publicized murder trial. Veronica had been buried under a term paper and tests that would wrap up her schoolwork. The phone rang shortly after breakfast. She didn't recognize the woman's voice on the other end of the line; there was an obvious effort at disguising the identity. Probably a handkerchief over the mouthpiece gave it the muffled quality. Later, Veronica thought it had been vaguely familiar and decided it was one of the wives in their circle of friends who had been trying to warn her. The muffled voice said, "I think you should know what's going on behind your back. Your husband is having an affair with Barbara Lange. If you want proof, drive to the Sunset Motel in Bayview and walk into your husband's room unannounced."

There was a click. The phone went dead. Veronica held the instrument in her numb fingers while icy moments ticked away. She was vaguely aware of the dull thudding of her heart.

Then she moved in a daze, scarcely aware of getting dressed and walking out to her car. She sat behind the wheel for several minutes as a dreadful battle was waged in her heart. She was suddenly faced with a choice that would have a terrible impact on her life. She could ignore the call, try to live a fantasy with Slade, pretending he was faithful, and try to stifle the ugly images that were searing her mind at this very moment.

She closed her eyes tightly against burning tears and shook her head. That would be burying her head in the sand—only delaying the humiliating time when Slade would ask her for a divorce so he could dump her and marry his law partner.

Blazing anger suddenly slashed through her. No, she wasn't going to take this meekly. She was going to find out the truth now and face it!

Furiously she slammed the car into gear and drove out of the yard with tires squealing.

Bayview was less than an hour's drive away. Slade had told her he had decided to get a motel room there rather than commute home every night because he couldn't spare the time lost in driving back and forth. Had she been a blind, trusting fool to believe him? Had he made up the excuse so he could spend every night in a motel bed with Barbara Lange?

She found out soon enough. At the front desk of the

Bayview motel she identified herself as Slade Huntington's wife and obtained a key to his room. By then it was past ten o'clock, and Slade, of course, was at the courthouse. But the evidence in the room was plain enough.

Across the unmade bed was carelessly tossed one of Barbara's dresses and a filmy negligee. Her lipstick smear was a scarlet mark on his pillow. At the foot of the bed, their suitcases stood close together.

Veronica stood there for a moment, torturing herself with the scene, burning every detail into her mind forever. She visualized in sordid detail what had taken place in that bed last night—the other woman clasped in an embrace of ecstasy in her husband's arms. The echoes of their whispered exclamations of passion seemed to linger in the air. The intimacy they had shared tainted the air like heavy musk.

Veronica covered her face with her hands, but the scene burned through her fingers. Shame, anger, and humiliation spun together in a fiery ball that blazed in her chest.

It was Aileen's tragedy being reenacted. Just as her sister had warned her. Slade had used Veronica exactly the way Aileen's first husband had used her. Slade had been desperate to get through law school. He found himself a trusting, naive girl, dumb enough to fall blindly in love with him and work to put him through school. Then, just as with Aileen's doctor husband, Slade had buried himself in his career and become involved with a woman in his profession. The drama lacked only the final scene, when Slade announced he was kicking Veronica out to marry his law partner, to make the scenerio identical to Aileen's experience.

Only, in this case, Veronica wasn't going to wait around for that final humiliation!

In a blind rage, Veronica ran from the motel. She drove home at suicidal speed. There, she tore clothes from racks in the closet, stuffed them in suitcases. One primitive urge controlled her . . . to run away and hide.

This was one crisis she couldn't share with Aileen. She would be too ashamed, after the way Aileen had warned her. And she was too humiliated to face their friends.

In the emotional storm that racked her, the child in her took possession of her actions. She thought of the refuge she had known, the happy, sunny days when she was a carefree child growing up on her grandparents' ranch. That was the place she would go now to escape the heartache of being a grown woman. She quickly made flight reservations. She drew only enough money from their joint bank account to pay for the trip. That much, at least, Slade owed her. But she didn't want another thing from him.

She scrawled five words on a farewell note to Slade. "Our marriage is finished—goodbye!"

Veronica's grandparents had started out as home-steaders in the great silent heartland of Australia. They had prospered and became one of the country's big landowners. Their station (ranches of their kind were called stations in their country) was a huge, sprawling area of rugged land, where modern cowboys in air-planes checked on their herds and often rode Jeeps and motorcycles at roundup time.

Their home, designed along colonial-type architectural lines, was comfortable, with large airy rooms and shady verandas and porches. It was built with heavy timbers. Miles from the cities and populated areas, the ranch nevertheless had all modern conveniences, including telephones, radios, and plumbing. They generated their own electricity on the premises. Hospitality was generous and sincere. Neighbors scattered hundreds of miles apart in these wide-open spaces often gathered at the big station for weekends of visiting and celebrations.

These warm, gentle people welcomed their granddaughter back into their home and encircled her with the kindness and love she desperately needed. She was like a wounded animal, creeping to the one safe hiding place where she could lick her hurt places.

She drenched herself with sunshine. She rode for hours, until her horse was tired and she was exhausted. Her grandparents knew her marriage had gone on the rocks, but they were wise enough not to ask for painful details.

She wrote a brief note to Aileen. After a few weeks passed, she was able to write a longer letter, explaining that she had left Slade and why. Aileen replied that Slade had gotten in touch with her, trying to locate Veronica, but she had obeyed Veronica's wishes that she tell him nothing.

The ranch life had been good medicine for Veronica during the first phase of shock and depression. But after a few weeks, she became restless and wanted to begin the process of starting a new life. Her college education had prepared her for a career in advertising and public relations, a field that had interested her since she'd helped her father during summer vacations in the small manufacturing firm he'd operated when they moved to the States. She'd decided to pursue that profession in one of Australia's larger cities, and she'd moved to Sydney. There, she'd gone to work for a public-relations firm, where she'd gotten two years of excellent practical experience.

During that time she'd had no contact with Slade at

all. She had steadfastly refused to allow Aileen to tell him where she was. She'd made no attempt to start divorce proceedings, assuming it would be too complicated with her being in another country. It was not a matter she wanted to think about. She'd pushed it to the back of her mind, assuming that Slade would have taken care of the legal business. It should have been a simple matter in their state with its no-fault divorce laws. Even if she wasn't there, she thought, there was some kind of legal procedure whereby Slade could get the divorce on his own. These days, in most states, divorce was simple and easy to obtain.

She had been shocked and dismayed to return after two years to find herself still very much married to Slade Huntington.

Why, in the name of sanity, had he not divorced her? Had she pricked his colossal male ego so much by deserting him that he had stubbornly refused to get the divorce, biding his time until he could get revenge? Perhaps he'd wanted to remain her husband so he could force this legal rape on her when she returned, satisfying his damaged male ego by humiliating and degrading her this way. Yes, that would make sense, considering his ruthless character.

And there was another, more practical explanation for his motives. He was being cold and calculating to further his political career. Perhaps he'd already had it in the back of his mind to go into politics when she was still living with him. Now he preferred not to have a messy divorce as a blot on his public image. Theirs was a conservative western state where voters could be swayed by such matters as a candidate's personal and family life. His opponent would certainly make the most of a personal scandal in his past.

But why would Barbara stand calmly in the wings,

content to remain his mistress while he remained legally married to Veronica? Again, she had to find the answer in the other woman's character. Barbara Lange was a modern, liberated woman, every bit as ambitious and conniving as her lover, Slade. She was ambitious for him, wanting him to climb the political ladder. She had the satisfaction of knowing he loved her. Perhaps she preferred that kind of arrangement, since it took nothing away from her role as an independent woman. Slade had no doubt assured her that he would divorce Veronica and marry her as soon as his political goals were reached. How far would his ambition carry him? To the governor's mansion eventually?

At this stage of his political career, Slade needed Veronica as part of his public image. As Aileen had put it, she was *useful* to him. But there was a side to him even more ruthless than Veronica had thought and perhaps Barbara had suspected. He might have told Barbara that the marriage would continue in name only. But he wasn't going to be content for her just to pose as his wife. He wanted his revenge, and he was planning to find it in bed. With a chill, Veronica heard his parting words echo in her mind: *"Get your things packed. Tomorrow night you'll spend in my home . . . in my bed."*

Was it a threat or a promise? A warning to keep her in line? All too soon, she realized with a sinking heart, she was going to find out. . . .

Chapter Three

V eronica spent that evening packing her suitcases. It was the most distasteful chore she'd ever faced. She had desperately tried to think of some way out of this trap. But she could find no escape from the heartbreaking weapon Slade held over her. No matter what the cost might be, she could not wreck her sister's life. Brian loved Aileen, but how would he react to being told that his wife, whom he adored and respected, had borne an illegitimate child and kept that ugly secret from him? Veronica shook her head tearfully. It would place a strain on any marriage. She couldn't take the chance of calling Slade's bluff. Aileen had suffered too much in her life.

She looked around the small, comfortable efficiency apartment that she had rented just a few weeks ago. She had planned for it to be her home for some time. Even in this short time, she'd begun giving it personal touches with plants, prints, family pictures, her favorite books and records in the bookcase.

Now she wished desperately that she had remained in Australia. Why had she foolishly returned to the United States? Her reasons hadn't been clear in her own mind. After two years away, she had begun to feel a powerful emotional pull drawing her back here. Part of it was missing her sister. As much as she loved her grandparents, Veronica felt closer to Aileen and her children. They were her real family. Her career had figured in her decision to return, too. She'd thought she would have more of a future here.

Had the memory of Slade unconsciously been part of the magnetic pull drawing her back, like a moth to the flame? As much as she loathed him, it had not been easy to erase from her memory the passion they had shared. She doubted if she would ever again find that kind of abandon in another man's arms. After all, they had lived together for over three years. A lot of bittersweet memories could pile up in that length of time—memories that one simply could not sweep out with last week's garbage.

Then she thought angrily that if some kind of perverse emotions over Slade had been partly responsible for her return, they had been purely unconscious, and she hereby renounced them! After the face-to-face encounter with Slade in her office today that had refreshed her memory of his ruthless macho nature, she had renewed her bitter fury toward him.

That made her plight all the more desperate. She jammed things into the suitcases with angry frustration. And when she was packed at last, she went to bed to toss restlessly on her pillow, alternating between tears and murderous anger.

The next day, Slade called to tell her he would pick her up late in the afternoon. She went to her office for a while but couldn't concentrate enough to accomplish anything productive. She returned to the apartment, and at five-thirty a sharp knock told her Slade had arrived.

When he entered the room, his brown-eyed gaze swept over her in a drenching glance, then made a quick survey of the apartment. Knowing well his ability to catalogue a storehouse of details in a glance, she was sure he could recite an inventory of every item in her apartment, plus a detailed description of the soft brown jersey dress she wore today.

"Well, all packed and eager to go, I see," he murmured with a quirk of his lips.

"Packed, but certainly not eager," she retorted. "I'm sure that condemned prisoners have been about as eager to walk to the gallows."

He raised an eyebrow. The golden specks swirled in his deep brown eyes as his gaze intensified. She could feel the electrical impact. It made a shiver race down her spine. He was a devil, but he could exert a powerful influence on other people.

He took a step toward her. Instinctively she shrank back. "You mean you don't have a welcome kiss for your husband?" The irony in his voice raked her.

"Certainly not! The only thing I'd welcome would be seeing your name in the obituary column."

Her verbal stab found a mark. His face paled, and the swift anger that flashed in his eyes matched hers. "Well, we'll see about that," he murmured softly. "Tonight, when you're naked, in bed with me, perhaps you'll feel differently. I seem to remember that for all your haughty, prim and proper ways, you can turn into a little pagan when we have sex."

Her face went from pale to scarlet. "The woman you're talking about no longer exists. Where you're concerned, Slade Huntington, I am a frigid statue made out of ice."

A pencil line appeared between his brows as he gazed at her with a puzzled expression, as if struggling to unravel a baffling enigma. Finally he shrugged. "We'll see. . . ."

"No, we won't *see*," she cried. "I want to get

something straight between us here and now, Slade. I'm not going to allow you to forget for one moment that you are forcing me to do this under the vilest kind of duress. You know I love my sister more than anyone else—that I'd do anything to protect her. You've used that to force me into this unholy role as your wife. I'll play the role in public because I have to, but when we're alone it's a different matter. I feel nothing but contempt for you and what you're doing!"

"Well," he said coldly, "at least you feel something. Even anger can turn into passion."

"Not in my case," she retorted, tossing her luxuriant chestnut hair as she raised her chin.

He looked at her with an expression of conflicting emotions, as if toying with an impulse to slap her. But instead he shrugged and picked up her suitcases.

They drove in cold silence across town. She saw that he had acquired a large, sleek Cadillac. Obviously, his law career had blossomed. He was rapidly becoming affluent.

Where was he taking her? Surely not back to the apartment they had shared when they were married. She would dread returning to those rooms filled with so many memories. Perhaps, she thought hopefully, he had moved into a bachelor's apartment. But when they arrived at their destination, she was astounded to find it was neither.

Slade turned into the driveway of a lovely two-story colonial-style home in an affluent neighborhood. The graveled driveway wound between flowering oleander bushes. Bougainvillea flowered in red splashes against the white columns of the home. In this arid climate it was necessary to irrigate, and sprinklers swished over the thick carpet of freshly mowed lawn.

"What are we doing here?" she asked curiously.

"We live here," he said, waving a suntanned hand at the spacious house. "This is home."

"Your home?" she exclaimed with genuine surprise.

"*Our* home, now that you're moving back in with me. Yes, I bought it a few months ago. A home is the best investment one can make to combat inflation. And I felt confident you would come back one day. I wanted to have a suitable home waiting for you."

She continued to stare at the elegant home with surprise that gradually turned into cold realization. "Now I understand," she suddenly exclaimed. "It's all part of the new image, isn't it? You want the voting public to see you as a solid, respectable, taxpaying, property-owning citizen, right? A wife and a home in a residential neighborhood are important ingredients of that image. But where did you ever get the money to buy a place like this? I knew you were doing well, but it must have taken quite a bit of money to swing a deal like this."

"The down payment," he said, choosing to ignore her cynical appraisal of his motives, "was a gift from a grateful client whom I kept out of jail."

Her gaze moved from the house to his face. "That was something I never could quite understand. How can you, in good conscience, defend criminals who ought to be in jail?"

"The Constitution," he pointed out, "gives all of us right to competent legal counsel. Every person accused of a crime is considered innocent unless a judge or jury finds him guilty. In the case of the client who gave me the down payment for this house, the man was innocent. It would have been a terrible miscarriage of justice to have put him behind bars for twenty years. I saved twenty years of the man's life. Is that something to be ashamed of?"

"I suppose not," she conceded, "if the man was innocent. But I've seen you at work in a courtroom. With your theatrics and dramatics and and spellbinding, you can twist most juries around your little finger. And I don't entirely mean that as a compliment."

"You don't? My fellow barristers would take it as quite a glowing compliment. However, I'm changing careers to become a public servant. Perhaps you'll find that more to your liking."

"I don't find anything about you to my liking, and I seriously doubt, knowing you as I do, that there is anything in the slightest way altruistic in your political career."

Again he gave her a curious, searching look and shrugged. He opened his door, slid from behind the wheel, came around to open her door, then took her suitcases from the trunk.

They crossed the broad veranda between the stately columns. Slade pressed the doorbell. The front door was opened almost immediately by a tall, middle-aged woman. Her prominent cheekbones and bronze complexion indicated an Indian heritage.

"Veronica, I want you to meet Mrs. Salinas, my housekeeper. Mrs. Salinas, this is the lady I told you about—my wife, Veronica, who has returned to be the mistress of the house."

"Welcome home, *señora*," the housekeeper said with a warm smile. "Please call me Josie."

"Hello, Josie," Veronica replied, reassured by the woman's friendly brown eyes. She needed all the emotional comfort and support she could find as she crossed the threshold of Slade Huntington's home. When the door closed behind her, it was like the final slam of a deadly trap from which there was no escape.

Veronica drew a deep breath, squared her shoulders

resolutely, and glanced at her surroundings. The home had been tastefully furnished. From the hallway she had a view of the living room. She saw a velvet couch, rich mahogany coffee and end tables, luxurious carpeting, an occasional chair upholstered with a lovely brocade material, tasteful prints on the walls.

"The client you saved from going to jail must have been extremely grateful," she said dryly.

"He was," Slade agreed, "as well as generous and, fortunately for me, quite prosperous."

For a moment a wave of sadness swept over Veronica as she thought of how things might have been for them. If Slade had been a faithful husband, she would have joyfully made this lovely house her home, grateful that their early struggles had rewarded them so well. But under the present circumstances, it could only be her prison.

Then, as she took in the scene around her, a fresh wave of bitterness assailed her. Slade could never have furnished the home so tastefully, choosing drapes with such a deft decorator's skill. She sensed a woman's touch here. Coldly she remarked, "I suppose Barbara Lange helped pick the furnishings?"

"As a matter of fact, she did," Slade said slowly, giving her a penetrating look. "You had disappeared on me. I was grateful for the help Barbara offered. If you don't like her choices you can make changes."

An acid retort rose to Veronica's lips, but, remembering the presence of the housekeeper, she stifled it and instead dismissed the matter with a silent, angry shrug.

"Go ahead with what you were doing, Mrs. Salinas," Slade told his housekeeper. "I'll take Mrs. Huntington's things upstairs."

Reluctantly Veronica followed Slade up the winding

carpeted stairway. He opened a bedroom door. "For the time being, you may use the guest room. After two years away from me, I can understand your wanting some privacy. But as soon as you're adjusted, we'll move you into my room."

She gave him a murderous glance that told him she'd never adjust to sleeping in his bed again. How could he have the gall to even suggest it? He had used her to finance his last year in college, just as Aileen's husband had done, and now he wanted to use her again to further his political ambitions. But that wasn't enough. He wanted to use her in bed, too. His ruthlessness knew no bounds!

Slade deposited her luggage at the foot of the bed. "Mrs. Salinas is preparing an evening meal for us. When she's through she can help you unpack."

"I can manage," Veronica said shortly. She looked around the room. Again, the furnishings, from the fluffy yellow curtains to the utterly feminine bed with its lacy canopy, were evidences of Barbara Lange's touch. Under other circumstances, Veronica would have loved the room with its sunny floor-to-ceiling windows and its cheerful decorator colors of yellow and white. But now she hated it. How she was going to despise sleeping in a bed Barbara had picked out! Had Barbara slept in it? she wondered. But of course not. Barbara would have spent her nights here in Slade's bed.

"I plan for us to have dinner here," Slade told her. "Then we're going to a meeting of my election committee. I'll introduce you to my campaign manager, and he can fill you in on the strategy he has planned. This will be your first public appearance as the candidate's wife. You'll want to dress up a bit."

Veronica felt a fresh wave of resentment and rebellion, but there was little she could do about her feelings. The weapon he held over Aileen's marriage was too deadly. She thought resignedly that she must practice silently gritting her teeth.

After Slade left the room, Veronica unpacked some of her things, hanging her dresses in the closet. That done, she inspected the adjoining bathroom. It was spacious. Her feet sank ankle deep in soft white carpeting. A mirror covered an entire wall above a tiled vanity. Soft shades of aquamarine tiles blended with eggshell-white walls.

Veronica stared at her reflection in the wide mirror. She was pale. Her mouth looked strained, her eyes tired. Small wonder! She felt drained emotionally and physically. A long, hot shower, she thought, might restore her so she could face tonight's ordeal.

She undressed, opened the frosted-glass shower door, and adjusted the water flow to a steamy warmth. She stepped in, welcoming the caressing heat of the shower. Tiny needles danced over her bare flesh, relaxing tense muscles, causing her nerve ends to tingle. She was wrapped in a cocoon of steamy fog. There was only the sound of splashing, splattering water. A dreamy feeling of being safe and pampered stole through her.

Suddenly a dark shadow fell across the shower door. The frosted door opened with a snap. Veronica screamed. She backed against the wet tile, her incredulous gaze riveted on the broad-shouldered form of a nude man stepping into the shower with her.

"Slade, get out of here!" she cried. "Have you gone completely insane?"

He gave her a brooding stare through the billowing clouds of steam. "Hardly. I think I'm acting quite rational for a man who hasn't seen his wife in two years." His gaze swept down her figure, scalding her with humiliation. "Still as lovely as I remembered," he murmured thickly.

She tried ineffectually to cover herself with her washcloth. "You're despicable! Get out or I'll scream for help."

He chuckled mockingly. "Who would come to your rescue? Certainly not Mrs. Salinas, even if she heard you all the way downstairs, which I doubt."

He took a bar of soap from its holder and began working up a thick lather in his big hands. "I remember you liked to have your back scrubbed," he explained. "When I heard your shower, I thought I'd take care of that chore for old times' sake."

"Never mind! I can manage."

But he moved toward her. She shrank even farther back against the wall of the shower. His soapy hands grasped her arms to turn her around. She struggled momentarily but only succeeded in slipping on the wet floor and falling against him. A fiery shock exploded inside her at the contact of their wet bodies.

Then he had her turned around. His soapy hands began sliding over her rigid back in a caressing motion. She stared wide-eyed at the tile inches from her nose, her wet fists clenched, her teeth clamped tightly together. This must be a bad dream, she thought frantically. The pounding water echoing from the tile walls around her, the billowing fog that now threatened to suffocate her, created a sense of unreality. She couldn't be standing here naked in the shower with Slade Huntington. She *couldn't* be!

But the touch of his strong hands told her otherwise. His fingers moved with familiar, expert skill around her neck and shoulders, then up and down her spine, gradually robbing her back of its stiffness in spite of everything. She tried not to allow traitorous memories to steal into her mind—memories of the many times his touch had known her body in intimate caresses like this. Yet, as his hands moved over her in a trip of exploration, they seemed to be recalling every curve, every contour, like a blind person's fingers tracing the Braille of a book once committed to memory.

Her heart began pounding wildly as his soapy palms slid under her armpits and found her breasts. She closed her eyes tightly. "No . . . no . . ." she whimpered between clenched teeth, but the protestation was directed more at the growing heat in her own body than at Slade.

Gently he turned her to face him. She refused to look at him. She could hear his deep breathing as he lathered her body, massaging her with a loving touch, relentlessly awakening responses that had slumbered for two long years.

Wildly, desperately, she battled with the growing tide of passion that threatened to sweep away her sanity. What a traitor her body was! Her legs grew weak. Strength ebbed from her muscles. Hunger became a molten flame deep within her. Slade had taught her body the meaning of passion . . . and it remembered well. . . .

Her breasts, glistening in the streaming water, rose and fell swiftly. She opened her eyes. His broad-shouldered football player's body filled the shower like a giant's, towering over her.

The emotions that had ruled her heart only moments ago—anger, humiliation, resentment—had been swamped by a flood of primitive desire. She no longer had the strength to fight the weakness of the flesh. She was incapable of rational thought.

Slade murmured her name. Then his arms were

around her in a hungry, crushing embrace. His lips found hers, and her mouth responded of its own eagerness. Every inch of her body was molded to his. Blood coursed through her arteries in hot, quick surges.

Then he swept her up in his arms, carried her out of the shower, their bodies still wet and slick with soap. Veronica was dimly aware of being gently settled on the thick white carpet. She was limp with surrender, giving herself up totally to emotions that rose to a blinding crescendo. . . .

Chapter Four

The shower spray again drummed against her body, but her emotions had experienced cataclysmic upheavals since she'd first stepped under the shower an hour ago. Now her body felt the imprint of Slade's lovemaking like an indelible tattoo that the shower could not rinse away, no matter how hard she scrubbed. In the aftermath of passion, her mind was icy clear again, and in that shocked sanity she was appalled at what she had done. She despised herself for being so weak, and she was furious at her traitorous body that even now felt relaxed and languorous in the afterglow of their violent lovemaking.

How humiliated she felt! Slade's look of triumph ground into her pride, making her grit her teeth. The last thing on earth she had wanted to do was to allow him to make love to her. How could she possibly have been so irrational, feeling toward Slade as she did? She tried to make some sense of her actions. It must have been a biological hunger stored up from two years of celibacy. Not just any man could have taken advantage of her vulnerability in that way. Probably no other man on earth. She had, in her young lifetime, been intimate with only one man, Slade Huntington, and though she would like to erase every shred of lovemaking from her conscious remembrance, the chemistry and biology of her body had its own needs, its own throbbing desires.

Slade's caresses had awakened a thousand sensual memories. Slade, damn him, had programmed her body to dissolve into a burning, quivering mass of desire when he unlocked her inhibitions with his skillful lovemaking. He knew how to make her shed all restraint, how to thrill her to mounting waves of ecstasy until the joy bordered on pain. He had spoken the truth when he said he could turn her into a pagan in bed. Her face burned as she seemed to hear her choked gasps and cries of ecstasy echoing from the walls of the bathroom, taunting her.

Slade was a sensual man, and he had made her into a sensual woman, awakened to every delicious thrill sensitive nerve ends could experience.

He had satisfied himself with her and he returned to his room, leaving her to face her self-recriminations alone. She had returned to the shower to scrub herself furiously, as if she could somehow wash away Slade's intimate touches. No longer did she languish under steaming billows of warmth. That had partly been her undoing in the first place! The shower had put her off guard, had made her feel relaxed and sensual even before Slade had so boldly joined her.

No more hot showers for her. She turned the handles all the way to cold and shivered under the icy sting that cleared her mind and shocked the last vestiges of weakness from her flesh.

Covered with goose bumps, she turned off the shower, stepped out, and dried vigorously with a rough bath towel until her body was a glowing pink.

She caught her reflection in the mirror. "You'd better feel ashamed, old girl," she said sharply. "Just make certain a bloody idiotic thing like this doesn't happen again!"

It was easy to make that firm resolution now, and to

believe it. But would Slade catch her off guard like that again?

He might not even try. She felt certain his had been more an act of revenge than one of seduction. His masculine pride had been injured by her walking out on him. This little sexual interlude had been a kind of victory for him. The look of triumph had been clearly defined in the way he'd looked at her afterward. He had conquered her, had made a mockery out of her rejection of him, and that might have satisfied him. Ambitious, power-driven men like Slade Huntington could be like that, she knew, and now perhaps he would return his energy to conquering his opponent in the political race. Any woman hunger he might have he would satisfy in the arms of his mistress, Barbara Lange.

She brushed her shoulder-length chestnut hair, applied makeup lightly, then decided on what to wear. Slade had suggested that she "dress up a bit" for the meeting with his election committee. She chose a knit suit. The cream-colored jacket was edged in black piping. It was a fitted style with slenderizing princess seams in front and back. The funnel-shaped neckline was styled with a V'd front and button-front openings. It was long-sleeved. The contrasting black self-fabric piping trimmed the neckline, front, and mock pockets. Also color-contrasted was the pull-on skirt designed with knife pleating all around to give her long legs walking ease.

Veronica tightened the elasticized belt around the jacket at her waist, stepped into black high-heeled pumps, then turned before the bedroom full-length mirror, giving herself a critical inspection.

Yes, she looked the part of the smart, stylishly dressed wife of a successful lawyer and political candidate. Then tears stung her eyes. That was exactly what she would be doing—playing a part. She felt like an actress about to go onstage. But there was none of the joy performers experienced. Hers would be a hypocritical role, an act of deception. And she was going to hate every moment of it!

With a sigh, she gathered her courage and started downstairs.

Slade was waiting for her at the foot of the winding stairway, drink in hand. Her face burned as his gaze fastened on her, watching every movement of her body as she descended the stairs.

The golden flecks swirled in the twin whirlpools of his intense brown eyes. His look drew her in, absorbing the essence of her being. "Making love agrees with you," he murmured. "Your face is flushed, your eyes are sparkling. You're lovely."

She returned a look of contempt. "My face is flushed because I'm ashamed. If my eyes are sparkling, it's from anger."

He sipped his drink, his brooding eyes refusing to release her. "I didn't get the impression you found lovemaking so repulsive."

Her flush deepened. "That was purely biological. You used me and I used you to satisfy a physical hunger. There was nothing spiritual involved. I'm ashamed it happened, and you can be certain it will not happen again."

He answered with a long, silent look of contemplation. Then he persisted, "You have to admit that sex is good between us. It was good from the start. Swallow that stiff-necked Aussie pride of yours, Veronica, and admit it—you like going to bed with me."

A bitter retort blistered her lips. Angry words welled up in her, clamoring to be spoken. She had learned the hard way that it took much more than physical attraction to hold a marriage together. It was true that she had once been under an almost hypnotic spell of physical attraction for Slade. *Correction*—she thought with a stab of humiliation—she could *still* be overwhelmed by that attraction, as she had found out to her regret this afternoon. Yes, it was true, sex had been great for them during their marriage, and still was. But a happy marriage demanded more than that from the couple involved. It demanded commitment, trust, mutual respect. Slade had killed that part of it. He had never been committed to their marriage. He had found himself a young, naive, trusting girl, Veronica, so blindly in love with him that she'd made herself a willing meal ticket for him while he finished school and got started in his profession. That accomplished, he had no further real need for her. He'd found another woman more appealing—perhaps his and Barbara's mutual involvement in the pursuit of their law careers had had something to do with it. Perhaps being thrown together in daily contact in their law cases, talking the same language, admiring each other's ability, had given Slade and Barbara Lange a closeness that he hadn't felt with Veronica.

She couldn't analyze their motives, and she wasn't sure she wanted to. She only knew that after she'd discovered their affair, any respect and trust she had once felt for Slade had died. He had killed that part of her, along with her young dreams. She hated him for that. Young dreams come only once in a lifetime.

If he'd let it go at that, it would have been bad enough. But now he had made himself even more despicable by ruthlessly forcing her to pretend they were happily married, just to further his political career.

She burned inwardly to launch into a verbal attack on him, to hurl it all in his face—his duplicity with Barbara Lange, his mistress, the heartless way he had used her. The bitterness of the past two years threatened to explode in her. She wanted to describe that sordid scene in the motel room where he had spent the night with Barbara, and how, after she had seen it, all of her feelings for him had turned into loathing and disgust.

But what little pride she had left kept the outburst bottled up inside her. Her stiff-necked Aussie pride, Slade had called it. Well, he'd left her precious little of that! What she still had, she was going to hold on to.

And what would be accomplished by any verbal accusation she might make? He knew quite well all the details of his affair with Barbara Lange. He knew all about the motel rooms they had shared while he was pretending to Veronica to be a faithful husband. There was no point in refreshing his memory. The man was without conscience. He was utterly ruthless. She wasn't going to give him the satisfaction of seeing her play out the part of a screaming, jealous, wronged wife. The best way to preserve her pride and strike back at him was to show him that she didn't need him, that she cared no more for him than he really cared for her. If he ever demanded an explanation about why she had suddenly deserted him and dashed off to Australia, she planned to tell him that she got bored with him and their marriage.

Let him put that in his pipe and smoke it! It would be the best wound to his swollen ego she could think of. It would salvage her pride, and might even give her the final, bitter victory.

He was glancing impatiently at his heavy platinum wristwatch. "I don't have time to stand here discussing your idiotic female whims. We're going to be late to the meeting if we don't eat at once."

He led her to the dining room, where the housekeeper had set an attractive table with fine china and crystal that sparkled on a white linen cloth. A flower arrangement graced the center of the table. Mrs. Salinas beamed as she hurried from the kitchen, bringing steaming dishes. "I hope you're hungry, Mrs. Huntington."

"Yes, starved." Veronica smiled, then blushed when she remembered that a session of lovemaking with Slade had always left her ravenous. "Oh, Josie," she said, "please call me Veronica."

"Thank you, *señora*," the housekeeper replied with a look of warm friendliness that struck a responsive chord in Veronica. She found herself liking Josie Salinas immediately. It would be good to have a friend in this house of icy hatred.

Mrs. Salinas had prepared a delicious meal of ham- and asparagus-filled crepes, a crisp salad, and hot rolls. Slade poured glasses of chilled white wine.

Veronica ate greedily, but Slade only sipped his wine and picked at his food absently while he poured over a sheaf of papers. No words were exchanged between the two of them during the meal.

She had barely finished when Slade impatiently hurried her out to his car. Their trip to his campaign headquarters was as silent as their meal. Slade was absorbed in his own thoughts. Veronica was content to sit quietly on her side of the front seat, as far away from him as possible. The less conversation she had with Slade Huntington, the better.

When they pulled up at the campaign headquarters, Veronica saw Slade's blown-up image smiling at her from a dozen huge posters covering the storefront windows. Inside, they were met by a noisy crowd, the key members of his campaign committee. It was the typical smoke-filled room.

There was much loud, jolly talk, backslapping, and hand pumping. Veronica found herself being hustled around the room, steered by Slade's firm grip on her arm. She mumbled perfunctory greetings as she was introduced to several dozen people, none of whose names she could possibly remember.

She was intrigued by the feverish devotion a political race could arouse in people. She gazed around at their intense expressions as they looked at their candidate. Slade was a hero to these people, she thought with a peculiar feeling of shock. He was more than an individual—he had become a symbol, a personification of their fervent political convictions.

Slade Huntington for the State Senate. He'll Make Our Government Honest Again.

How ironic was that slogan! If these people knew Slade as she knew him, how disillusioned they would be. . . .

One of the men Slade introduced her to was Jake Foreman, his campaign manager.

Foreman was a tall, slender individual. His face was long, homely, lugubrious. He had glittering black eyes that moved in constant restless glances, like those of a wary soldier on patrol in enemy territory. A heavy diamond ring sparkling on his left hand and a costly wristwatch appeared to be displayed as symbols of financial success. But his obviously expensive suit did not seem to fit comfortably on his lanky frame. He gave Veronica the impression that he wished he could take his coat off and loosen his collar.

He was polite when they were introduced, speaking in a voice that was unusually soft and mellow. He had an air of old-fashioned courtesy. Yet, at the same time, his bright eyes were scrutinizing her closely.

"Perhaps the missus and I could have a private chat?" he asked Slade.

"Sure," Slade replied. "I'll circulate around while you two get acquainted. You'll have a lot of planning to do. . . ."

Slade wandered into the crowd. With a polite bow, Foreman ushered Veronica into a small back room.

The room was furnished with chairs and a table and had a small sink and drainboard and refrigerator.

"Would you care for something to drink, Mrs. Huntington?" Foreman asked, going straight to the refrigerator, which was well stocked.

"Yes, if there's a diet soft drink."

He held up a frosty can. "Will this do?"

"That's fine."

He opened the can with a soft pop and handed it to her along with a paper cup. Then he poured a glass of milk for himself.

"I always keep milk here," he explained. "My ulcer invariably acts up during a political campaign." He chewed an antacid tablet, washed it down with the milk, then took a seat across from her at the table.

"This is your profession—managing political campaigns?" Veronica asked.

He chuckled. "Lord, no. I do get some pay for my services because I believe a man sacrifices some of his worth and dignity to just give away his talents. But the money I earn as campaign manager couldn't begin to support me. Fact is, most campaign managers, even on a national level, are business or professional men who take time off from their jobs to manage a campaign."

"Then you must love politics."

He sipped his milk thoughtfully. "I do find it intensely rewarding and fulfilling, though it can be dirty business at times. Politics, Mrs. Huntington, deals with our society's destiny. As a campaign manager, I can help shape the society in which we live. Not many pursuits provide that opportunity."

He leaned back, his glittering eyes fixed solidly on her. "The American system of democracy is one of mankind's supreme accomplishments. The world has never witnessed so grand a design before . . . a system in which a man is limited only by himself. I was born under extremely poor circumstances. My father was the town drunk. My mother took in washing to keep us from starving. I began my career as a business entrepreneur while still in grammar school. Sold newspapers, washed cars, did yard work when other guys my age were playing football. I dropped out of school in the sixth grade to work. By the time my contemporaries were graduating from high school, I'd saved enough money to open a small hamburger stand. Now I own a chain of fast-food restaurants. My accountant tells me I'm worth a million or so.

"The point of all that is," he went on, "that probably nowhere else in the world would I have had such an opportunity to pull myself up by my bootstraps. In another country, another system, I might have been locked for life into the poor-class stratum in which I was born. This is a land where a man has the freedom to succeed or fail according to his own ability without being enslaved by class or government. I read books constantly, sometimes two a day, and the more I study history and other governmental systems, the more I fall in love with the American system of individual freedom."

She was beginning to get an insight into the character and motives of this soft-spoken, long-faced individual who was directing Slade's political fortunes. Jake Foreman was a success-oriented man, a man driven by inner demons planted in his nature when he was a child. He needed goals to reach for, or he would perish. That, combined with the streak of old-fashioned idealism in his makeup, had produced a man who would be tough to reckon with in the political arena. She could understand why the campaigns he handled were usually successful.

"Forgive me for boring you with so much personal history and philosophy, Mrs. Huntington," he said, "but I believe it is important that we get to know each other well, because I am going to let you in on a little secret: The success or failure of your husband's campaign will largely rest in our hands—yours and mine."

He smiled at her reaction. "You look surprised. Well, let me explain. The campaign manager brings experience and skills to the race that the average office seeker doesn't have. It's the manager's job to build an efficient, effective machine. He has to manage the candidate's funds to the best advantage. He must know the constituency, the mood of the people, their problems, their political prejudices. He needs to understand the media, get along well with people. He has to be cold-blooded and hard-nosed about how to spend campaign funds. He must know how to schedule the candidate's speaking time to the best advantage. There are no college courses you can take to train you for this job. It comes from experience. Winning an election can be a trying, sometimes brutal task, and the campaign manager bears most of the burden.

"So much for the manager—in this case myself. Then we come to you, the candidate's wife. In this state, with its lingering frontier values, a candidate's family life can be either a considerable asset or a dreadful liability.

You must be prepared for our opposition to pounce on any hint of scandal surrounding you and your husband and start a whispering attack, if not an open blast."

Veronica cringed inwardly. What was she letting herself in for? Or, more accurately, what had Slade gotten her into?

"Slade has been evasive whenever I questioned him about you two being separated the past two years," Foreman continued. "Is there anything about the matter you'd care to discuss with me, Mrs. Huntington? I can assure you it won't go any further than these walls."

Veronica withdrew behind her own defenses. She was not about to discuss with Jake Foreman, or anyone else, the painful, humiliating details of her marriage breakup. Coldly she replied, "There was no scandal. I simply left Slade and went back to Australia. Our relationship had disintegrated—"

"It was a trial separation?" Foreman asked with a note of hopefulness. "And now you've patched things up and your marriage is back on solid ground?"

She was at a loss for an answer. How could she tell him the truth, that Slade had blackmailed her into coming back to him? She didn't dare reveal to anyone the dark secret that could destroy her sister's marriage.

But Foreman apparently took her silence for an affirmative reply, for he waved away further discussion. "I've intruded on your personal life too much. We'll simply present a picture of a couple who had some problems in their marriage but overcame them, and now you're back at your husband's side in this important political race. I think voters will accept that and feel sympathetic toward you. But there is one more thing I must know, and please be completely frank with me, Mrs. Huntington." He paused, impaling her with his black-eyed stare. "I need from you your assurance that you'll stick with Slade through the campaign. It could be disastrous for him if you walked out on him again once the campaign gets heated."

Anger flashed through her. He made it sound as if she were the guilty one, as if she had deserted Slade and he were the injured party! But again she had to fight down the bitter denial that boiled up inside her. How she'd love to crucify Slade with the truth! But fear for her sister's happiness made her stifle the words. Slade was ruthless enough to strike back at her through Aileen.

Through stiff lips she forced herself to say, "I—I assure you I'm going to stay with Slade through the campaign."

The lanky campaign manager settled back in his chair, an expression of relief crossing his long, mournful countenance. "Good! You'll be a tremendous asset to him, Mrs. Huntington. You're an attractive, stylish woman with an air of respectability. Voters will like you. And Slade tells me you are trained in the field of public relations. Good! That can be a practical help. You and I can work together to put across a dramatic appeal to the voters of this state."

A sudden mood of nervous energy seized him. "We must defeat Kirk Malden!" he exclaimed. "The man is corrupt. He will do this state a great deal of harm if he remains in office. Unfortunately, he has built a strong political base through his political favors. He's a shrewd politician. He knows how to vote the right way for bills that affect organized groups, such as labor unions, and thus win their endorsement. He has a well-financed campaign. We believe the money is coming from organized crime, though as yet we can't prove it."

Foreman's eyes grew even more brilliant until they

shone like black marbles in his sallow face. "But we're going to give him a run for it! Slade, too, has strong financial backing. Are you familiar with the Clayton family, Mrs. Huntington?"

Veronica frowned thoughtfully. "I believe I have heard the name. They have something to do with a big ranch in the state, don't they?"

"More than one big ranch. The Claytons," Foreman explained, "own vast amounts of property, both ranch-land and oil fields. They are one of the wealthiest, most powerful, most influential families in the state. They are contributing heavily to get Slade elected. The ruling patriarch of the family is Elijah Clayton, a huge, powerful man. Next in line is his son, J. D. Clayton. J.D. is a big, strapping fellow. He dresses and talks like someone out of a John Wayne movie. But don't let his home-on-the-range manner fool you. He's smart, and he's perfectly at ease in the finest hotels in Europe; he's a member of the jet set. I think he puts on that cowboy image for effect. The Claytons will be here tonight, and I want you to meet them. I also want to introduce you to Jim Baxwell, publisher of the *Morning Sun* and a strong supporter of Slade's. He's blasted Kirk Malden in his editorials and has strongly endorsed Slade. He's a powerful ally."

Then he paused. "Any questions, Mrs. Huntington?"

She shook her head.

He smiled. "Then, shall we rejoin the others?" He rose, winced, and rubbed his stomach. He chewed another antacid tablet as they returned to the outer room, where the crowd had grown even larger.

The Claytons had arrived. Jake Foreman took Veronica to meet Elijah Clayton. He was an imposing figure of a man. In his sixties, he had a thick shock of white hair, a florid complexion, eyes like blue diamonds, and a rumbling voice that could rattle windows.

His son, J.D., was equally striking, a blond, blue-eyed broad-shouldered, handsome man in his thirties. As Jake Foreman had predicted, he wore western attire: cowboy boots and a stitched shirt. But his rugged complexion implied that he was no drugstore cowboy. He was escorting a lovely, red-haired young woman. His blue eyes expressed approval as they swept over Veronica with obvious interest.

"I'm mighty pleased to meet you, Mrs. Huntington." He offered to shake hands in the style of western informality. His palm was firm and callused, more evidence of a vigorous outdoor life. Veronica wondered if his western accent was an affectation. She sensed more sophistication in his style than his cowboy speech mannerisms indicated.

"I'd like for you to meet Miss Nichole Clayton," His white teeth flashed against his suntanned complexion. "Nichole is a distant member of the family. That's why we have the same last names."

"Kissin' cousins," Nichole murmured, giving Veronica a sudden, challenging female look, obviously piqued because of the interest J.D. was showing in another woman. She was holding a drink in one hand. From the thickness of her tongue, the way her red hair had tumbled over one eye, and the way she was listing slightly to starboard, Veronica deduced that it was not the first drink she'd had that evening.

A slender young man who bore a striking resemblance to Nichole wandered over to join them. He turned out to be Nick Clayton, Nichole's twin brother.

Veronica was conversing with the Clayton family when she glanced toward the doorway and felt her stomach suddenly cramp in a painful spasm.

Slade had apparently left the building while she was in the back room talking with Jake Foreman. Now Slade was walking back into the room, but he was not alone. Close at his side was a familiar tall, beautiful woman—Barbara Lange! Their heads were together in earnest, intimate conversation. They appeared to be oblivious to anyone else in the room. Veronica felt momentarily paralyzed. She had hoped never to come face to face with Slade's mistress again. Now there was no avoiding her.

Barbara had not changed in the past two years, except perhaps to become even more glamorous. Her raven hair was smartly styled. Her olive complexion was smooth and clear, emphasized by a tiny beauty mark near the left corner of her mouth. Her figure was voluptuous. She was elegantly attired as usual, tonight in a designer creation of clinging red fabric that emphasized the sleek lines of her long legs and the seductive curves of her generous bosom.

Veronica tortured herself with imagining how familiar that bosom and those supple legs must be to Slade.

White-hot fury slashed through her. Slade was worse than contemptible! He had blackmailed her into playing this hypocritical role as his wife, had been sexually intimate with her only a few hours ago, and now he was blatantly flaunting his mistress before her eyes. How she despised him!

She mumbled an excuse and fled to the rest room. She fought hard against bitter, angry tears, but they scalded her eyes and ran down her cheeks. She hid in the room until she regained her composure. Then she washed her face with cold water and repaired her makeup.

At last she felt able to cope with facing other people again and started out. But the door opened. She drew in her breath sharply. Barbara Lange had entered the lounge.

For a deadly moment the two faced each other without speaking. Then Barbara's lips moved in an insolent smile. "Well, the candidate's wife, I see. You're looking well, Veronica. Australia must have agreed with you."

Veronica's heart was thudding painfully. Her clenched fingers were icy. "I really don't have anything to talk with you about, Barbara," she said in a tensely controlled, frigid voice. "Now, if you'll excuse me . . ." She tried to move around the tall, black-haired woman.

But Barbara remained in her path. "We may have to put up with each other for a bit, Veronica. It seems that Slade needs you for the campaign. So we'll probably be seeing one another quite often during the next several weeks."

"That's too bad," Veronica returned cuttingly. "My deepest wish was that I would never have to see or talk to you again."

"And I had the same hope about you. I was so happy when you had the good sense to get out of Slade's life and go back to Australia. Why didn't you stay there?"

"That," Veronica retorted, "is really none of your business, is it?"

"Perhaps." Barbara shrugged, her gaze smoldering darkly. "Except that anything that affects Slade affects me. I had thought you were the naive type. But it was pretty clever of you to turn up here just when Slade is beginning his campaign. You may have more sense than I gave you credit for."

"I didn't plan it this way!" Veronica gasped.

Barbara's winged eyebrow over her left eye raised slightly. "Oh, no? Perhaps you have Slade fooled. But I'm a woman. You don't fool me. You've returned to try and get Slade back, and you knew this would be perfect timing. You knew it would be a political liability for Slade to have an estranged wife on the scene at a time like this, or, even worse, a divorce. You gambled on his needing you to play at being his wife again. You rolled the dice and you won—this round at least. But don't delude yourself into thinking you've won the game."

Barbara's words caused emotions to churn inside Veronica. Part of her felt like laughing at the ridiculous scenario Barbara had concocted. And yet one thing she'd said touched a nerve somewhere deep in Veronica's heart. *You've returned to try and get Slade back.* Was there any truth to that at all? Certainly not in a conscious sense. But had that been a motive deeply buried in her subconscious? She remembered her reaction when Slade walked into her office yesterday—that familiar trembling in her knees, the flush suffusing her body, telling her that the old magic Slade brought with him was still there, as strong as ever. And that spontaneous sexual explosion between them in her bathroom certainly had been dramatic proof that she didn't have Slade entirely out of her system. If she had no more feeling for him at all, why had she come so unglued when she saw him with Barbara tonight?

It was too confusing to sort out. Maybe love was gone, but had passion and anger lingered on, one fanning the flames of the other?

In time, perhaps that, too, would burn itself out and she could safely erase Slade from her life forever.

But as for her deliberately timing her arrival to coincide with Slade's political race in a Machiavellian ruse to get him back, that was pure nonsense! She did derive some satisfaction from Barbara's jealous outburst. It was pleasing to know that the other woman could suffer a bit over Slade, too. Veronica was human enough to accept some profit from this cruel situation.

"It does look like I'm important to Slade right now," she said slowly, testing Barbara's reaction.

The other woman's eyes narrowed. "Slade is just using you," she fired back. "The way he used you to help him get his law degree. You mean nothing more to him than that."

Veronica turned pale. Barbara had won their skirmish by a vital stab. Her pride was mortally wounded. With a killer's instinct, Barbara had struck her most vulnerable spot. It hurt all the more because it was true!

Pushed to the ragged edge of breaking down, Veronica blurted out, "Well, you can put your mind to rest. I don't want Slade back. I despise him. After this race is over, you are more than welcome to him!"

With that, she fled the room, leaving behind a smug Barbara Lange.

Veronica went straight to the bar that had been set up on one side of the room, pushing her way blindly through the crowd. Normally she avoided alcohol. But after her encounter with Barbara, she was in need of a stimulant. "Bourbon and Coke, please," she said to the bartender.

She had just taken her first sip when a strong masculine hand touched her arm. She looked up at the tall, broad-shouldered form of J. D. Clayton. "Mrs. Huntington, I know a quiet place a few blocks from here where they serve really good cocktails. If you'd do me the honor of joinin' me for a drink there, I'd be most grateful. I'd really like to have a talk with you in private."

Surprised Veronica searched his face, uncertain how she should respond. Her gaze turned swiftly to the people around them and picked out Nichole, some distance away, who was giving them a sullen, glowering stare. "I don't think your date would appreciate it if I left with you," Veronica murmured.

The big rancher responded with a smile and a shrug, not taking his gaze from her. "Nichole is family," he said softly. "She's been followin' me around since she was no bigger than a puppy. I'm just like a big brother to her."

Veronica smiled. "She doesn't exactly look at you like a sister. What was it she called you—kissin' cousins?"

J. D. chuckled in his deep baritone. "Lordy, ma'am, don't pay any attention to that. Nichole is just a child with a few romantic notions. She's at the age when she's in love with love."

"Well . . ."

Veronica's gaze turned to the crowd again. And then she saw something that brought back a tight knot of anger inside her. Barbara had rejoined the crowd and was at Slade's side again, so close her hip brushed his in a secret, intimate manner as they laughed and chatted with Jake Foreman.

Veronica flushed, and her gaze swung back, bright with anger now. She gathered up her purse. "All right, thank you, Mr. Clayton. I'd like very much to have that drink with you."

She strode out of the room with the tall man, holding his arm. As they left, she caught sight of Slade's eyes, suddenly aware of her leaving with J. D. Clayton, and she saw an expression of anger knot his jaw.

Chapter Five

*P*lease call me J.D., Mrs. Huntington. That's what all my *amigos* call me. Is it okay if I call you Veronica?"

They had been transported in J. D. Clayton's large, sleek Cadillac several blocks to a private Petroleum Club, which catered to individuals in the oil and ranching business. An elevator had whisked them to a penthouse floor where the club was situated. Now they were seated close together at a small, secluded table. The rich paneling, deep carpets, and quiet, efficient service surrounded them with an air of affluence. It was the kind of club millionaires belonged to. A combo played sophisticated Nashville music in the background.

She sipped a dry martini. "Yes, you may call me Veronica."

"Good." He smiled. "I reckon we're going to be seeing each other quite a bit while this race is going on. Might as well be on a first-name-calling basis. Seems more neighborly."

Veronica settled back, feeling somewhat relaxed as the alcohol sent a sensation of warmth stealing through her body.

She was conscious of J.D.'s steady gaze. It was not unpleasant; rather, her bruised ego felt warmed and flattered by the look of interest she was receiving from a virile, handsome man. Considering how rich and attractive J. D. Clayton was, he could no doubt have his pick of dozens of women. His distant cousin Nichole, for example, a lush nineteen-year-old, beautiful by any standard, appeared to be his for the asking. Veronica's shattered self-esteem drew some nourishment from the thought that J.D. would desert such a lovely young companion for a few stolen moments with her. And the expression in his eyes made it clear that he had not brought her here only to discuss politics.

"I notice that you have a British accent, Veronica," J.D. observed.

"It's Australian," she replied. "Somewhat different from what Americans call British. I'm afraid my speech has never become entirely Americanized."

"I like it. It's one of the many pretty things about you."

Again she felt a flush of pleasurable response. Why she asked herself, should she feel guilty? After the way Slade had treated her, she owed him nothing, least of all faithfulness. Not that she was forming any romantic inclinations toward J. D. Clayton. For the moment she was satisfied to bask in the attention of such a desirable man. Slade had wreaked vicious damage to her self-assurance as a woman.

"You Yanks are dreadful scoundrels at flattery," she countered, trying to keep the conversation light.

"No, I mean it. You are a heck of a good-lookin' woman," J.D. persisted. "I haven't been able to take my eyes off you since we met."

So I've noticed, she thought. Then she met his eyes with a challenging look. "Do you think you should be saying things like that to a married woman?"

He studied her face silently, then murmured, "I kind of wonder if you are a happily married woman. There's a look of sadness about your eyes that I reckon wouldn't be there if you were satisfied with your marriage."

Veronica was disconcerted. The conversation had taken a direction that made her uneasy. She made an attempt to change the subject. "Speaking of accents, you have quite a western accent, J.D. Is it real or put on?"

He laughed. "It's real. I just naturally grew up talkin' this way. By the way, you bein' Australian, maybe you can interpret something for me that only Australians seem to understand. I've always wondered what in thunderation the words in your national folk song 'Waltzing Matilda' mean. I figure it must be something about dancing with a girl named Matilda."

She laughed. "The lyrics are a combination of Australian dialect and slang. 'Waltzing Matilda' means carrying one's bundle or swag on the back . . . sort of backpacking in modern terms."

"Well, what do you know about that! I was a mile off. And then there's something about a 'jolly swagman.' That sure has me stumped."

"Yes, it goes like this." She softly sang the familiar words:

"Once a jolly swagman camped by a billabong
Under the shade of a coolibah tree,
And he sang as he watched and waited till his billy boiled,
'You'll come a waltzing Matilda with me.'"

J.D. grunted. "Catchy melody. But the words are Chinese to me."

She explained. "A swagman is a tramp. A billabong is a water hole. Watching his billy boil—well, a billy is a tin can used to boil water over a campfire for tea. The story of the song is a rather sad tale about the swagman getting caught stealing jumbuck—sheep—from a large landowner, and he commits suicide by jumping into a billabong before the troopers arrest him."

"The poor swagman. But that's what he gets for being a sheep rustler. Over here, we used to hang cattle rustlers on the nearest tree."

They both smiled, but then she felt his gaze become intense again. "Now that you've cleared up the mystery of 'Waltzing Matilda' for me, how about clearing up the mystery of Veronica Huntington?

"What do you mean?" she asked, her uneasiness returning.

"The mystery of the unhappiness in the eyes of such a pretty lady."

Nervously she replied, "Veronica Huntington is a boring subject. It would be more interesting to hear what J. D. Clayton, the son of the richest man in the state, is like."

He chuckled. "Why don't *you* tell me what you think I'm like?"

She cocked her head slightly to one side, studying the tall, bronzed man. He was a handsome brute. His thighs strained at his western-style trousers as if trying to split the seams. His waist was slightly heavy, evidence of rich food and expensive liquor. His face was cut in classic lines, with a Roman nose and a jutting chin. But there was a somewhat spoiled look around his mouth, which was not surprising.

"I'd say," she began, "that you're a man used to having what he wants out of life . . . a bit spoiled, perhaps, but quite charming."

His eyes smoldered. "And suppose I decided I wanted you?"

Her gaze didn't waver. "Well, I'd say you might not *always* get what you want."

"But then again, I might?" His voice had a bantering tone, but an underlying note of resolve that disconcerted her. She realized she must be on guard. Slade had made her quite vulnerable to this kind of attack.

Again she steered the conversation to safer ground. "You really haven't answered my question. What does a rich man like J. D. Clayton do to keep busy?"

He smiled. "Being rich, as you call it, is a full-time job. I'm Daddy's right-hand man in seeing over the ranches and in our other investments. Daddy might have spoiled me, but he's always made me work hard—just as hard as the other hands. I'm often out there on the ranch fixing fences, branding cattle, or roughnecking on one of our oil rigs."

"And when you play, I suppose you hop a jet to Paris, or ski at an exclusive resort, or gamble at Monte Carlo?"

J.D. threw back his head in uninhibited laughter. "Well, you pretty much hit the nail on the head, little lady. Got to admit, I do like to see those dice roll once in a while, or play a hand in an all-night poker game with high stakes. That's part of good livin', right? But that's enough talk about ol' J.D. Let's talk about Veronica Huntington. I'd say you like the outdoors as much as I do. Your complexion has the healthy glow of fresh air, and those freckles across your nose look like they were put there by the sun."

She squirmed. "I don't consider my freckles one of my strong points. But, yes, it's the outdoor life for me, too. I also grew up on a ranch, my grandparents'. And I rode horses by the time I could walk."

"Did you!" he exclaimed enthusiastically. "Then you'll have to go riding with me sometime on our ranch. If you like horses, you'll sure enjoy some of the fine animals in our stables. How about it, Veronica?"

"It's . . . tempting," she admitted, picturing herself riding beside this big man who could make her feel so feminine and desirable by the attention he was showering on her. She felt instinctively that he was spoiled and self-centered and probably trained by his father to be utterly ruthless in his business dealings. But he could also be extremely charming and self-confident. And he had a certain air of urban sophistication in spite of his western appearance. He was also, obviously, experienced with women, a dangerous advantage.

"But," she added, "I am going to be very much tied up with my husband's political campaign in the coming weeks."

"Yes, we sure do want to get Slade elected," J.D. responded slowly. "But maybe you'll have a little time to spare. In any case, I'm going to be working closely with Jake Foreman and your husband in the coming weeks, too, so I hope to get to see a lot of you, Veronica."

His fingers closed over hers. Nervously she withdrew her hand. "Why are you so eager to see Slade win this race? Jake Foreman tells me that your father is spending a lot of money to help him get elected."

J.D. shrugged. "We have the money to spare. And it's in the best interests of the state. We need to have an honest man from this district in the senate."

"And you think Slade is honest?"

J.D. looked surprised. "Sure—isn't he?"

Uneasily Veronica realized she had allowed her personal prejudice against Slade to show. Maybe, she thought, he was only dishonest in his marriage. Perhaps on a political level he was more sincere.

"Is there some reason you don't think Slade is right for this office, Veronica?" J.D. persisted. "After all, you know him better than anyone else, being his wife."

I once thought I did, she reflected sadly. *Then I discovered I didn't know him at all.* Aloud, she said, "J.D., being Slade's wife does not give me any special judgment about his ability as a legislator."

She wished he'd change the subject, but he had backed her into a semantic corner and refused to ease up. "We've all heard that you and Slade were separated. You must have been havin' some trouble in your marriage—"

She colored. "You're beginning to be rather personal, aren't you?"

He nodded. "Forgive me, I am. I'm just interested in knowing what kind of man we're backing. And now that I've met you, I have a personal interest in the matter." His direct gaze made the intent of his words plain enough.

She withdrew her own gaze and gathered up her purse. "Listen, we must get back to the meeting. . . ."

But before she could rise, his hand closed over hers, making her pause. "Before we leave, I want you to know that from the minute we met tonight, Veronica, you have had me under your spell. I hope we're goin' to have the chance to become a lot better acquainted."

She had no answer for that and was relieved when he scribbled his initials on the check and arose to escort her to the elevator.

On the way down, in the privacy of the carpeted, padded cubicle with its soft lights and wired music, he placed his hands on her shoulders, forcing her to stand closer. He tipped her chin up, bent, and brushed her lips with his. "Now, that's just a friendly kiss," he told her softly. "I'm not tryin' to get you to be an unfaithful wife. But I want you to be thinking about that kiss in case your marriage isn't working out and to remember you've got a good friend hangin' around. All you need to do," he said, gazing directly into her eyes, "is crook your little finger at me, and ol' J.D. will come running."

They returned to the campaign headquarters as Slade was beginning to address the gathering. Veronica and J.D. slipped in quietly and stood in the back of the room. They were not noticed. All eyes were directed to the side of the room where Slade stood.

Veronica listened to the resonant voice that filled the room. She gazed at the striking figure Slade cut, with his shock of wavy silver hair and his physique that towered over almost everyone else in the room. He was a spellbinder, all right, she was forced to admit. He appeared relaxed, confident, imposing. His eyes flashed and he gestured smoothly as he made his points and then nodded as the audience applauded enthusiastically.

Yes, Slade was in his element here . . . a born leader. Whatever her personal feelings, she had to give the devil his due. Even she felt herself falling under the hypnotic spell of his magnetic personality. But then her gaze shifted slightly from Slade to the dark-haired woman on the fringe of the crowd nearest him, Barbara Lange, gazing at Slade with luminous eyes, and Veronica felt a burning sensation in the pit of her stomach.

Slade gave a short, rousing speech designed to inspire the group to work hard as the campaign got under way. His followers responded with feverish applause and cries of "Slade's our man!"

The candidate's brief address was the climax of the evening. When Slade finished talking, the election committee gathered around him, eager to shake his hand and slap his back.

As the meeting broke up, Slade threaded his way through the crowd to where Veronica waited. His face was flushed, his eyes bright with excitement. He took her arm and led her outside to his car, nodding and speaking to friends on the way.

"You look like a man who is in his element," Veronica said with an edge of bitterness when they were settled in his car.

He started the powerful engine and smoothly guided the machine from the parking lot. "Why do you say that?"

"It's pretty obvious. You thrive on being the center of attention. You like the thrill of speaking to crowds, basking in their response. You looked like Caesar triumphantly receiving an ovation from the Forum. You're a born politician, all right, Slade Huntington."

"Is that so bad? Our government depends on our political system to make it work. If you're going to have a political system, you have to have politicians to run it."

"That's all right, I suppose, as long as the politicians are honest men with some character."

He gave her a curious look. "Are you implying that I am dishonest?"

She felt the smooth vibration of the big car, the muffled whisper of the tires on the pavement. She gazed out the window at the streetlights and buildings that passed by them. She thought, you were dishonest with me, Slade, in the worst way—the way no woman can accept. What other kind of indiscretions would you pursue if you go to the capital? Will you turn into one of those legislators who are so notorious with women, making a sexual harem out of your office staff, your secretaries? Will you accept sexual favors from female lobbyists? Or are you really in love with Barbara Lange, and will you be faithful to her?

And she thought about how he had ruthlessly used her to get his law degree, how he was using her now to further his political ambition. He was a man who made use of others to get what he wanted. Would he use his political power as selfishly?

The accusations stung her lips, but her pride kept them unspoken. Her outward response to his question was just a sullen shrug.

"Well," he said lightheartedly, "I'm not going to let your antagonistic mood spoil the evening. Sure, I enjoyed tonight. Those people believe in me and what I stand for. They're ready to sacrifice a lot of time and money to back me all the way. That would give any man a thrill."

They rode in hostile silence for several blocks. Slade, still glowing with the success of the evening, was humming softly to himself, ignoring Veronica's coldness. Then he suddenly asked, "By the way, where did you and J.D. go?"

She shot him a narrowed glance. "So you noticed?"

"Of course. You left together and were gone quite a while."

The opportunity to strike back at him for the way he had humiliated her by having Barbara Lange at the meeting tonight now became irresistible. "I noticed you gave me a dirty look. Did you think we were slipping out to the parking lot to neck?"

He laughed. "Don't be silly. I know you too well for that."

"Oh, yes? Perhaps you don't know me at all, Slade Huntington."

"Yes, I do," he said smugly. "I know all about your conservative, puritan upbringing, the private religious school your grandparents sent you to. You were a virgin when we married. A bit stuffy and uptight about sex until we went to bed and you discovered you liked it. But I know you well enough to know you wouldn't go hopping into the back seat of a car with a stranger you had met less than an hour ago."

He was making her madder by the minute. "Then why did you give me that dirty look when you saw us leave together?" she fired back at him.

"I was irritated. You know how careful a candidate's wife has to be not to start gossip about her conduct."

"That was the only reason?" she asked furiously. "You were just worried about your precious campaign image?"

"Sure."

"Well, don't be so darn sure about me, Slade. What if I told you that these past two years in Australia I've been bed-hopping with a whole string of men?"

"I wouldn't believe you," he said calmly.

"Suppose I told you I felt an instant attraction for J. D. Clayton? He is an attractive man. I decided to have a good time. We went out to his car and I took my clothes off and we had sex."

They had arrived home. He pulled into the driveway of the stately colonial house and parked in the dark shadows of a flowering bougainvillea. "I wouldn't believe that, either," he said, switching off the engine and turning to her with a look of sudden intensity. "But that does give me an inspiration. Sex can be fun in a car. Makes you feel young again, like a couple of teenagers on a date."

She backed away from him. "Oh, no!"

Before she could open her door, he had captured her in his arms. The flush of the night's events was still on his face.

"No, you don't, Slade Huntington," she gasped, struggling with him. "I'm not going to be degraded this way. You are all stirred up and sexually aroused by the excitement of the evening. Now you need a woman—any woman. A prostitute off the street would do. . . ."

"What difference does it make?" he retorted. "You have made it abundantly clear that you no longer love me. And yet passion is still here. We proved that this afternoon. Even if you don't love me, in fact might even hate me, you don't find me physically replusive. We're still legally married. So why not enjoy the most basic delight a man and a woman can share?"

His words were low, intense, spoken against her unwilling lips. She was aware of a multitude of sensations as he pressed her against the car seat, holding her captive until their mouths were locked. She was aware of the heat of his body in the close quarters, the masculine smell of his suit fabric, the faint, clinging aroma of cigar smoke, the scent of his aftershave lotion. She could hear the faint night sounds outside, magnified and intensified by the hush of the late hour . . . the ticking and swish of a water sprinkler, the rustle of a bird in a nearby tree, the distant chiming of a steeple clock.

His lips on hers became more insistent, then brushed across her cheek, and he whispered her name in her ear. She felt the beginning stubble on his cheek that touched hers, and it somehow awoke a sting of excitement in her. The fabric of his coat sleeve brushed her arm, raising a prickling of goose bumps.

Her nerve ends became acutely attuned to the moment, like stringed instruments vibrating to a high pitch, betraying her and canceling out her reason.

Her head began swimming, her senses reeling, as his lips trailed to the hollow of her throat. She bit her lip and inhaled deeply. She grasped for her receding fringe of sanity and twisted away from him, but he relentlessly kept her wrapped tightly in his arms. His mouth found hers again, drawing resistance from her. A shudder coursed through her.

Then a door handle dug into her back, awakening her to an avenue of escape. She wrenched away from him, grasped the handle, and stumbled out of the car. Her high heels crunched on the gravel driveway. She kicked off her shoes and ran across the lawn.

Laughing, Slade caught up with her.

"Let me go!" she gasped.

"This is fun. Brings out the primitive instincts."

"Slade, you're a bloody idiot."

She struggled futilely. He scooped her up in his powerful arms and carried her to the edge of the lawn near a row of hedges.

For a dangerous moment Veronica slipped back in time, to an earlier period of their lives, when their moments of lovemaking had been light and gay. Slade's mood tonight reminded her of the carefree Slade she had once known. His lighthearted banter made her think of the man with whom she had once willingly shared her bed. Was he behaving this way to charm and seduce her? she wondered. Or had Slade, too, taken a nostalgic step back in time. Tonight, his tone of voice and his teasing manner were ghostly echoes of the Slade Huntington who had captured her heart, who had carried her to the heights of ecstasy in his strong arms.

Veronica fought to keep a hold on the present, to remember the kind of man Slade had become. But his nearness, the warmth of his body, the sound of his beating heart, all conspired to blot from her memory the years that had left her heart shattered.

She was treading dangerous ground, fantasizing that she was once again the new bride in the arms of the man she loved.

"Put me down," she insisted. "I'm tired. I want to go to bed."

"Sounds like a terrific idea. Let's go to bed together —right here."

"Now I know you've taken leave of your senses," she retorted coldly.

"Why not here?" Slade insisted, his mouth curled in a wicked smile. "The hedge gives us privacy. Look around you. It's like a secluded Garden of Eden here, and I'm Adam and you're Eve. How about it—Eve?"

It was true that they were surrounded by lush tropical vegetation: palm trees, a grove of banana trees. Flowering beds of gardenias and rosebushes saturated the night with perfume. And filtering down through the leaves were platinum shafts of moonlight, creating an aura of romance.

Gently he laid her on the damp grass and knelt beside her. In a low voice he said, "If we're going to play Adam and Eve, we should dispense with the fig leaves, don't you agree?"

Slowly, as he knelt beside her, his hair glowing silver in the soft moonlight, Slade reached up and with a casual jerk opened his tie. He slipped off his coat, tossed it aside. Then, with the grace of a jungle cat, he slipped out of his shirt.

Veronica tried to look away, but her eyes were

magnetically drawn to him, to the powerful bulge of his muscles, the matted hair on his broad chest. His tawny skin glistened with a golden sheen in the shafts of moonlight that caressed his bare skin.

Desire rose in Veronica, a beating, rhythmic pulsation that pounded through her and left her breathless. No matter how evil Slade had become, he still held a dangerous power over her that knocked the wind out of her, leaving her breathless.

In spite of herself, Veronica's eyes traced the outline of his broad shoulders, his rippling biceps, the deep chest tapering to a trim waist with its ridges of firm abdominal muscles, the thighs straining at his trouser material. He was one college athlete who had not allowed himself to go to pot. He jogged, swam, and lifted weights regularly. The result was a rugged physique glowing with health.

An involuntary tingle shot through her as she gazed at the familiar body exposed before her.

She tried to turn away, to get to her feet and run to escape the ravaging torment that was tearing through her. It was torture to be this close to Slade, to ache to feel his arms around her and recapture the love they had once shared. But could she give herself willingly this way, after all the anger that had passed between them—after Slade's deceptions and lies and, what was worse, his ruthless use of her just to further his political career?

It was insanity to lie here and allow Slade to work his magic on her.

But even as she told herself that, Slade's fingers were slipping her jacket from her shoulders, and her muscles were growing weak.

"No, Slade . . . please . . ."

"You can't think of a single good reason not to," he murmured in a low voice that caressed her with the same seduction as his hands moving over her body.

She gulped deep breaths of the night air. "Slade, this is insane," she trembled. "Out here in the open like this—"

"I told you. Nobody can see us here."

"Just the same—"

There was a whispered rustle of her garments. Slade's fingers opened buttons with consummate skill.

"I'll never forgive you for this, Slade."

"On the contrary . . . you'll thank me."

Their voices became husky whispers in the darkness.

"Slade, please don't do that . . ."

"Why not? You know you like it."

"Yes, but . . ." Her voice trailed off in a soft gasp. She dug her fingers into his hair. Her body was turning into molten flame.

She could no longer keep her hands off him. Her palms moved over his broad chest. Her fingers dug into the matted hair. She felt the strength of his shoulders and shuddered when her caress roved over his rippling biceps. Her hands became avid for the touch of his bare flesh. They moved back down his chest to his belt buckle.

He carried a scar on his shoulder from his football days, a jagged white line that ran down over a collarbone that had been broken during a game. She kissed the scar; then her mouth tasted more secrets of his deep, moving chest. His breath was hoarse in her ears as her lips and hands moved over him.

In return, his relentless fingers sought her. Reality slipped away. She was in a state of dreamy rapture. She felt the night air caress her body and realized vaguely that Slade had undressed her, but she hadn't been aware of it happening.

She welcomed the fierce embrace of Slade's arms crushing her yielding breasts against the hard planes of his chest.

She seemed to be sinking downward. All will to resist had been drained from her. Her heart was beating like a steady drum, the pounding of a primitive rhythm.

Then an icy shock jolted them out of paradise. Slade jerked upright, spluttering. Veronica uttered a gasping scream. The cold water sloshing over her evaporated her dream state in a flash. Within seconds she was drenched. Her hair was turned into dripping strands plastered to her cheeks and neck.

She clambered to her feet, hugging herself, shivering. "What is it?" she cried.

"The sprinkler system!" Slade shouted. "The damn sprinkler system!"

All around them fountains of cold water were erupting from sprinkler heads buried in the grass, shooting in a fine spray of rain from which there was no escape.

Veronica began laughing, half hysterically. "Saved by a cold shower!" she exclaimed. "What poetic justice!"

With the jolt back to reality came realization of how she had been moments away from surrender. Again Slade would have seduced her, feeding his ego with the triumph of proving to himself that she couldn't resist him.

But the sprinkler system had saved her. Her sanity had been restored. Slade was going to have to find himself a different Eve. She had only one thought in mind now—escape!

Veronica darted away, running through the fountains

of water. She felt the spray on her legs, felt the splash and sting on her body. Now she welcomed the mind-clearing shock of the cold water.

In seconds she had slipped between a space in the hedge, finding a hiding place in the darkness. Slade was stumbling around in the man-made torrent of rain, calling her name.

Quietly, feeling like a hunted cat in the jungle, she moved through the hedges. The leaves brushed her bare skin. She had slipped around to the area where Slade had carelessly tossed his clothes. She reached through the hedge, groped in his pockets until she found his keys.

She drew a breath, gathering her courage. I hope none of the neighbors call the police to report a naked lady running across the lawn, she thought grimly. Then she made a wild dash for the front door of the mansion. With trembling fingers she fumbled with the keys, got the door open, then ran up the stairs, leaving a trail of wet footprints.

Once in her room, she slammed and locked the door and fell against it, panting. When she'd gotten her breath back, she ran to the bed and threw herself across it with a bounce and began laughing hysterically.

Presently she heard Slade pounding up the stairs. Then he rattled her doorknob. "Veronica, let me in," he ordered.

"Go away, Slade." She giggled.

He pounded on the door.

"Slade, it's not going to do you any good."

"You're not going to leave me like this, are you?" he pleaded.

"Go take another cold shower," she suggested.

"That's not funny."

"I think it's hilarious. What beautiful timing! Tell

me, Slade, what kind of bloody idiot waters his lawn at midnight?"

"The timing mechanism got fouled up somehow. I had it set to begin sprinkling at noon, but the darn thing went off at midnight."

"That's what you say. I think heaven had a hand in it to save me from your clutches."

"I didn't think you wanted to be saved. You were as eager as I was."

She blushed angrily and sat up, gathering the bedspread around her. "You caught me in a weak moment. It's not going to happen again. I'm not your wife anymore, Slade. The fact that we're not divorced is only a technicality."

There was an ugly silence. Then Slade muttered, "I've brought your clothes with me. Don't you want them?"

"I'm not going to open the door, if that's what you mean."

Another silence.

Veronica said, "Slade, if my dress is ruined, you're going to buy me another. It was your fault."

More silence. Finally Slade hit the door with his fist in an angry gesture of frustration. Then she heard him go down the hall to his room, cursing to himself.

She went to the bathroom, washed the wet grass blades from her body under the shower, dried on a rough towel, and slipped into a nightgown.

In bed, she gazed at the moonlight filtering through the lacy curtains at the window. She tried to savor tonight's victory, but it slowly turned to ashes and left sad loneliness in its wake. She went to sleep with tears trickling down her cheeks.

Chapter Six

*B*reakfast the next morning was a cold event. Beyond a brief, impersonal greeting, no conversation was exchanged. Slade confined his attention to glancing through a handful of papers as he ate. Veronica nibbled at a piece of toast. She was acutely aware of Slade's sullen preoccupation—the aftermath of his frustration and her victory last night.

She savored the triumph, knowing it had been a blow to Slade's ego. Until she had turned the tables on him, he had gloried in his power over her. He'd been convinced that she didn't have the strength to resist him, that she would go to bed with him whenever he desired.

It was true that Slade had taught her the meaning of lovemaking. When they married, he had awakened slumbering passions in her that she hadn't known existed. She had been his willing love slave, happy to give him pleasure in any way he desired, and receiving a like measure of fulfillment in return. Her body had been tuned to his. She had been hooked on him, a love addict, craving more and more of him.

That physical hunger had still existed in her even after her love and respect for him had died. It had been deprived and starved for two years and had overwhelmed her when he surprised her in the shower. Afterward, she had felt betrayed by her own emotions.

She had felt degraded, humiliated, and she had despised her own weakness as much as she despised Slade.

But last night she had regained control of her actions and her emotions. Her pride and self-esteem had been restored.

Then a small inner voice warned her that she had won only a round last night. The battle was far from over. Living under Slade's roof, she was certain to face more encounters. Would she win the next round? Or, she wondered with a sudden chill, would her weakness where Slade's physical attraction was concerned defeat her resolve?

She was constantly walking a tightrope when she was near Slade. Even now, her emotions were mixed. His presence in the room was like a force field, affecting the chemistry of her body, intruding on her thoughts and feelings. She was aware of everything about him—the small, tightly curled black hairs on the back of his suntanned hands and broad wrists, the strand of silver hair that had tumbled over his forehead, the faint aroma of talcum he had dusted on his freshly shaved jaw and cheeks.

Slade drained the final swallow of coffee from his cup, placed it back in the saucer with a click, and rose from the table. He gathered up his papers. "There will be a news conference here at the house early this afternoon," he said in a cold, businesslike tone. "We're expecting representatives from all the news media: TV, radio, newspapers. Jake Foreman will be here, too, and some of the others. I expect you to be here, properly dressed and prepared to meet the public. We want to give the media a picture of a devoted wife in a solid, respectable home to counter the gossip my opposition is bound to stir up over our separation."

She met his eyes in a level gaze. "More deception, right?" she said icily.

He flushed angrily. "Just keep your hostile attitude to yourself. Remember there's a lot at stake—for both of us."

Their eyes locked in a long moment of bitter conflict. They were separated by the look, divided into two worlds with a void of remote, frozen space between them. Gone was the exuberance Slade had exhibited last night. He looked grim and forbidding this morning, an impersonal stranger.

Veronica felt a pang of sadness. Life could be so cruel. Love brought a man and a woman together with a rush of warmth, a joyful union of all their hopes, dreams, plans. They shared little daily experiences, private jokes; they knew one another so intimately they could almost read each other's thoughts. Then, this terrible estrangement—wrenching them apart, turning love to hate. And the two who had been so close became distant strangers, realizing they had never really known each other at all.

Part of her regretted the change in Slade from the lighthearted, almost boyish mood he had been in last night. He could be extremely charming when he was like that.

But then she reminded herself who was responsible for the sad state their marriage had fallen into. She grieved for the innocent, trusting young wife she had once been. That person was a stranger to her now. She had been disillusioned, embittered, made hard inside. And Slade had done that to her—and to their marriage.

"Very well," she finally said in a brittle voice, raising her chin. "I'll remember to play the part of a loyal, devoted wife. Perhaps, with a bit more practice, I'll become a pretty good actress."

He nodded abruptly. "See that you do." And then he turned and strode briskly from the room.

That morning, she faced a task that she dreaded as much as the news conference. She had to tell Aileen that she had moved back in with Slade. How could she possibly explain that to her sister? She dared not give Aileen a hint of Slade's blackmail. It would devastate her sister if she found out that Slade was using her past indiscretion to force Veronica to live with him again.

No, she had to keep up the masquerade for Aileen's sake.

In her bedroom, Veronica donned a comfortable sports outfit, red slacks and a frilly white blouse. She was seated at the vanity when a tap at her door announced the housekeeper.

"Buenos días, señora. Can I make your bed?"

"Certainly. Come in, Josie."

The tall woman entered the room, tugging a vacuum cleaner after her. She placed her hands on her hips, giving Veronica a critical look. "That's a pretty outfit. *Muy bonita.* Looks good on you."

"Thank you, Josie." Facing the mirror, Veronica brushed her hair vigorously. Highlights shone like bronze streaks in the luxuriant chestnut mane that tumbled around her shoulders.

The housekeeper began arranging the bedclothes. "I'm glad to see you in this house, ma'am. A house is nothing but a building without a woman living in it. That's what Mr. Salinas used to say."

"Your husband?"

"Sí. A fine man." Her lustrous brown eyes shone proudly. Then she crossed herself. "I pray for him every night."

Veronica laid her brush down and turned. "Is something wrong with him? Is he ill?"

"The government people, the *inmigración*, sent him back to Mexico. But he'll come back across the river again. He always does. Then we'll have a fine time. All our friends will come over, and we'll drink beer and dance and laugh, and finally all our friends will go home, and then Mr. Salinas will carry me into the bedroom and make me feel like a woman." She rolled her eyes. "He's a real man . . . what we call *muy macho*. He stands straight and looks every man in the eye. Nobody better get funny with Mr. Salinas, I'll tell you. He's got a knife scar here—" She drew a line with a forefinger across one cheek. "Makes him look fierce —*muy malo*." She laughed.

She was bustling around the bed, furiously shaking the pillows. She said, "You got a real man, too, *señora*. That Mr. Slade." She rolled her brown eyes expressively. *"Muy macho."* She put down the pillows and looked at Veronica with a penetrating expression, placing her hands on her hips again in a characteristic gesture. "This bed—it's not very comfortable."

"It's all right."

Josie Salinas shook her head. "The one in *Señor* Slade's room is much better."

Veronica blushed. "This one is just fine. . . ."

The housekeeper persisted, "This room is too small. The light is not good here. You would be happier in the big bedroom."

Veronica wavered between amusement and irritation. "Josie, I really think our sleeping arrangement is our private concern. We're—quite comfortable this way."

Josie shot her a disapproving look and went back to fluffing the pillow. She grumbled, half under her breath, "Well, it's none of my business. I'm just the housekeeper. But Mr. Salinas sure wouldn't put up with *me* sleeping in the guest room, I can tell you that. I raised six kids. We didn't get 'em by me sleeping in the guest room. I told all my daughters, 'When you get a good man, you keep him busy in the bedroom if you want to hold on to him. . . .'"

Veronica started to say something, but Mrs. Salinas cut her off by switching on the vacuum cleaner, ending the conversation.

Veronica fumed inwardly. *Now he and the house-keeper have ganged up on me, trying to get me into his bedroom!*

She finished applying her makeup, then went downstairs. She reminded herself that when Slade moved her here from her apartment the day before yesterday, she had left her car in the apartment parking area. She would have to call a taxi to take her there to retrieve her own car. Even though she had brought her clothes and some personal belongings with her, she had no intention of giving up the apartment completely. When the political campaign was over, no matter who won, she planned to get out of Slade's house. She could see no reason why Slade would want to blackmail her into staying with him any longer than he needed her for political purposes.

Getting her car took the better part of an hour, and then she was on her way to her sister's home. Aileen and Brian now lived in a comfortable, rambling ranch-style home in a suburban residential district.

On the way, Veronica practiced breaking the news to Aileen that she and Slade were back together again. She tried several explanations but discarded them all as too implausible. She had to admit that there wasn't any sane, convincing reason why she should try to patch up her marriage.

She parked in Aileen's driveway and walked slowly

up to the front door, dreading the lies she was going to be forced to tell her sister.

"Veronica! Where have you been?" Aileen exclaimed upon opening the door. "I've called your office and apartment a dozen times the past two days. I was on the verge of contacting the police!"

"Well," Veronica began, "it's rather a complicated matter."

"Come in, for heaven's sake. I'll put on some tea. You *are* all right, aren't you?" Aileen asked, looking at her anxiously.

"Sure, I'm okay," Veronica muttered.

Over cups of tea in Aileen's comfortable living room, Veronica gathered her courage to explain about Slade, but she hedged. "How is Brian?"

"He's fine."

"The kids?"

"All right. Michael had the sniffles last week, but he's okay now. They're at school now."

Veronica nodded.

Aileen sipped her tea, watching Veronica expectantly. Veronica knew her sister would not press her but would wait patiently until she explained where she'd been since the day before yesterday.

Glancing across the room, she saw their reflection in a mirror and was struck by the difference in their outward appearance. No one would ever take them to be sisters. Aileen was tall and willowy. Like their father, she had straight dark hair, which she wore long, gathered at the nape of her neck with a ribbon. Her complexion was extremely fair, almost pale. Her nails were immaculately groomed. She moved with the fluid grace of a professional model. There was a slightly reserved, formal air about her. She had always seemed mature for her age.

Aileen was like an indoor plant, unaccustomed to direct sunlight, carefully tended and pruned. By contrast, Veronica was like a healthy flower that grew on a hillside, thriving on wind and rain, raising her face to the sun. So much about her facial structure was like her mother's, the tawny eyes, the blunt nose, the high cheekbones, the generous, wide mouth with lips slightly bowed upward, the sprinkling of freckles across her nose and cheeks, her chin, slightly cleft, with a proud, stubborn thrust. Where Aileen's hands were slender and delicate, Veronica's were strong for a girl's, with long, tapered fingers.

Veronica was leggy, rangy, somewhat above average height. Aileen was the taller of the two, however, and seemed even more so because of her slender, willowy build.

Their personalities and character traits were as different as their physical appearance. Veronica was well organized and efficient. She kept her office and apartment immaculate, orderly, with everything in its place. She had some artistic talent and had sketched since she was a child. She liked hiking, riding, swimming, collecting old bottles, and buying shoes. She was gullible, a patsy for a sales pitch. She trusted people and believed what they told her, to the point of being a sucker at times. Anybody could sell her anything.

Aileen, on the other hand, was at a loss in dealing with housekeeping. Fortunately, Brian could afford a maid, or they would live in a constant state of clutter covered by a film of dust. What she lacked in Veronica's athletic stamina, she made up in a certain hardness in dealing with people. She trusted no one. Veronica felt sure that Aileen's disillusionment over her first marriage had left her embittered and suspicious of human motives. In her quiet, refined way, she was the strong extrovert of the two. Veronica was thoughtful, introspective, somewhat shy. While Aileen's formal, reserved manners at first gave that kind of impression, one soon discovered a core of iron under the pale, delicate exterior.

Aileen could be kind and generous, but Veronica knew her sister could also carry a grudge if someone has mistreated her or a loved one. She did not forgive easily. She was as bitter toward Slade as she was toward her first husband, declaring them to be two of a kind. She was not going to accept a reunion between Slade and Veronica with much pleasure.

But Veronica couldn't evade the issue indefinitely. She made small talk until she ran out of subjects. An uncomfortable silence ensued. Finally Veronica blurted out, "The reason you haven't been able to reach me the past two days is that I have moved back in with Slade."

Her statement was like a glass shattering on a tile surface, followed by a shocked silence. Aileen's eyes widened, her pupils spreading and growing darker. She held her breath for a moment, then carefully put her teacup in the saucer and placed them on the glass-topped mahogany coffee table situated in front of the green velour sofa where they were seated. "My," she breathed, "that is surprising news."

Veronica fumbled self-consciously with her cup. She could sense her sister's mental processes adjusting to this incredible development, testing it as her reactions gathered momentum.

Finally Aileen said, "I really don't understand, Veronica."

"Well," Veronica blundered on, "Slade came to see me. He asked for a second chance to patch things up.

—I thought I owed it to our marriage to give him that. . . ."

"Your marriage? But aren't you divorced?"

Veronica sighed. "That's another thing. I was certain Slade had filed for divorce while I was in Australia. Turns out he didn't, and we're still very much man and wife—in the legal sense."

Aileen gazed at her with critical appraisal. "Veronica, it's awfully easy for people to talk you into things. I hope Slade hasn't talked you into something you're going to regret." She hesistated. "You know, of course, that he's running against Kirk Malden for the state senate."

"Yes."

"And has it occurred to you that Slade could be politically motivated—that he's just using you to improve his public image, knowing that being divorced could cost him some votes?"

"Yes, I know," Veronica said miserably. She felt trapped. She must sound like a naive child or a hopeless masochist, but how else could she explain the situation without revealing the ugly truth to Aileen?

Her sister's lips had drawn into a disapproving line. "I—I don't exactly know what to say, Veronica. You were so bitter toward Slade, and for good reason. Frankly, I'm stunned that you'd want him back."

"I know," Veronica admitted. "But I was very much in love with Slade in the beginning, and—"

"He used you," Aileen said coldly, "to put himself through school, exactly the way my first husband used me. And then, that thing with his law partner—"

"Well, he did pay me back for the schooling. Remember, he put me through my last year in return. And as for the other—well, that's in the past, and—"

"Are you sure?" Aileen asked, looking at her sharply. "I've seen them together on the television news."

Veronica had no answer for that, knowing with deadly certainty that it was true.

Aileen reached for her hand. "You've been through so much. You're my kid sis. I feel responsible for you since—well, since we lost Mom and Dad. It was us against the world there for a while. I couldn't bear to see you hurt again."

Veronica sighed. "Slade does have some good qualities. He came through for you that time you were in trouble. And he introduced you to Brian. . . ."

And the evil side of him has canceled out the good several times over, she added to herself bitterly.

"That's true," Aileen replied. "Maybe I'm being too hard on him. But it's going to take some doing before I'll trust the bloke again."

They talked for another hour. When they parted, Aileen sent her off with her blessing and wishes for happiness with Slade, but her voice had a hollow ring.

"Can't say I blame you, sis," Veronica muttered to herself, getting into her car. "What a gullible little sap I must seem to you!"

Slade was pacing around the living room when she returned to his house. He looked impatiently at his watch. "Where have you been?"

"To visit Aileen."

"How is she?"

"Surprised that I'd go back to you. She thinks I should have my head examined. Of course, I didn't tell her why I'm here, that you resorted to such rotten blackmail."

"We don't have time to start a fight now. The reporters will be here soon."

"It will just take me a few minutes to freshen up and

change into something appropriate," she said coldly. She hurried upstairs and changed into a skirt, blouse, and blazer jacket. She had chosen the deep green outfit because it flattered her tawny eyes and chestnut hair.

She made quick repairs to her makeup and ran a comb through her hair. When she rejoined Slade, the main room of the house was crowded with reporters, TV camera crews, and photographers. She was greeted by a volley of electronic flashes.

Veronica struggled against a wave of panic. Her innate shyness made her cringe. She fought a desire to bolt and run. At this moment she was grateful for Slade's strong arm that went around her. She shrank against him.

This was going to be harder than she'd realized. She hadn't anticipated the full extent of being thrust into the limelight. And she soon discovered it was to grow even worse.

The press conference began with Slade delivering a brief prepared statement. Veronica marveled at how calm and relaxed he appeared. But then he was used to being in the public eye. He obviously enjoyed the limelight.

At the close of his statement, reporters began firing questions at him. "Do you expect this to become a dirty race, Mr. Huntington?" a reporter asked.

"That's entirely up to my opponent," Slade smiled. "We'd prefer to campaign on the issues."

"Senator Malden has called you a shyster upstart, not dry behind your ears, with no experience in state government. How do you respond to that, Mr. Huntington?"

"When the air in a room becomes stale and contaminated, you open a window for some fresh air. I plan to be that breath of fresh air this state government so badly needs. Being an attorney, I am certainly as well acquainted with our state statutes as Senator Malden."

"Why are you so opposed to the Three Oaks Canyon location for the new state reservoir? Most of the business leaders agree with Senator Malden that it's by far the better location."

"For some business interests it might be. But not for the state as a whole. Numerous studies have shown it would be a bad ecological choice. It would benefit the larger urban areas in the northeastern section of the state, but not the rural areas and smaller towns in the southern half. The Crystal Falls area would be more centrally located. It would do less ecological damage."

Veronica was regaining her composure, relieved to stand silently while Slade drew all the attention of the reporters. But suddenly her blood ran cold when she heard her name spoken.

"I—I beg your pardon?"

A woman reporter repeated her question, "Mrs. Huntington, our readers would like to know if you and Slade Huntington have agreed on a permanent reconciliation?"

Again panic assailed her. Her mouth felt dry. She looked frantically at Slade, who smiled easily, putting his arm around her again. "Why, of course it's permanent," he said. "Veronica will be by my side throughout the campaign and will go to the capital with me when I'm elected, right, dear?"

The answer did not satisfy the woman reporter. She persisted. "Would you comment on the reason for your separation, Mrs. Huntington?"

Veronica stared at the woman. She was middle-aged. Her gray hair was worn in a short style. Behind severe, horn-rimmed glasses, her eyes were sharp and penetrating, and they were fixed on Veronica with stubborn tenacity.

Slade again began to answer, but the reporter interrupted. "Our readers would like a quote from Mrs. Huntington. She's going to attract a lot of interest in this campaign."

Again the penetrating eyes were riveted on Veronica. With a sinking feeling, she knew she had to answer the question. The TV cameras had suddenly swung in her direction. The other media people were staring at her. Several microphones were thrust at her. She looked around like a trapped rabbit and caught a glimpse of the campaign manager, Jake Foreman, standing in the doorway. He was munching on one of his stomach pills, his glittering black eyes watching her intently.

The female reporter kept digging at her. "There are rumors that the breakup was the result of your husband's philandering. Do you wish to comment on that?"

Out of the corner of her eye she saw Slade's jaw knot, his face pale slightly. It was the first time during the news conference that she'd seen him begin to lose his grip on his smooth self-control. He was obviously furious at the reporter but frustrated. An angry outburst at this point would score against him.

Veronica felt herself on the verge of tears but fought them down. She was trapped. She had to answer. "It was nothing like that," she forced herself to say.

"Could you speak louder, please? I couldn't hear you."

Veronica drew a deep breath. Her fists were clenched in icy knots at her sides. "My husband and I separated because I needed some time to be by myself, to work out some personal problems. We married young, when I was in college. I didn't really know who I was. I went to Australia for a while to get a better perspective on my life. Now I'm back, and—and everything is all right. . . ."

The reporters were scribbling notes as she spoke. Her statement appeared to satisfy them, because there were no further questions aimed at her. Slade replied to a few more raised hands, and the press conference ended.

Jake Foreman joined them. He patted Slade's back. "Nicely done, my boy. You made points with the press today. So did you, young lady." He smiled, taking Veronica's arm. "Can I borrow your lovely wife for a few mintues, Slade? I think we need to have a little council of war."

"Sure," Slade replied, moving off to speak to one of the TV reporters.

Foreman guided Veronica into the library and closed the door behind them. Her legs gave way. She sank into a chair, tears running down her cheeks.

The campaign manager poured two drinks at a portable bar. "I prescribe a little bourbon and branch water for you, my dear. For myself—" He poured a dollop of whiskey into a glass of milk. "The milk is for my ulcer, the booze is for me."

He raised his glass. "A toast to a brave little lady. They gave you a bad time out there. And you handled it very well."

Veronica gulped her drink, holding the glass in trembling fingers. Her nerves were shot. She welcomed the feeling of warmth that spread through her body, the calming effect of the alcohol on her emotions. "Who *was* that woman?"

"Selma Davenport. A real barracuda. But a good

reporter. Back in the old days, we used to call her kind sob sisters. They go for the human-interest angle, the gossip. And it would appear that you are going to be a prime target. I'm sorry."

"Oh, my God, no!" Veronica choked. "Slade didn't tell me I was going to have my private life paraded before the entire world."

Foreman sat beside her, taking her hand. "In politics, no one has a private life, Mrs. Huntington." He patted her hand gently. "I'm old enough to be your father, my dear. And I'm going to talk to you like a father. I think you should know what's in store for you. Slade should have told you, but I see he didn't. But let's not be too hard on the boy. He's new to politics, too. He probably didn't realize himself what you were in for.

"You see," Foreman continued, "most people lead very dull, routine lives. Husbands are fat and paunchy, and wives lose their figures when the kids come. They get out of the trap of their lives by reading about celebrities. Especially young, good-looking celebrities."

"I'm no celebrity," Veronica gasped.

"Well, you're certainly in the public eye now. You'll be the smart, attractive young wife they'll see at Slade's side on TV newscasts, in newspaper stories, in public appearances. And the fact that there's a hint of scandal about you and Slade will make you all the more interesting—the subject of gossip and speculation. Why were you and Slade separated? Was he running around on you, or were you running around on him? They'll conjecture about that. Some of the scandal sheets will make up their own answers."

Veronica felt the contents of her stomach rising up in her throat. Desperately she fought down the wave of nausea. She shook her head. "I—I can't—" she choked.

"Well, that's what we must decide now," Foreman said gently. "I asked you before if you were going to stick with Slade through the campaign. It would be rough on his chances if you left him now. It would be fatal if you deserted him later in the campaign."

Veronica looked at him hopelessly. She drained her glass, then rose, went to the bar, and poured a second drink, stronger than the first. She had no way of replying. How could she tell him that Slade had her in a hopeless trap with his cruel blackmail threat?

Jake Foreman said, "I also told you before that I'm not going to pry into your private life. The reason for your separation, whatever it was, is none of my business, except as how it might affect the campaign. Now, I thought you gave a splendid explanation. They may not believe you, but if you stick with that, they won't have anything else concrete to go on. What I don't like are surprises. I don't want to get halfway through this campaign and have somebody come up with some juicy scandal about you two that I don't know about."

Veronica shrugged sullenly. "There's no scandal in my past. As for Slade, you'll have to talk to him."

Foreman nodded. "All right, I will. Now, we'll drop this subject for the time being. I wanted to have this chat to prepare you for what's in store. Now I think you know."

He sipped his drink, leaning back on the sofa and crossing his legs. "Let me tell you how elections are won, Veronica. The general public thinks it's the loyal party members, the Democrats or Republicans, or what have you, who swing the elections. But that isn't the case. You see, in every election, whether it's for the mayor of some small town or president of the United

States, we have a percentage of voters that we call the undecideds and the indifferents. This is the group that decides the outcome of an election. Loyal party members, voters committed to a candidate, are not the deciding factor. The undecideds and indifferents may be only a small percentage of the total voters, less, perhaps, than ten percent. But in a close election it's that nine or ten percent that swings the outcome. You probably know that Truman defeated Dewey by a small margin of the popular vote and Kennedy won over Richard Nixon by only a bit more than a hundred and eighteen thousand votes."

The drink was enveloping Veronica's nerves in a warm, relaxing cocoon, diminishing the horror she had felt at the news conference. "It would appear," she murmured, "that I'm going to learn a lot about American politics."

"Well, we Americans have learned a few things from you Australians." He smiled. "For example, the secret ballot got its start in Australia in the last century. But getting back to what I was talking about, the voters who are undecided right up until election day are usually pretty well-informed individuals who have a certain independence. They study the issues and the candidates. They're not Democrats or Republicans just because that's the way their parents voted. Because there are so many complexities in campaign issues, they have trouble making up their minds.

"The indifferents are people who often don't vote at all or, when they do vote, do so on an emotional basis. They don't like the color of candidate X's neckties, so they vote for candidate Y. Or their vote is swayed because of a rumor they heard that candidate X drinks, kicks dogs, or beats his wife. Has nothing to do with the issues or the ability of the candidate.

"Now, that indifferent group can easily decide an election. Smart politicians go after them with carefully planned campaign techniques, usually an emotional appeal."

"I think what you're telling me," Veronica deduced, "is that Kirk Malden is a smart politician, and he's going to dig into this matter of our marital difficulties for all it's worth, so I'd better be prepared."

"You're an astute young lady," Foreman smiled. "Now, let's see what we can do to win over that group of undecideds and indifferents. We'll work on recruiting cell groups and individual foot soldiers. Slade, obviously, can't knock on every door and shake every voter's hand, so the next best thing is to send personal emissaries to knock on doors and shake hands. That part will be up to me to arrange. What I want to talk with you about is television. Television has become a powerful influence in contemporary politics. Now, that's in your field of public relations. I'd like to hear your views on how to make the best use of our TV spots. Bear in mind that we have the funding to buy some prime-time half-hour segments. Slade is an excellent public speaker. I think he'll come across on TV better than Malden, who looks like the thug he is. I thought we could make use of some of Slade's best speeches."

"Yes, but not for the entire half-hour," Veronica said. "You'd lose all but your most committed viewers. The public wants to be entertained by television. They won't sit still for a half-hour speech, no matter how good, unless it happens to be an address by the president on some matter of vital national concern."

"Go on," Jake Foreman said, listening with interest.

Why am I doing this? Veronica wondered. I couldn't

care less if Slade gets elected. The only thing he has going for him is that he might be somewhat the lesser of two evils.

But the campaign manager had asked her professional opinion on a subject in which she'd had training and experience. So she gave him an answer.

"You'd need to dramatize the half-hour," she said. "Show Slade walking over the proposed dam site. Have some action, dialogue. Perhaps use film clips. If Senator Malden argues that legalized gambling will bring revenue to the state and lower taxes, you'll want to counter with an emotional appeal. Make an issue out of the organized-crime angle. You could have film clips of violent crimes, police cars with lights flashing, that sort of thing. Then a fade-in to Slade warning voters that they would trade lower taxes for higher crime. Slade's speeches would be fine, but they need to be broken up and tied in with other visual production."

Foreman's bright eyes registered growing respect. "Obviously you know your business. We'll see that you take control of producing all our television spots." Then he glanced at his watch. "Now we must get moving. We're scheduled to go to a political rally and barbecue at the Clayton ranch this afternoon."

Veronica groaned inwardly. The press conference had left her emotionally drained and bone-weary. She didn't want to go anywhere.

But the campaign manager arose, smiling. "The next few weeks will be hectic for you, Mrs. Huntington. Be prepared to be on the go constantly. As the saying goes, on the rubber-chicken circuit!"

Veronica changed into a casual outfit, a fringed skirt and shirt with pearl buttons, suitable for a ranch barbecue.

She rode beside Slade to the Clayton ranch, stiff and silent. Slade made one attempt to break through the icy wall that separated them. "That reporter put you on the spot. You handled yourself well."

She shrugged, conscious of a fresh wave of resentment. "When you forced me into pretending to be your wife again, you didn't tell me my private life was going to be bared before the entire state."

"I honestly didn't know it would become such a public issue. Apparently the media have decided to make a big thing out of it."

Veronica looked away at the countryside passing by the car window. She was not in a mood to talk with Slade.

They drove down a private road and into the landscaped yard of the Clayton ranch. It was obvious that the Claytons must be numbered among the richest landowners in the state. Irrigation had transformed the grounds into a lush garden with terraced lawns, giant oak trees, winding graveled paths between neat hedges, fountains and garden statues. On a slight elevation above the grounds was the ranch house, a sprawling mansion with stucco walls and red-tiled roof in classic Spanish style.

Picnic tables had been set up under the oak trees. The air was filled with the aroma of giant slabs of beef being barbecued over open coals. A strolling band of mariachi musicians, attired in Spanish costumes of tight black trousers, black vests and wide-brim black sombreros, all trimmed with gold filigree and sparkling buttons, was serenading the guests. A large crowd was already present, and more cars were arriving by the minute.

The Claytons formed a welcoming committee when Slade stepped out of his car. Elijah Clayton, patriach of the clan, greeted Slade with a hearty handshake and a slap on the back.

Veronica saw J. D. Clayton, resplendent in cowboy boots, a red western shirt with black shoestring bow tie, and a costly white Stetson hat. A warm flush spread up her cheek as she remembered his kiss in the elevator. He opened her door with a flourish and offered his hand to help her out. "You are certainly beautiful today, Veronica," he said warmly, his gaze sweeping over her.

Standing a few paces behind him was the lovely red-haired girl Veronica remembered from the election-committee meeting the night before. Like the others, Nichole was dressed in western attire, blue jeans that hugged her slender hips like a second skin and a dark shirt left carelessly open to the valley of her proud young breasts. Veronica envied the girl's huge brown eyes and fair complexion.

"Hello, Nichole," Veronica smiled, wanting to be friends with the girl.

But J.D.'s kissing cousin merely gave her a sullen look, turned, and walked away.

"It's goin' to be a hot afternoon, Veronica," J.D. observed. "How about a cold glass of beer? We've got a bunch of kegs iced down over here."

"That sounds good."

She remembered as she sipped the beer that she'd had nothing to eat since breakfast and had already had two drinks before leaving Slade's home. Her head was beginning to swim. But she recklessly drank the beer, wanting to numb her feelings.

Slade had been whisked off by the crowd and was somewhere out of sight, mingling with the guests. She couldn't see him, and she didn't care. But then she saw a new arrival, Barbara Lange, looking cool and glamorous in a white linen outfit, moving purposefully through the crowd in Slade's direction, and Veronica felt a surge of anger.

"How do you like being the wife of a popular candidate?" J.D. asked.

"I hate it," Veronica said grimly. "I don't like being shoved into the limelight against my will this way."

"But I'd think that a wife who truly loved her husband would be raring and chomping at the bit to help him."

She felt his gaze on her, testing her reaction, and she knew he was fishing for her true feelings toward Slade. J.D. had made it obvious last night that he had designs on her. Now he was continuing to put out feelers to determine how loyal she was to Slade, and how far he could get with her.

As much as she despised Slade for what he'd done to her, and as angry as she was about the situation that had been forced on her, she was not ready to encourage another man, so she said nothing.

She did wish she had a friend in whom she could confide. There was no one she could talk to about Slade's cruel blackmail, certainly not Aileen or Jake Foreman. Perhaps, as she grew to trust J.D. more, she could talk with him.

Soon loudspeakers were blaring as political luminaries were introduced.

"They're goin' to want you up there on the platform with Slade," J.D. reminded her.

A shudder ran through her. "That's the last thing I want," she moaned. She was drinking another beer. Her head was swimming and her tongue was becoming thick. The thought of sitting up there beside Slade, again forcing herself to smile at him, playing the hypocritical role of the faithful wife as hundreds of eyes were directed toward her, was more than she could cope with today, and she gulped the beer to further numb her mind.

"I was just through a ghastly press conference," she mumbled, tears burning her eyes. "I'm still unnerved by it. I—I just can't get up there in front of all those people . . . everybody staring at me . . . the TV cameras . . ."

J.D. put a comforting arm around her. "Tell you what," he said in a conspiratorial tone, "why don't we just sneak off? We can slip up to the house. Jake and Daddy would skin my hide, but we won't tell anybody. . . ."

She looked at him gratefully, trying to get him in better focus. The alcohol was affecting her vision along with other things. She was vaguely aware of J.D.'s strong arm guiding her along a graveled path between a row of hedges. Then they were inside the big house. She had a jumbled impression of Mexican tile floors, spacious whitewashed walls, and great, open beam ceilings. The cool breath of air conditioning washed over her.

They sat at a bar, where J.D. mixed her another drink. A warning voice in a fuzzy part of her mind told her it would be foolish for her to drink any more. But she ignored the warning.

"Let's take our drinks over here, where we can be comfortable," J.D. suggested, leading her to a long couch. "You look tired."

Veronica sank in the luxurious fabric, welcoming the relaxing comfort. She was surrounded by fluffy pillows. A Navajo rug spread before her on the tile floor. The couch faced a giant fireplace made of stone. Above the fireplace was a set of the longest steer horns she had ever laid eyes on.

J.D.'s arm had gone around her. She was aware of her thigh pressed against his. She knew she should move away, but her muscles were like lead. It was too much of an effort to move. And the human contact was comforting.

J.D. said softly, "I keep getting signals from you that you resent being a politician's wife, almost like Slade had somehow forced you into being at his side during this campaign."

Veronica nodded. She pushed a strand of her hair back from her forehead, but it tumbled back over one eye. She was too tired to bother with it. She leaned her head back against J.D.'s arm, gazing up at the beamed ceiling. "He did force me into it," she said.

Perhaps the alcohol had loosened her tongue, or perhaps she was at the point that she had to confide in someone or she would break down completely. "I didn't want to go back to Slade. I certainly didn't want to go around the state pretendin' to be a loyal wife, fighting to get her husban' elected."

"Then why did you come?"

She frowned. "Can't tell you that part."

"But Slade isn't using physical force. Has he threatened to hurt you physically?"

She shook her head. "Not that way. Slade wouldn't abuse me physically."

"Then what?"

Again she shook her head. "Don't want to talk about it."

Her mind was swimming, her senses reeling. She closed her eyes.

J.D.'s lips were close to her. His breath was warm against her cheek as he whispered in her ear, "Veronica, I told you last night how attracted I am to you, right from the first minute I saw you. I want you more than any other woman I have ever met. I don't know what kind of weapon Slade is holding over your head to force you to stay with him. But I want you to know that as soon as you can get free of him, I'm here waiting for you."

He kissed her ear, and then his lips trailed across her cheek to her mouth.

His kiss was not unpleasant, although she felt no physical response. She just liked being here with someone who was comforting and sympathetic.

She felt his caress on her body.

"No, J.D.," she whispered. She squeezed his hand. "Not that, yet. . . ."

The drinks on an empty stomach had hit her hard. She was not accustomed to alcohol, and unable to gauge her capacity. In her present state, she felt detached, as if she were in a dream, only partly aware of what was taking place.

She struggled to a sitting position. "J.D., I'm not being a tease, but I'm not ready to have an affair. Please don't force it on me now. Maybe sometime later. I do like you, and you're an attractive man. But . . . not now. My life is in too much of a mess already without another problem to cope with."

J.D. did not press the issue. Gently he said, "I can wait, Veronica. You're sure worth waitin' for, believe me. Just keep rememberin' that I'll be around, waiting. Anytime you need anything . . ."

"Thank you." She gave his hand another squeeze. "Right now, what I'd like better than anything in the world is just to stretch out here where it's quiet and go to sleep for a while. I'm so tired."

"You go right ahead. I'll see that nobody disturbs you."

She kicked off her shoes. J.D. helped arrange the

pillows as she made herself comfortable on the couch. In seconds she had fallen into a deep sleep.

She had a vivid dream. She had been stripped naked and tied to a stake with leather thongs. Slade, dressed in black western clothes, with a bandit's mask over his eyes, was piling wood around her ankles. He struck a match. Just then J.D. dressed all in white, came riding up on a great white horse. He drove Slade away, untied Veronica, swept her up in his arms, and was riding off across the prairie with her.

The jogging motion of the horse disturbed her slumber. It finally awakened her, and she realized someone was shaking her. She opened her eyes and looked up at Slade's angry face.

"So this is where you sneaked off to," he said furiously. "Don't you realize it was important to be on the speaker's platform this afternoon? It was very awkward for all of us. Something like this is all it takes to get nasty rumors started."

Veronica sat up, looking at him sullenly. "That's all you care about—your precious public image. Does it make any difference to you at all that I was exhausted? I needed some rest."

His eyes narrowed. "Exhausted? More like passed out, if you ask me. I saw you gulping beer with J.D. All we need now is for word to get around that Slade Huntington's wife has a drinking problem."

"The only problem that I have," she shot back, "is being Slade Huntington's wife!"

The political rally had ended. When they left the house, Veronica saw that the sun was setting. She had slept away the afternoon. Except for a few stragglers, the grounds were deserted. She didn't see any of the Claytons.

They drove back into town in frigid silence. At

Slade's home, Veronica went straight to her room, where she took a shower and put on a dressing gown. Hunger pangs and a wave of dizziness reminded her that she hadn't eaten anything all day.

She opened her door. The house was silent. Down the hallway she saw light under Slade's bedroom door. Silently she moved past his room and down the stairs to the kitchen, where she turned on some lights.

Exploring the pantry and refrigerator, she discovered that Mrs. Salinas had the home well stocked with food. She put on a pot of coffee and prepared a cheese omelet.

A sound at the doorway suddenly brought her around. She felt a quickening of her pulse as she saw Slade standing there, staring at her with brooding eyes. He, too, was in a robe. His shock of silver hair was rumpled. The golden specks in his brown eyes seemed to swirl like the currents of a whirlpool as he gazed at her. "I smelled the coffee," he said. "Do you have a cup to spare?"

She shrugged, nodded toward the electric pot that was beginning to bubble. "Help yourself," she replied coldly.

She returned to her task at the stove.

Slade moved into the room behind her. She was aware of his presence nearer to her. Her hand holding a spoon suddenly trembled.

"I see you're making one of your famous omelets," he murmured. Dishes rattled as he took a cup and saucer from the cabinet. "You were always an excellent cook, as I remember."

He poured his coffee, then sat at the kitchen table, sipping the pungent beverage. He was making her nervous and self-conscious, watching her as she cooked.

"This reminds me of the first year we were married," he continued. "We were living in that little garage apartment, remember? I'd be at school all day, and you had your secretarial job. Then I'd come home and study. We'd finally get around to a late supper, maybe ten o'clock. You'd make an omelet the way you're doing now. Then we'd sit and chat over the meal, telling each other about our experiences that day."

Veronica felt a painful lump in her throat. She dashed the back of her hand across her eyes. Why did he have to bring up painful memories like that? She kept her face turned away from him, concentrating on making the omelet.

When it was done, she took her plate to the table, sitting as far away from Slade as possible.

"Young couples usually have a struggle those first years," he mused sadly. "They dream about how things will get better when they're making more money, when they move into a bigger house. It isn't until it's too late that they look back and realize that those early days when they're struggling, when they own few material things and are living in a tiny rented apartment, are really the best times they'll have. They are more carefree and in love then than they'll ever be again. . . ."

Veronica's head was bent over her dish. She ate because her body needed food, but her meal had become tasteless. She struggled to hold back tears. This was the first indication she'd had that Slade had any feeling of nostalgia for the closeness they had once shared and remorse that it was over. Was it possible that a shred of human feeling existed somewhere in his ruthless, ambition-driven nature?

She didn't trust herself to speak. She quickly finished her meal, rinsed her dishes, and returned to her room.

She was barely in bed before Slade knocked at her door. "Veronica, I want to talk to you."

"No," she said in a muffled voice. "Leave me alone, Slade. I want to go to sleep."

"I will not meekly go away," he said stubbornly. "This is my house. You're my wife. I want to talk to you."

"We've been all through this before," she replied in a strained voice. "The matter of my being your wife is only a legal technicality. I am living here under duress."

"Veronica, I need you tonight," he said threateningly. "I'm not going to sleep a wink, thinking about you in bed in the next room. The other day, in your shower, when we made love . . . it was good . . . as good as it has ever been for us. It was as exciting for you as it was for me, you can't deny it."

Her face burned in the darkness. The truth of his words shamed her.

He rattled the doorknob. "Unlock the door, Veronica."

"You know you don't just want to talk to me," she said.

"Of course not. I want to make love to you."

"Well, I don't want you to. And I'm not going to unlock the door." Her heart was thudding painfully.

"I'm losing my patience," he said with growing anger. He rattled the knob loudly.

She drew her bedcover closer around her, a chill entering her bloodstream. Slade had a ferocious temper.

Suddenly there was a splintering crash! Light from the hallway cascaded into the room. Slade had kicked the door open!

His dark frame filled the opening. A shaft of a soft

light glimmered in his silver hair. He stood there
motionless for a moment, as if considering his options.
Veronica huddled into herself on the bed. She had
never before been scared of Slade, not physically. But
for a brief, frantic moment she realized the depths
of Slade's anger. The air crackled with the fury of
Slade's emotional intensity. Veronica stopped breathing.

Then Slade began stalking over to the bed, like a
jungle cat after its prey. Veronica sucked in her breath,
realizing it was not fear she experienced in that moment, but anger. Her nerves were an open wound, raw
and painful. Conflicting emotions stormed inside her. It
was a romantic fantasy come true, being overwhelmed
by a powerful man whose magnetic attraction she had
never truly been able to resist. But the reality was much
different from the fantasy. In her fantasy, she was safe.
She could turn off the picture anytime she wanted to.
She was in control of the action. But this time Slade was
in control, and they both knew it. That knowledge gave
a new, exciting, yet frightening dimension to what was
happening.

He stood over her bed, his face dark with fury. "This
business of locking me out of your room is going to
end!" he stormed. "You're my wife. A wife does not
lock her husband out of her bedroom. Not in my
household."

With that, he scooped her out of the bed. She
struggled furiously, but his arms were like steel.

He carried her down the hallway to his room, where
he dumped her on his bed. Her emotions were boiling
between anger and fright. She felt his gaze slashing at
her, drinking in the vision of her body barely concealed
by a flimsy, transparent nightgown. A hot flush suf-
fused her flesh.

She covered her breasts with her arms. Her eyes returned his gaze with blazing fury.

He switched off the lights. The bed sagged with his weight as he settled beside her. He pulled her stiff body close to him. She felt a thousand pinpricks of sensation where her pliant curves yielded to his hard ridges and muscles.

She stiffened as he impatiently slid the gossamer nightwear from her shoulders. She was rigid, gritting her teeth against the emotional storm that threatened to break through a dam within her.

Now he was cuddling her close against his own nakedness. He seemed content to merely hold her close for the time being. Minutes ticked by as he gently stroked her bare back, easing the tense resistance of her body almost imperceptibly. She felt the tension gradually drain from her muscles. Moment by moment, she slipped into a kind of hypnotic relaxation.

Her consciousness became centered in sensation, the tactile warmth of his body, the soothing caress of his hands, the warm closeness of their flesh. A distant part of her mind cried No . . . no! even as her hips began to move in the rhythm of his lovemaking. . . .

Long afterward, when Slade was asleep beside her, Veronica stared at the dark ceiling above her. Finally she arose, slipped on a robe, and went downstairs. She opened the liquor cabinet and mixed a drink. As she sipped it she thought that Slade's trap around her was now complete, and there was no escaping him. It had not been enough to force her into the role of his wife for the sake of his public image. He would use her body to satisfy his lust whenever he wished.

It was close to dawn when she finally fell into a troubled sleep on the couch downstairs.

Chapter Seven

*B*eginning the following morning, Slade Huntington's campaign for the state senate moved into high gear. For Veronica, life became a jumbled kaleidoscope of political meetings, hasty airplane flights with Slade to speaking engagements, lunches with civic organizations, keeping a forced smile as she appeared in public beside Slade, writing his speeches, and very little sleep.

Jake Foreman had wasted no time in putting together a loyal, hardworking campaign organization. First, he had assembled an advisory group of knowledgeable experts, including several party officials, newspaper editors, lawyers, and a few veteran politicians. They were chosen for their experience in other campaigns, their firsthand knowledge of the various voting factions in the district, and their loyalty to Slade. This panel became a sounding board that could brainstorm ideas and suggest ways to attack and counterattack the opposition.

Next, the campaign manager sent out letters to enlist supporters into cell groups around the district. These were volunteers who enjoyed the excitement of the political battle and were energetic supporters of Slade Huntington. They became a valuable weapon. They passed along information about Malden's tactics, worked to enlist other supporters, and distributed campaign materials such as bumper stickers and electioneering posters.

Jake Foreman quoted Mao Tse-tung, the Communist revolutionary leader, "Give me just two or three men in a village and I will take the village." Foreman grinned. "Now, that was a Communist talking, but it isn't bad advice for a campaign manager in a democratic election race. A few loyal, hardworking key people can swing the votes in a precinct."

In a short while Foreman had several hundred cell groups around the district, hard at work to get Slade elected.

Veronica found herself listening to, and learning from, Jake Foreman. Whatever her feelings about Slade, she found the political process fanscinating and Jake Foreman a brilliant campaign manager. The man was a dynamo of energy. He seemed to go without sleep and to get his nourishment from the battle. Under other circumstances, she would have put herself heart and soul into Slade's campaign. As it was, she worked on speeches, direct mail, television, and other public-relation strategies, but only because she was forced to do so.

Foreman was convinced that a small percentage of undecided and indifferent voters held the key to victory. "The indifferents," Foreman philosophized, "may be productive, law-abiding citizens, but they are not much interested in what goes on politically. Many times they are wrapped up in their work or career, professional people like doctors or research scientists who are too busy to read about or care about the candidates and the issues. They may be businessmen who travel most of the time and are not much in touch with local issues. Or, on the other side of the coin, they might be semi-recluses or eccentric little old ladies who are out of the mainstream of the real world.

"Our task," Foreman went on, "is to find out who those indifferents are, and the second step is to think of ways to reach them and get them to vote for our man. These are people who often can be swayed by personal contact and by emotion."

To that end, Slade's campaign manager worked hard to put together an army of what he called foot soldiers. "The indifferents and undecideds have to be reached," he said. "But there is no way Slade can knock on every door of his district and say 'Please vote for me.' If he could, the election would be in the bag. Since Slade can't do it all himself, we'll send substitutes in his place. These people will be our foot soldiers. It's been my experience that a candidate who has the right kind of foot soldiers out beating the bushes for him never fails to win an election," Foreman said confidently.

He explained further, "If a neighbor comes knocking on your door, he's not going to influence you if you are a staunch Democrat, or a firm Republican, or whatever your political choice might be. Our foot soldiers are not going to waste their time trying to change the mind of someone who has a firm political conviction. They're not out to start political arguments or convince anybody by logic.

"On the other hand, if you happen to be one of the undecided or indifferent voters and somebody knocks on your door and says, 'Hello, I'm your neighbor down the street, and I just wanted to tell you that I think Slade Huntington is a fine man, and I just wanted to ask if you'd please vote for him,' why, you're going to get a percentage of folks who will be flattered and moved by this personal appeal. We're living in a lonely, dehumanized society, and personal contact can mean a lot, specially if it's from a neighbor who will take time to all on you and chat a bit. This approach will work with only a percentage of possible voters—but remember we're dealing in percentages.

"The kind of people who make good foot soldiers," Foreman explained, "are extroverts who are often active in civic drives, like appeals for the United Way, Boy Scouts, or Heart Fund. Those kind of folks usually know their neighborhood pretty well, too."

Veronica discovered that Foreman had a specific program for recruiting his army of foot soldiers. He obtained maps of the areas to be covered and had the blocks counted. That gave him the number of volunteers he would need. "I like to have one person per block, although we don't always get them," he said.

Next, he set up a room for telephone callers. He had ten telephones installed, and he hired twenty professional operators, women with pleasant, friendly voices, to make the calls. They worked in thirty-minute shifts so they could be fresh and poised when they spoke. Volunteer workers had made lists of telephone numbers.

The operators had brief, prepared speeches. An operator would introduce herself, then say, "I'm calling for Mr. Slade Huntington, who is running for state senate. He asked me to call to see if you would be willing to help in his campaign. Would you be willing to help him win the race?"

The operators were instructed to be cordial with negative replies, but when they had an affirmative response, they explained that a packet of information would be sent to the volunteer and he or she would be asked to call on neighbors.

In this manner, Foreman constructed his army of volunteers who were out beating the bushes for Slade.

These tactics, along with direct mail, newspaper advertising, billboards, posters, and television and radio spots, cost a great deal of money. But Foreman seemed not concerned with expenses. The Claytons, he assured Veronica, had promised all the money they needed.

When the campaign manager delegated the task of speechwriting to Veronica, he talked about the issues and how Slade should address them in his speeches.

"You see, Mrs. Huntington, there are two kinds of promises a political candidate can make in his campaign: the promise to do something, or the promise not to do something. It's a heck of a lot easier to be against something. You remember the old story about the shipwrecked victim who was washed up on the shore of a tropical island. When the natives dragged him out of the surf, he asked, 'What kind of government have you got here? Whatever it is, I'm agin it!' That's human nature. Some voters can be more strongly influenced to vote against something or somebody than for something.

"Usually the incumbent points to his past record and promises to do more or give more if reelected. The challenger criticizes the record of the incumbent and promises *not* to do what the incumbent promises to do.

"Now, let's apply that to the race between Slade and Malden. Senator Malden wants to legalize gambling in the state, saying it will bring in revenue and lower taxes. Slade is against that, warning it will invite organized crime. He needs to back up his warning in his speeches with statistics and quotes from law-enforcement people.

"Malden is working hard to have that new dam and reservoir situated up at Three Oaks Canyon. Slade is opposed. He needs to talk about the damage that location would do to the ecology. Get some biology professors and wildlife people to give him quotes, and have some conservation groups make statements he can use. A lot of the land up around Three Oaks Canyon is owned by a development company called New Land Horizons. We think they are lobbying strongly for that Three Oaks Canyon location because they stand to make a bundle if it's situated there. We feel sure they are making a big, secret payoff to Malden, but we haven't been able to prove it, yet. We feel sure the New Land Horizons outfit is corporate-owned by some greedy businessmen around the state, but the whole thing is so well masked that we can't get a finger on it. So Slade can't make any direct accusations, but you can put some innuendoes in his speeches about 'special interests' backing that Three Oaks Canyon location. 'Special interests' covers a lot of territory, and it has become a kind of buzzword, has the ring of 'villain' about it.

"Now, there are other issues that are important, too, such as teachers' salaries, raising the gasoline tax, liberal or conservative aid to education. Malden has tried to give himself the image of a liberal. His voting record shows he's strong for welfare, labor unions, increased state spending. Slade is running on a more conservative ticket, wanting to cut government spending, reduce taxes, and fight inflation. There are pros and cons on both sides. Folks are running scared of inflation and mad about taxes, so that's a plus for Slade. But, at the same time, a lot of voters have come to depend on state jobs and state social programs, and you can bet they're going to support Malden. The labor unions are going to back Malden because he wants to repeal right-to-work laws. But this is a western state with a good many voters in favor of right-to-work laws, so Slade needs to take a definite stand on that."

Veronica, who had been taking notes, said grimly, "I can see I have my work cut out for me."

"Yes, and you'll do a fine job! So far, the speeches you have written for Slade have been excellent. Slade is a fine public speaker, a silver-tongued orator of the old school, sort of a modern Daniel Webster or William Jennings Bryan. You provide him the material, and his resonant voice and polished delivery turn the words into sheer poetry. The two of you make a winning combination."

Veronica blushed and looked away. *More like a losing combination,* she thought bitterly. The wall between her and Slade was growing higher every day.

But Foreman seemed oblivious to the chasm between Slade and Veronica. He said enthusiastically, "Having you actively working on Slade's campaign is an asset to us in two ways. First, we have the benefit of your talent and expertise. Second, it helps allay any gossip Malden might be trying to stir up about your separation and reconciliation.

"I wish," Foreman went on, "we could pin Malden down to a public debate. Slade would rip him to shreds. But Malden is too shrewd for that. His style is more that of the old Huey P. Long demagoguery. He does better at the grass-roots level, going around in shirt-sleeves, shaking hands at labor union meetings, on street corners, and in fraternal lodges. Have to give the devil his due; Malden is an old master at that. His campaign manager, Dade Tolliver, is one for the books. He wears a shoestring necktie, suspenders, and white socks, and he chews tobacco. But he's a shrewd one. And dangerous. His specialty is starting ugly rumors, using derogatory innuendoes. He's been the moving force behind some vicious campaigns. But he's kept Malden in office all these years. Have to give him credit for that."

That week, Veronica went on the road with Slade again in a swing through the district. A heavy schedule of public appearances and speeches had been lined up for him. On Friday, they were in a small town several hundred miles from home base. Slade was to make a key address that night. Malden had been in the town earlier that week to address a labor group. Jake Foreman considered this a strategic area, and he was eager for Slade to counter any gains Malden might have made. A hall had been rented and considerable effort had been made to publicize a town meeting. Jake Foreman and several members of his campaign advisory board flew into town that morning with J. D. Clayton in one of the Claytons' private airplanes. Veronica had been given the task of writing the speech Slade would deliver that evening.

At midmorning, Slade received an urgent telephone call from Barbara Lange. A knotty problem had arisen in his law firm. She pleaded with him to return for a few hours to help her straighten the matter out.

A hasty meeting was called. J.D. offered the use of his airplane. It was agreed that Slade would fly home, take care of the problem there early in the afternoon, and be back in time to deliver his speech.

Veronica spent a tense, angry afternoon locked in their motel room as she slaved over the speech. She felt certain the "urgent problem" in the law firm was Barbara—she hadn't see Slade all week. They were no doubt locked in Slade's private office. Her imagination supplied lurid details of what was going on there.

She communicated some of her frustration and anger to her speechwriting. The job was completed late that afternoon. She had been at her typewriter without a break for four hours. When she wearily stood up, her back ached and every muscle in her body was tense with fatigue. She felt gritty and utterly exhausted.

She took the speech to the room Foreman occupied. He read it through without comment, then looked up, his bright eyes sparkling. "Terrific! Mrs. Huntington, you filled this one with fire and brimstone—exactly what we need!"

Fire and brimstone. She had been seething with it all day since Slade went flying off to Barbara Lange's arms. She wasn't surprised that some of it had spilled onto the paper in her typewriter.

"Read this," the campaign manager exclaimed, handing the speech to one of his advisory members. "This is going to be Slade's best speech to date. You'll be at the hall to hear Slade deliver it tonight, Mrs. Huntington?"

Veronica shook her head. "I have a blinding headache. I'm going back to the room and collapse. One of the local stations is televising it. I'll watch it on the tube."

She returned to her room where she gulped two aspirins, washing them down with a shot of straight bourbon. Then she sprawled across the bed and was asleep almost at once.

It was dark when she awoke. Her headache was gone, and she felt rested. When she looked at her wristwatch, she realized with surprise that it was time for Slade's speech to be going on. Apparently he had returned just in time to be whisked from the airport to the town meeting. She assumed Jake and the others must have met him at the airport with his speech, and he had read it over while they drove him to the meeting hall.

She switched on the television set and turned to the local channel. Slade's image flashed on the screen. She heard the words she had written that afternoon being spoken as smoothly as if Slade had rehearsed the speech all day. He was a silver-tongued scoundrel, all right, just as Jake Foreman had described. The words rolled off his tongue like music. He seemed to savor each phrase, then deliver it with relish and power. He breathed life and fire into the words she had written.

His television image was striking. With his mane of silver hair contrasting with his tanned complexion, his strong profile, broad shoulders, and magnetic personality, he made an impact on the TV audience.

That included Veronica. She felt herself slipping under his hypnotic spell. And then, with a cold jolt, she remembered where he had been all day—secluded with Barbara Lange. And the warmth that seeing him so vital and handsome on the television screen had sparked in her suddenly turned to dead ashes.

Angrily she switched off the set. She needed to work off her churning emotions with physical exertion. Quickly she stripped off her clothes, yanked a brief bikini swimsuit from a drawer, and dressed for the pool.

She ran outside to the courtyard and dived into the motel pool. She lost all sense of time as she swam hard, churning the water with angry strokes. She kept it up until she had worked the burning anger from her body. Then she floated for a while.

An hour later, in better control of herself, she clambered from the pool and headed back to the room, dripping water as she walked. She opened the door and froze with a gasp.

"Lovely," Slade murmured, his look appraising her dripping, scantily clad body.

He was sprawled in a chair, his tie loose, drink in hand, looking relaxed and immensely pleased with himself.

Veronica's face was stiff, her voice cold. "I thought you'd still be at the meeting hall."

He shrugged. "Finished the speech fifteen minutes ago. I came back with Jake and the others. We're going to have a celebration in his room in a little while. The speech was a rousing success." He raised his glass to her. "Thanks to my talented little wife who wrote it."

She looked away. "I'd like some privacy while I change, if you don't mind," she snapped.

She started toward the bureau. Slade rose from the chair, his big body moving with the speed and liquid smoothness of a panther. She felt his strong fingers catch her arm. "Don't be in a hurry," he said huskily. "I like you in that bikini, with your body all shiny and glistening. You look like a mermaid."

"Slade, let go of me," she said sharply.

He shook his head. "Why don't we have our own celebration here, before we join the others? You're almost dressed—or should I say, undressed—for it."

Hot blood rushed to her cheeks. "Don't start that now, Slade. Leave me alone."

"That's not easy when you suddenly come walking in here seminude. Do you have any idea how good you look in a bikini?"

"I never would have worn it if I'd known you'd be here when I got out of the pool."

"Then I'm glad I surprised you."

The desire to fling a scorching remark about Barbara Lange was almost overwhelming, but her stubborn ride choked back the words. Instead, she raked him with a scathing look and tried to pull away from him.

But his strong arms kept her his prisoner. He drew er wet body closer.

"Slade, don't! Let me go."

She pulled away from him and tried to run to the athroom, but, laughing, he caught her, and they umbled on the bed. She struggled, but Slade held her own. Grinning, he tickled her. In spite of her anger, he was forced to laugh.

"I know all your good tickle spots," he warned.

As on that first night after the election-committee meeting when they got caught in the sprinkler system, Slade was in a jubilant, boyish mood, a mood that was hard to resist.

"You're high because of the good reception you got onight."

"Right." He grinned. "I'll confess. I'm a terrible nam. I love to hear the applause of a big crowd. It's ntoxicating. It pours adrenaline into my blood, awakens my hormones, makes me passionate."

"Well, I'm not your crowd. To me you're just a bloody ear basher."

"That's Australian for a talkative bore, isn't it?"

She shrugged. "If the shoe fits . . ."

"Well, we'll see about that." He grinned dangerously and tickled her again.

She was forced to laugh until her stomach hurt and tears ran down her cheeks. "Slade, please . . ."

"Still an ear basher?"

She shook her head. "No," she gasped.

"Care to elaborate?"

He had tickled her until she was on the verge of hysteria. "You're a—a regular William Jennings Bryan." She giggled.

"That's more like it. Are you proud of your husband?"

"You're not my husband."

"I have a marriage certificate that says different."

"It's just a meaningless piece of paper."

"We'll see about that," he threatened. Gently he kissed the drops of water left from the pool off her throat and shoulders.

"Slade, don't . . ."

His tickling had left her weak. She knew, considering the mood he was in, that resistance was useless.

"There's no sprinkler system to save you tonight," he murmured, nuzzling the hollow of her throat. The masculine stubble on his jaw tickled her sensitive flesh and awakened a rash of goose bumps. Her choked protestations were directed more at her own traitorous emotions than toward Slade.

How could she hate him so and still feel response like a flash of fire throughout her being? The answer was basic and biological. He was an extremely attractive, sexy man. And she had a woman's normal appetites. She was far from frigid, and Slade, damn him, knew it well, just as he knew how to awaken her slumbering passions.

He hooked his thumb in the halter top of her bikini and stripped it from her with a gesture. He buried his face in the shadowy valley between her lush breasts, murmuring her name softly. Then his lips trailed up the golden mound and found a throbbing nipple. Her blood began coursing through her arteries in heated, pounding surges.

Veronica showered. She dried herself angrily, scouring her body with fierce rubs, as if hating the flesh that had clung to Slade so avidly. To her image in the mirror she hurled her pet Australian slang term for a fool, "You drongo!"

To go to the party in Jake Foreman's room, she had selected a pullover tunic in a lush tropical print and black pants. The tunic had a button-trimmed V neck, and its drop sleeves had button-tab detailing. She fastened a gold slave-chain bracelet on her slim bare left ankle, thinking grimly that its symbolism accurately described the relationship Slade had forced on her. She stepped into gold high-heeled sandals and gave her appearance a final check in the bathroom mirror.

She left the bathroom. Slade was standing before a dresser mirror, fastening his gold cuff links. He turned and smiled. "You look lovely."

She shrugged off the compliment coldly as she gathered up her purse.

Slade said, "I want to tell you again what a fine job you did on that speech. It was inspired."

"Let's get one thing straight right off," Veronica fired back. "Anything I contribute to your campaign is only because I'm being forced to do it. I am not one of your devoted constituents. It's only a job to me, which I happen to know how to do well. . . . And, win or lose, you'll get a bill when I'm through."

His eyes glazed over. "Of course," he said calmly. "Let's keep everything businesslike. You'll be paid well for your services . . . all your services." He gave the tangled bedclothes a meaningful glance that sent a scarlet flush of humiliation and anger to Veronica's cheeks. A furious reply rushed to her lips, but she swallowed it, realizing the futility of pursuing the subject.

He tucked her reluctant arm in his and led her down

the hall to the room where glasses were clinking and voices were humming.

When they entered, they were greeted by a smattering of applause. "To the next senator from this district!" Jake Foreman exclaimed, raising his glass.

"Hear, hear!" one of the men in the room agreed. "That speech should bring you a lot of votes, Slade. It was excellent. Very stirring!"

"Then my lovely wife deserves the credit," Slade said with a forced smile, "since she wrote it."

Veronica felt more embarrassed than complimented. She felt like a hypocrite. The room was filled with men who sincerely wanted to see Slade win this race. She was an unwilling contributor to his efforts. Whether Slade won or lost was of no interest to her. She only wanted to see the end of the race so Slade would release her from bondage. But she had her role to play and remembered to murmur the correct responses to comments directed her way.

She was the only woman at the small gathering. These were members of the inner circle of Slade's campaign forces, the party men and the experts who made up his advisory committee. Jake Foreman had believed tonight's speech to be so critical that he had asked them to be on hand to assess the effect of Slade's address.

J. D. Clayton was in the room. He smiled when Veronica walked in, his eyes signaling a special message of greeting. She was pleased to see him again. She sensed a growing fondness for and trust in J.D. He was a friend she knew she could lean on if the going became rough.

The room was murky with cigar smoke. Veronica felt threatened by the return of her headache. Someone handed her a drink. She toyed with it, listening to the ice cubes make tiny rattling, clinking sounds that were almost lost in the rumble of male voices around her.

The conversation turned to the opposition. Veronica half listened, wishing the meeting would end so she could take another aspirin and go to bed.

She heard Foreman say, "Malden is speaking in Sanderson tomorrow. I think some of us should go hear him first hand. Slade, this might be a good opportunity to again challenge him to a debate. The media will be there in full force. If they spot you, they're going to pounce on you. You could hammer away at the debate issue. Sooner or later, Malden is going to begin looking bad if he keeps ducking a debate with you."

Slade frowned. "I don't like to disappoint you, Jake, but I simply have to get back to my law office tomorrow. We've got a real snafu there. I didn't get it all untangled today. Sorry."

Veronica shot Slade a deadly look. This was more evidence of the powerful hold Barbara Lange still had on Slade, to be able to divert his attention from the campaign to spend another day with her. Evidently the time they spent together today had not been enough for them.

J. D. Clayton spoke up, "I can get over there to hear Malden's speech, Jake."

A sudden inspiration seized Veronica. "I'd like to go," she blurted out. "I haven't had the opportunity yet to see Slade's opponent." She looked straight at Slade and said, "After I hear him speak, I might decide to defect to the other side."

Laughter followed her quip. But Slade didn't laugh. He was the only person in the room besides herself who understood that truth had been spoken in jest.

Boldly she swung her gaze to J.D. "Would you have room for a passenger?"

Clayton responded with an expression of surprised pleasure. "Why, certainly! Plenty of room in our private jet. We can leave the airport here after breakfast and be in Sanderson in an hour."

When Veronica glanced at Slade again, she delighted in the look of controlled displeasure in his face.

Veronica had good reasons for wanting to go to Sanderson with J.D. She welcomed any excuse to get away from Slade. Besides, she had no desire to endure the humiliation of returning home with him, knowing he would go straight to his office to spend the day with Barbara Lange. This time Veronica would challenge him at his own game. She would spend the day in the company of another man, J. D. Clayton.

Later, in their room, Slade demanded, "What kind of smart-aleck stunt are you pulling?"

Her eyes widened innocently. "Whatever do you mean?"

"You know very well what I mean—dashing off across the country with J. D. Clayton."

She smiled sweetly. "But you told me I was far too much of an inhibited prude to ever get involved with another man, remember?"

He nodded. "That's not what has me concerned. I'm not sure it looks good for you to be seen taking a trip with another man when I'm someplace else."

Twin spots of anger burned on her cheeks. "Your precious public image again!" she cried. "That's the only thing you're worried about. Thanks for reminding me that your only interest in me is what I can do to help you win the race—write speeches, produce your television spots, convince the public that you're a respectable married man, and provide a convenient body when you are sexually aroused! I have a good notion to have an affair with J.D.!"

His fingers clamped painfully on her shoulders. He shook her as he would a rebellious child. "I've had enough of your temper tantrums for today. I'm too tired to deal with your infantile notions. You made it clear enough what you thought of me when you ran off to Australia."

I hope I did, Veronica thought, but you don't seem to accept it. Perhaps, as you Yanks put it, you need a house to fall on your head. And, she suddenly added to herself, J. D. Clayton might just be that house!

Slade refused to continue the fight. He undressed and went to bed. Veronica turned out the lights and followed suit. She wished the motel had separate twin beds. But it did not, so she spent the night as far away from Slade in the double bed as she could without falling off the edge. He kept to his side, too, much to her relief. A wide, silent gulf separated them.

She had trouble falling asleep. As always, when they fought, later she felt a backwash of regrets and a painful flood of memories of how different their relationship had once been. In those early months of their marriage, she had always slept in his arms, feeling warm and safe, and they would awaken to make love, then fall asleep again in the middle of a kiss. And now they were strangers, sharing the same bed, but a world apart.

Slade was up early the following morning. He gulped a cup of coffee for breakfast and left while Veronica was still dressing. She had breakfast in the motel dining room with J.D. and Jake Foreman.

Over coffee and orange juice, the campaign manager said, "Let me give you a little background information on Senator Kirk Malden, Mrs. Huntington, so you'll know something about the man you're going to hear speak today. You see, part of the business of conducting an election campaign is researching the opposition. We have several volunteer investigators who are gathering information on Senator Malden. They go through newspaper morgues, study legislature records, interview people. I'm sure Malden has a task force doing the same kind of investigative snooping on Slade. A good campaign manager needs to know the opponent as well as his own candidate. 'Know thine enemy' is good advice for anybody running for office. That includes digging into your opponent's private, business, and public life. We want to understand his psychology, his emotional makeup, his personality, and his economic picture. We try to learn all we can about his family life, who his friends and business associates are, how he made his living before getting into public life, what his record was in school, his military record, if he had one, what connections he might have with special-interest groups and lobbyists, where he gets his campaign funds, his voting record, how much property he owns . . . his net worth."

"Have you found out all that about Kirk Malden?" Veronica asked curiously.

"We've got a pretty big filing cabinet filled with data about Senator Malden. I wish we had more. There are several important questions about him that we haven't been able to answer.

"I'm not going to bore you with all that material, but here are a few facts. Kirk Malden is fifty-two years old, and a confirmed bachelor. He's short, stocky, partially bald, and very talkative. He did some amateur boxing as a young man, and still lifts weights to stay firm. He likes to act tough, something of a bully. His passion in life is good food and drink. You'll see him almost every night in one of the better restaurants, surrounded by political hacks who feed his ego by listening while he talks about himself."

Veronica found herself growing interested, despite her resentment at being involved in Slade's campaign.

Jake continued. "Malden comes from a small-town family. His father did a bit of farming and owned a feed store. Kirk Malden graduated from high school in the bottom half of his class and went into business in his hometown. For a while he worked in his father's feed store, then operated a used-car lot and sold real estate. Apparently he did pretty well as a salesman. He likes to use that rural, small-town background to put himself on the grass-roots level with voters, and he's good at that. He can go around in shirtsleeves, talking with farmers about their crops, with small-town businessmen and rural folks. He deliberately talks in a down-home manner, pretending to be the voice of the common man. But don't let that earthy populist image fool you; he's plenty shrewd and sophisticated when it comes to getting bills through the legislature.

"Malden got elected to the city council in his hometown, and that seemed to whet his appetite for politics. He was drafted into the military during the Korean conflict. When he got out, he went to school on the GI bill, earning a law degree from a small college near his hometown. But he never did practice much law. He went back home and immediately got back into politics. This time he was elected a county commissioner, and from there he moved up to the state senate, and he's held that office ever since. He's put together a strong constituency that sends him back to the capital term after term. Consequently, he's built up a strong seniori-

ty in the senate. He's chairman of several powerfu
committees. He's such a solid fixture that most of the
time nobody even bothers to run against him. Slade i
the first serious opposition he's had in years, and we've
got him running scared."

"Slade keeps hinting that Senator Malden is dishon
est," J.D. observed. "Have you found any proof o
that?"

Jake sighed. "We feel sure Malden has gotten kick
backs and payoffs over the years, but he's so clever we
can't prove a thing. We know he has quietly gone abou
buying up a lot of valuable farmland. How could he d
that on the modest salary a legislator earns in this state
The New Land Horizons Development Company has a
big stake in locating the dam and reservoir up at Three
Oaks Canyon. They have been buying up land in tha
area for years. If the dam goes in there, they'll sell a big
chunk of their land to the state for a whopping profit,
and after the lake is filled, they'll still own private
recreation and development sites all around the lake,
and you know what lakefront property can bring. With
his influence as chairman of several committees, Malden can single-handedly do a great deal to have the
dam situated at Three Oaks, so we feel confident the
New Land Horizons Development Company is paying
off Malden in a big way, but we can't prove a thing. We
can't even get a handle on who really owns that
development company, it is so well hidden behind
parent corporations and silent partners and investors."

They talked politics during breakfast, then drove to
the airport, where Clayton's sleek private jet was ready
for takeoff.

Veronica was swept aloft on a carpet of luxury. The
plane was expertly piloted, flying smoothly. J.D. made

Veronica feel like a VIP. The jet had a lounge section where they were served drinks.

"Well, you've been gettin' a pretty heavy dose of American politics since I saw you at the ranch that day, Veronica." J.D. smiled. "I got the impression then that you weren't so happy bein' forced into it. Still feel the same?"

Veronica blushed, remembering how intimate she had allowed J.D. to become with her on the couch in the big ranch house. "I really wasn't myself that day," she murmured. "The press conference had upset me, and I'd had a lot more to drink than I should have. But as for this particular bit of politics, I still feel the same. So far, it's been nothing but a lot of hard yakka for me."

"'Yakka'?"

"A lot of hard work. I've been at it night and day, doing Slade's speeches, working on a direct-mail campaign, TV spots, all that malarkey."

"It seems to be payin' off. Slade is runnin' a good race."

"Well, the polls seem to indicate he's slightly ahead of Malden, if you can believe the polls." She made the statement with no particular emotion.

Her lack of enthusiasm was not lost on J.D. He searched her face, raising an eyebrow. "Then I take it you're still the reluctant politician's wife?"

He was putting out feelers again. And she felt a need to respond. She was growing genuinely fond of J.D. His lazy smile and laconic western drawl were somehow soothing. She felt there was something solid and dependable about him. She was seized by a strong impulse to confide in him and was on the verge of doing so when the pilot announced over the intercom that they were circling for a landing and instructed them to fasten seat belts.

J.D. looked disappointed. Obviously, he, too, had been aware of the moment. It was lost in the flurry of landing and the distractions of the next two hours.

Senator Malden was also arriving by plane. A speaker's platform had been set up in front of one of the hangars at the airport. It was covered with flags and bunting. A loudspeaker system was blaring the music of a country and western band, playing to keep the crowd entertained while waiting for Malden's plane to land.

Veronica and J.D. took an unobtrusive position on the outer fringes of the crowd.

Soon Malden and his entourage arrived. He was accompanied by a number of prominent figures: political leaders, the local mayor who was supporting him, a well-known pro football player. It was a cast cleverly designed to put on a good show for the public.

"Jake said Malden has a clever campaign manager," Veronica murmured. "I can see he knows political hoopla."

Several dignitaries were introduced; then Senator Kirk Malden began his address.

He fit the picture Jake Foreman had drawn of him. He removed his coat. Soon he was waving his arms, his voice thundering with the fervor of an evangelical minister. There was a marked contrast between Slade's polished delivery and Malden's style. But Veronica suspected that Jake Foreman had misjudged Kirk Malden's ability as a speaker. In his way, he was every bit as much an orator as Slade. Only his approach was different. He used poor grammar and regional colloquialisms, punctuated at times with vulgarities, and Veronica was convinced he did it deliberately. He came across is a man of the poor working people, a fist-pounding evangelist who used the flag, motherhood, the Bible, and poverty liberally in an emotional appeal that built to a feverish climax.

Jake Foreman had described Malden as a shirt-sleeve Huey P. Long type of demagogue. Veronica decided that description fit him well.

"Friends and neighbors," he ranted, "I'm here to talk to you about the man who's runnin' against me in this senatorial race—Slade Huntington. I want to warn you that that he's a smooth-talkin', big-city shyster with a bunch of crackpot ideas that's goin' to do nothin' but put honest, hardworkin' folks out of work and send your taxes sky-high!"

Malden pounded his fists and waved his arms, working himself into a frenzy. The crowd responded, interrupting him repeatedly by applause. At times he would shout; then his voice would sink to a whisper. He'd tell earthy jokes, and the audience would burst into laughter. Then he'd grow deadly serious, leaning over the speaker's rostrum, gazing directly at the people before him.

"You people are my friends, my family. Look at my record and see what I done for the laborin' people of this state, the poor, and the needy. Look at the bills I sponsored that built bridges and roads and improved the school system. You look an' see the bills I wrote that helped out the poor with a whole bunch of social services. An' now we got this smooth-talkin' Philadelphia-lawyer type that's out wantin' to wipe out the progress we made. Slade Huntington." He spoke the name with a sneer. "He's one of them highfalutin egghead types that uses big words nobody can understand and ain't got the practical sense to find the end of his nose. He don't care that much about you folks." He snapped his fingers. "He's not my enemy. Friends, he's *your* enemy!"

Again there was a roar of response from the crowd.

Veronica had listened to the speech with whirlpools and crosscurrents of emotion. At first she thought she was going to be amused by the rantings and ravings of a buffoon. And then she began to realize how deadly clever Kirk Malden was. He was a political animal who instinctively knew mob psychology. Under his pose as an earthy man of the people was a calculating, razor-sharp mind. In spite of how she felt about Slade, she felt her blood boiling at the personal attacks Malden made on him.

Later, when the speech had ended and Veronica was back on the plane with J.D., he asked, "Well, what do you think of the opposition, now that you've heard him in person?"

"He plays rough," Veronica said grimly. "I think Jake has underestimated Kirk Malden's ability as an orator. He's every bit as much of a spellbinder as Slade, though in an entirely different way. He knows exactly how to get a crowd worked up emotionally. And I don't for one minute believe that hayseed cracker-barrel image. His audience today was largely blue-collar workers. I bet he smooths out considerably when he's talking to a bunch of industrialists. Did you notice he didn't address the issues at all? He spent most of the time in personal attack on Slade. He's making Slade the issue. He's avoiding the big issues—the location of the dam, the matter of legalizing gambling in this state."

"Then you think he's going to be tougher to beat than Jake believes?"

"I think they're all underestimating him. He actually had that crowd believing that Slade is against social services for the poor, aged, and needy, and that's an outright lie. Slade just wants to eliminate some of the waste, corruption, and unnecessary bureaucracy in administering those services."

J.D. was giving her one of his slow, searching smiles. Then he drawled, "Looks like hearin' Senator Malden has stirred up political fever you didn't know you had. You'll probably want to go back now an' work your head off to get Slade elected."

His words brought her thinking processes up short. She analyzed her deeper feelings, then slowly shook her head. "No, it's just the bloke got me ropeable— Australian slang for being very, very angry," she explained. "What I said before goes. I'm sick and tired of politics, and let's stop talking about it."

He grinned. "That, as we say in America, is a swell idea. Hey, here's another idea. It's early. If you're not in a big rush to get home, we could stop off at the ranch. Remember you promised to go for a horseback ride with me sometime? I'd sure like to show you some of our horses. I have a hunch, if you admire good horseflesh, you'll be thrilled at some of the fine-blooded animals we've got in our stables."

Veronica found the invitation extremely tempting. There was nothing waiting for her at Slade's home but more bitter conflict. She grinned. "Okay. To use another bit of Australian slang, that's an onkey-dorey idea."

J.D. had not exaggerated when he bragged about the horses in the Clayton stables. Veronica went into ecstasy over the beautiful, spirited animals. Some were racehorses. Some had aristocratic lineage from a family of winners who were used for breeding purposes. Veronica estimated that several million dollars were tied up in the Clayton string of horses.

J.D. paused before one of the stalls. "Veronica, I

want you to meet Vagabond Lady. The two of you ought to hit it off. She's a roan with reddish chestnut hair almost the color of yours."

Veronica stroked the big mare, who nuzzled her. "Oh, I love her!" she cried.

"Would you like to ride her?"

"Could I?" Veronica exclaimed, her eyes sparkling.

"She's a bit spirited. Likely to be frisky and buck a bit," J.D. warned. "I don't let anyone ride her unless they're pretty good in a saddle."

"I can handle her," Veronica said confidently. She gazed into the huge brown eyes of the roan mare. "It's love at first sight, isn't it, Vagabond Lady, you beautiful creature!"

J.D. found a pair of blue jeans and boots that fit Veronica and had Vagabond Lady saddled for her. He rode a big black stallion. Astride a horse, he was a good-looking man, riding tall with ease and grace.

As J.D. had warned, Vagabond Lady reacted to the saddle and bridle bit with a saucy independence. She shook her head and threatened to buck. But Veronica spoke soothingly, patting her neck while controlling her firmly, and they soon came to an understanding. The roan began trotting obediently.

J.D. grinned. "Didn't take long for you two to make up. I can see you grew up in a saddle, all right."

They rode for an hour across the beautiful rolling prairie. When they reached a grove of spreading oak trees beside a clear stream, they stopped to rest.

They tied the horses and strolled to a grassy spot on the creek bank. The clear water of the stream bubbled musically over the rocky bed.

"What a beautiful place!" Veronica exclaimed.

They sat on the creek bank. J.D. propped himself on an elbow, chewing a grass stem, watching her. Veronica lay back on the grass, her arms folded behind her head for a pillow, gazing at puffballs of clouds in the azure sky. She smelled the perfume of wild flowers and listened to the song of a bird. It was a peaceful interlude in the hectic drama she'd been caught up in for the past weeks.

As she gazed at the sky her thoughts roamed to Slade. Hurting memories crowded her heart and put a lump in her throat. Their first earthshaking kiss. The searching of each other's eyes to the depths of their being. Slade's tanned body, the rippling muscles, strong thighs, broad shoulders. The feeling of safety in his protective arms. And the feeling of heart-pounding awareness when his gaze roamed over her body as if devouring every secret, the shivery touch of his caress on her trembling arms and legs. The whispered, intimate secrets, shared in the darkness, and the peaceful afterglow of lovemaking, when they lay silently, their shoulders touching, their hands clasped, their hearts in rhythm.

Now all of that was gone. There remained only the memory of a man she had once known, a love she had once shared. Slade had destroyed it, and now he was a stranger. Perhaps it wasn't altogether his fault. Had there been something lacking in her to drive him into the arms of another woman? No matter how much she blamed Slade, and hated him at times, she felt a sense of her own inadequacy, too. Every woman was haunted by that sense of failure when her marriage went on the rocks.

With an effort, she returned to the present, aware that J.D. had spoken. "I'm sorry. What did you say?"

"Just wondered where you'd gone." He smiled.

"Only daydreaming. Looking up at the sky does that to me."

"I'd rather look at you," he said in his soft, drawling manner.

She returned the gaze. His presence was comforting. She liked being with him.

He bent slowly and kissed her. She circled his neck with her arms and returned the kiss lightly. "I'm growing quite fond of you, J.D., but I don't want to give you the wrong impression. I'm still a married woman."

"But not a happily married woman," he insisted, and she had no reply to make to that.

She felt languorous, almost without will. She fantasized what it would be like to lie here and have sex with J.D. in this secluded glen, feeling somehow detached, as if standing apart from herself. She had grown fond of J.D. He was an attractive man, and the unpleasant situation with Slade had made her vulnerable. There would be none of the thundering passion Slade could arouse in her. But J.D. wanted her, and a woman could be tempted to give pleasure to a man who ardently desired her.

But then a sudden cold panic brought her to a sitting position.

Slade, damn him, was right. He had spoken the truth when he said she was not capable of having an affair. Her strict moral upbringing had erected barriers that were not easily brushed aside. They were ingrained in her character, and to ignore them would be denying her own worth. She had made a point of telling Slade that all that was left of their marriage was a technicality— but the fact remained that they were still legally married. More than that, as much as she fought against it, she was still sleeping with Slade.

It was infuriating that Slade knew her so well. She ardently wished she could shock that smug attitude out of him. It angered her that he so confidently took her for granted.

"I'm sorry, J.D.," she said, squeezing his hand. "I don't want to let you get all worked up and then not deliver. I am fond of you. You're a swell, dinkum friend. I feel comfortable with you. But not up to having an affair—at least, not at this point."

"An affair?" he murmured slowly. "I guess you misunderstood. I'm serious, Veronica. I want you to divorce Slade and marry me. I realize it would have to wait until after the election. . . ."

She gazed at him with a surprised confusion of emotion. "I—I don't know what to say, J.D. I didn't expect this."

"You're not happy with Slade, are you?"

She shook her head. "Slade ruined that for me." In halting, painful words she told him the whole, ugly story about Slade's affair with Barbara Lange, how Veronica had discovered it and the pain and bitterness that followed. "I finally realized the truth, that Slade uses people to get what he wants. He used me to finish getting his law degree. Now he's using me again to help win this election."

"It looks to me," J.D. said, "like Barbara Lange is still very much in Slade's life. She's a partner in his law firm now. I see them together a lot."

Veronica nodded miserably. "He's with her today."

"Then I don't reckon you owe him any loyalty."

"I suppose not. But technically we are still married." She reached out and touched J.D.'s hand. "I need to think about what you said today. I—I really didn't know you were getting this serious. You've caught me off guard. I have to think about all this. . . ."

He gazed at her searchingly, as if by looking deeply enough into her eyes he could read her thought processes. Then he drawled softly, "When I was no more than a little button, I wanted a horse of my own in the worst way. Had my eyes on a beautiful palomino pony my father had added to our stables. He said I was too young, had to wait until I was more grown up. Well, I waited patiently. I hung around that pony, wantin' her, wishin' and waitin'. And one day, on my birthday, Dad took me out to the stables. Said the time had come—that pretty little palomino pony was mine. That taught me a lesson that sometimes you have to wait for somethin' you really want."

She smiled at him tenderly. "I don't want to lead you on or give you false hopes. Right now I'm still a bit mixed up. A part of me, I suppose, is still involved with Slade. I have to get my mind clear about that, be sure he's out of my system entirely. . . ."

"I can wait," J.D. promised.

She plucked at a blade of grass with a nervous gesture, her mind a tumult of confusion. She asked, "Why me, J.D.? A man like you could have his pick of women."

"Okay, so I picked you."

"But I'm not a glamorous model, an actress, an international beauty. Those must be the kind of women you associate with."

He shrugged. "Maybe it's because you're different. I wanted you from the first minute I laid eyes on you."

As they rode together back to the stables Veronica tried to get a handle on her feelings about J. D. Clayton. Could she fall in love with him? He was a colorful and intriguing man. Any woman would find him attractive. And yet he was still something of an enigma to her. She didn't know him all that well, yet. Perhaps, when she did, she would find she could fall very much in love with him. She was glad for their friendship at this point. He provided a strong shoulder to lean on. She needed someone like him, although the nature and extent of that need was not yet clearly defined in her heart.

When they arrived at the stables, J.D. suggested, "Why don't you go on up to the big house and have a drink? I need to see about a few things here, and then I'll join you there and drive you on into town."

Veronica entered the cool, air-conditioned interior of the spacious ranch house, remembering the time she had been here before at the barbecue political rally.

When she strolled into the high-ceilinged den with its open beams, Mexican tile floor, giant fireplace, and bar, she saw a familiar mop of red hair. Nichole Clayton turned from the bar, giving her a cool, level gaze.

"Hello, Nichole." Veronica smiled, trying to melt the younger woman's cold stare.

Nichole slowly swirled the ice cubes in her glass. "Been ridin' with J.D.?" she murmured.

"Yes. He certainly has some beautiful horses."

"The best money can buy," Nichole said with an edge in her voice. She downed her drink, took a package of cork-tipped cigarettes from her purse, and lit one. She inhaled deeply, then waved her hand in a gesture that took in the room. "Clayton money everywhere you look. This house cost a mint to build and keep up." She snapped her fingers. "Petty cash to the Claytons."

Veronica joined her at the bar. "You sound bitter, Nichole. There's nothing wrong with being rich, is there?"

"Guess not," Nichole said, her lovely young mouth curving downward. "If you happen to be one of the rich Claytons. I'm one of the poor relations."

Veronica poured a soft drink into a glass with ice cubes, aware of Nichole's measured gaze. "The Claytons usually get what they want. Has J.D. gotten you yet?"

Veronica flushed, giving the girl a sharp look. "Nichole—"

"I know," the redhead said, raising her hand. "None of my business. Sorry."

There was a moment's stiff silence. Then Veronica said, "Listen, Nichole, J.D. and I are good friends. Nothing more than that. I'd like to be your friend, too."

Nichole gazed at her. For a moment tears filled her eyes. "Sure." She shrugged. "We can be friends. I don't have anything against you. Why should I? It's J.D.'s guts I hate."

"Why?" Veronica exclaimed, surprised. "What has he done to you?"

Nichole sullenly poured another drink. "A lot of things. You wouldn't understand. You'd have to be a poor Clayton livin' on the charity of the rich Claytons to understand."

"Charity? No, I guess I don't understand."

"It's a long story." Nichole downed another drink. Veronica realized she had never seen the girl when she wasn't drinking. Nichole said, "Someday I'll tell you all about the Claytons. Maybe you could write a book about them . . ." She broke off.

Veronica suddenly became aware of J.D.'s tall figure in the doorway. He was giving Nichole a stern look. She returned his look with a sullen glare and then turned her back on him, facing the bar and refilling her glass.

"Ready for me to take you back to town, Veronica?" J.D. asked.

"All right. I just have to change out of these riding clothes."

A short while later they were in one of the Claytons' air-conditioned Lincoln Continentals. Again Veronica felt surrounded by plush luxury: soft leather, wood-grained dash, the strains of background music from a multiple speaker system.

"I have to apologize for my little cousin Nichole," J.D. said. "I suppose she was bending your ear."

"Well," Veronica said, "she wasn't making a whole lot of sense."

"The child has a drinking problem, as you can see," J.D. said. "We've had to haul her to a private sanatorium to have her dried out on several occasions."

"For some reason, she seems bitter about being related to the Clayton family."

He nodded. "I suppose that's part of her problem. Her family is dirt-poor. My dad felt sorry for Nichole and her twin brother, Nick. He took them under his wing, practically adopted them. He paid for their clothes, their schooling. In Nick's case, it worked out fine. The boy now has a degree in engineering and a brilliant future. Nichole has been a problem, though. She drinks too much. Smashed up a couple of cars . . ." He shook his head.

"Part of the problem could be that she's in love with you," Veronica said thoughtfully.

J.D. gave her a curious glance. "You mentioned that before, the first time you met her. What gives you that idea?"

"I'm a woman. It's obvious to me she considers me a rival."

His suntanned face broke into a smile. "That part would certainly be true if she had any claim on me. I told you before, Nichole is too young to be in love with anyone. She's just a kid in love with the idea of love."

"Don't be too sure," Veronica murmured. "I have a feeling Nichole is a lot older than you think."

When the car drew up in front of Slade's home, J.D. turned to Veronica. "I'll be spendin' a couple of days in town. Have some business to take care of here. I have reservations at the Holiday Inn, room two-twelve. Please give me a call there when you're able. We could have a drink, or have dinner together."

"I'll—I'll try," Veronica said nervously. Once again, she felt the victim of events that were rushing her in an unexpected direction faster than she could think.

The big house greeted her with silence. The housekeeper had left for the day. Slade, she thought with a pang, was no doubt somewhere with Barbara Lange.

She glanced at her watch. It would soon be dark. She had a lonely sandwich in the kitchen, keeping herself company with a mental review of the day's surprising events. Heading the list was J.D.'s proposal. She struggled to get an emotional understanding of that surprising development. How did she really feel about it? Could she fall in love with J.D.? The proposal had given her damaged ego a boost. It was good to know that an attractive man would want her, and she felt a warm flood of emotion toward J.D. for that. Slade had made her feel degraded, humiliated, and somehow lacking as a woman. J.D. had restored her feeling of worth, and she could almost fall in love with him out of gratitude.

Her confused feelings about Slade were still in the way of her becoming intimate with another man. If she could ever wipe Slade entirely out of her life, she would be ready for love again, and why not J.D.?

The loneliness of the big, silent house pressed down

on her. She wandered into the den, switched on a console TV, but found nothing worth watching. Attached to the set was a videotape recorder. Slade had a library of videotapes, including several movies, but none of the titles interested her.

She searched the bookshelf, found an anthology of short stories, and settled down with it. She was avoiding going upstairs now that Slade was forcing her to share his bedroom.

She was in the middle of a story by Dorothy Parker when the telephone rang. It was Slade. "How was your day?" he asked.

"All right," she replied coolly.

"You heard Senator Malden speak?"

"I certainly did."

"Well . . . what did you think?"

"He's a formidable opponent. Jake Foreman may have underestimated him. He's going straight for your jugular vein, by the way. As far as he's concerned, there is only one issue—Slade Huntington."

There was a moment's silence. Slade said, "Yes, that's Malden's style. But I'm not worried. Our polls tell us we're ahead."

Silence again, and then Slade said, "What I really called about was to see if you were safely home and to tell you that I'm still not through here at the office. Looks like it will be close to midnight before we are finished."

This time the silence dripped ice. When Veronica could control her anger enough to speak, she said, "Well, I'm sure that you and Barbara will complete what you set out to do," and she hung up.

She picked up the book of short stories and hurled it across the room. She wished she had Slade for a target.

Furiously she paced from room to room, her heels

echoing in the silent house. She stopped at the liquor cabinet, poured a drink, swallowed it, poured another. Tearfully she exclaimed, "The bloody no-hoper is driving me to drink!"

She didn't care anymore. She gulped the straight bourbon, choked, gasped, and wiped tears from her eyes. If it took getting drunk, she had to stifle the emotional turmoil that had become an unbearable, crushing pain.

The silence of the house shrieked at her. Loneliness became a stifling blanket. She felt on the verge of an indefinable panic. Her hands were trembling. She clamped her teeth together to keep them from chattering.

"Steady, girl," she gulped. "Don't go off the deep end."

Suddenly, she grabbed up the telephone directory. She leafed through the pages, found the number she wanted, dialed it. An impersonal female voice said, "Holiday Inn."

"Mr. J.D. Clayton's room, please."

"Just a moment." A brief silence. Then: "He's in room two-twelve. I'll ring."

He won't be there, of course. He'd be in the bar, or at the Petroleum Club with business friends. . . .

But she heard his voice say, "Hello?"

She held the receiver tightly. She really had no business calling him. She should hang up. But she looked around the room that mocked her with its silence. She touched her tongue to her lips. "It's—it's Veronica."

"Well, hey, this is a nice surprise!"

"Yes. . . . I—I really didn't think I'd catch you in your room—"

"You just did. I finished dinner a few minutes ago."

"You're probably going out. I—don't want to hold you up. . . ."

"Nonsense. Nothin' I could possibly do that would be more important than talkin' to you."

"Thank you, J.D.," she said tearfully. "A few more statements like that, and I *will* be in love with you."

He chuckled. "I'll have to try and think up some more." Then his voice became solicitous. "You sound kinda upset. Is something the matter?"

"Oh, I'm rattling around this big old house all alone. Slade will be tied up until midnight. I got myself into some kind of nervous funk. Bloody silly of me, but there it is. Had to talk to somebody or start screaming."

She left out the ugly, humiliating reason for her emotional state—the fact that Slade was using business reasons for spending the evening with Barbara Lange.

J.D. said, "Listen, why don't you come over here? We can have some drinks and talk. I'd come get you, but my dad came into town with some friends and then decided to borrow my car for the evenin', so I'm afoot. Do you have transportation?"

"Yes. I have my car."

"Then you'll come?"

She hesitated but then rebelliously brushed caution aside. "Yes, I'd like that. J.D., you're a dinkum friend."

"You keep calling me that. Is it good or bad?"

She smiled through her tears. "It's very good."

"How long do you think it would take you to get over here?"

"I have to change and put on some fresh mascara. What I have on seems to be running down my face. Then there's the drive across town. About an hour, I should guess."

"Fine. You be careful, now."

In her car, she had waves of misgivings and was on the verge several times of turning around. Then the thought of spending the evening alone in the big house with visions of Barbara Lange in Slade's arms reawakened her fury, and she kept going.

She knocked timidly on J.D.'s motel-room door. He opened it at once, smiling warmly. "I'm glad you came, Veronica. To tell the truth, I've been pretty lonesome, too. Kept thinking about how we spent the day together."

He kissed her.

Nervously she moved away from him. "This is pretty scandalous, visiting you in your motel room. If anybody saw me come here, it could start a rumor that would be dreadful for Slade's campaign. Could we go someplace else?"

"We could go to the bar if you don't mind gettin' a headache. They've got a rock band playin' there. Besides, if you're worried about startin' a rumor, we'd be more likely to be seen together in a public place, don't you think?"

She nodded. "Yes, I suppose that's true."

"Relax," he assured her. He moved to a bureau where a bucket of ice and some bottles had been placed and mixed two drinks.

She accepted the glass he handed her and sat stiffly on the edge of a chair. J.D. took a position on the side of the bed.

"Have you thought about what I told you today—how I feel about you?" he asked, giving her a long, steady look.

She nodded, lowering her eyes. "Yes, but that's not why I'm here, J.D. Please don't get the wrong idea. You see, Slade called early this evening, said he was

oing to be tied up until past midnight. I know it's just
n excuse. He's been with Barbara Lange all day. I'm
ure they're together tonight. I was upset, angry . . .
onely. You're the only person I could think of that I
ould talk to."

He smiled in his slow, relaxed manner, his blue eyes
ontinuing to gaze at her. "Obviously, Slade is runnin'
round on you, havin' an affair with Barbara Lange.
You might as well accept the truth."

"Oh, I accepted that a long time ago," she said. "But
still feel angry and humiliated—especially since he's
orcing me to pretend to be his wife. He could have the
lecency to stay away from her until my part in this farce
s over." She downed her drink in a gulp.

"I still can't figure out what he's doin' to force you to
tay with him."

"I'm sorry, J.D. That's the one thing I can't talk
about."

"Not even to a dinkum friend?" he asked with a slow
mile.

"Not even to a dinkum friend." She sighed. "Maybe
ne day I'll tell you, but for now please don't ask me."

He refilled her glass. The drinks relaxed her. She
ettled back in the chair.

They talked about other things; the election, the
orses, J.D.'s family. Her nervousness faded. She was
glad she'd come. At one point, she rose to put her
mpty glass on the bureau. When she moved past J.D.,
e caught her arm and gently pulled her down beside
im on the bed.

Talking out her problems had helped, but words were
ot as comforting as a man's strong arms. She rested
er head on his shoulder, not wanting to think. She felt
lesperately weary of the battle her life had become.

Then she sighed, "I'm going to have to leave now.

Thank you, J.D., for listening to all my troubles and for being such a good friend. When this election is over and I'm free of Slade, perhaps I'll feel more like being a woman again."

She gave him a friendly good-night kiss of gratitude.

The door burst open. There was a blinding flash.

Afterward, Veronica could remember screaming.

She leaped to her feet. She heard J.D.'s muttered curse.

Through half-blinded eyes she made out the vague image of the man in the doorway. Then he turned and ran. J.D. thrust her roughly aside and dashed out the door in pursuit of the intruder.

Chapter Eight

*W*ell, he got away," J.D. said furiously as he stormed back into the room. "I chased him to the parking lot. He jumped in a car and took off before I could grab him."

Veronica's heart was pounding wildly. "Who was he, J.D.?"

Clayton frowned darkly. "Some kind of photographer. Newspaperman would be my guess."

Veronica turned deathly pale. She was drenched with horror. "Oh, no!" she gasped. "How could this have happened?"

The rancher scowled. "He must have followed you here and was hangin' around outside the door, waitin' for just the right moment." He shot her a searching look. "Did you notice a car following you over here?"

She shook her head, too bewildered and stunned to think clearly. "I—I don't know. There was a lot of traffic. It's certainly possible."

J.D. nodded. "That's probably it. He was staked out around your house, saw you leave, and followed you."

She again shook her head like a dazed shock victim. "I just don't understand. . . ."

"It's plain enough," J.D. said grimly. "Either a hungry free-lance photographer or an eager reporter is out to grab a hot scandal item. Kirk Malden is fast makin' this a dirty race. You heard him speak today. There's already a lot of speculation about you and Slade in the gossip columns, over your separation and the way you suddenly patched things up when this political race started. It would be a big, juicy scoop for some newspaper or tabloid to blast a story about you havin' an affair, and usin' the picture he probably got of us in a motel room, kissing—"

"But it was an innocent good-night kiss," she said tearfully. "We weren't having an affair."

"You an' I know that. It won't look that way when the newspapers do the story."

Veronica sank into a chair, her legs feeling like rubber. She remembered the merciless woman reporter Selma Davenport, who had probed into her private life with such relentless determination. The media, she knew, could turn into a pack of hungry wolves when they smelled blood.

"This is a disaster," Veronica whispered. "It could wind up costing Slade the election."

J.D. stared at her with brooding eyes. "I never should have asked you to come over here. But I never dreamed—"

Veronica looked up tearfully. "Don't blame yourself, J.D. I'm the one who called you, remember? You didn't twist my arm to come over here."

He sighed. "No use in either one of us blamin' ourselves. It won't undo what's happened. The question is, what do we do now?"

"I have to tell Slade."

He nodded. "I'll go with you."

She shook her head. "I think it would be better for me to talk to him first. He's going to be furious. Slade has a temper at times."

J.D. shrugged. "I'm not afraid of him."

"That's not the point. It isn't going to help anybody for the two of you to get in a fight. If the newspapers found out about that, it would only confirm that something was going on between the two of us, don't you see?"

He muttered slowly, "Yes, I guess you have a point."

"Let Slade cool off first a bit. I doubt if he'd care all that much about my sleeping with another man. It's the damage this might do to his precious election chances that's going to set him off."

Veronica drove home, clutching the steering wheel with icy hands, her thoughts in a turmoil. The implication of what had happened was striking her with sickening force.

The lights were on in the big colonial-style house. Slade's car was parked in the driveway. She stopped her little car behind his, then walked up to the door, her heart pounding heavily.

When she let herself into the house, Slade came into the hallway from another room. He was frowning darkly. "Where in tarnation have you been this time of night? I was about to call the police."

She drew a deep breath, summoning her courage. "Slade, I have something to tell you. You're not going to like it."

His frown deepened.

There was a moment of painful silence. Veronica forced herself to speak. "When you called and said you wouldn't be home until after midnight, I was angry and lonely. I knew J. D. Clayton was spending the night in town at the Holiday Inn. I went over there to talk to him; I couldn't stand being here by myself. We—we had some drinks and talked. Then, as I was about to leave, the door burst open. A—a man took our picture. . . ."

Slade's face turned white. His shocked gaze wa
riveted on her.

Veronica licked her dry lips. "J.D. chased the ma
out to the parking lot, but he got away."

Slade crossed the hallway in furious strides, menac
ing her. Veronica stiffened. His face was black wit
rage. She thought for a horrifying moment that for th
first time he was going to do her physical harm.

His fists were balled granite. His eyes were searin
her like twin flames from a blowtorch. "What exactl
were you doing when the picture was taken?" h
demanded.

"I told you. I was with J.D.—"

"What do you mean, 'with J.D.'? You were in be
with him—making love?" He spoke the words wit
brittle fury.

"Of course not. We were sitting on the edge of th
bed. I was giving him a perfectly innocent good-nigh
kiss. . . ."

Slade began pacing the hallway. His eyes had becom
battlefields of raging emotion. "Then you had *bee*
making love," he said in a voice that snarled wit
bitterness. "Had you put your clothes back on?"

Her face whitened. Through stiff lips she said, "
know how the situation looks, but, no, we had no
made love. We had talked, as I told you, and I wa
about to leave. I'm fond of J.D., and it was just
normal impulse to give him a friendly good-nigh
kiss—"

He whirled, facing her again. "And I suppose yo
expect me to believe that?"

For a long moment their eyes clashed. "No," sh
whispered, "I don't suppose I really do."

How ironic, she thought. This should be a moment o

poetic revenge for her. At last Slade was getting a dose of his own medicine. Now he was feeling all the jealous, hurt rage that had torn her apart the day she discovered he had slept with Barbara Lange. But the revenge was not sweet. Rather, it turned bitter. Instead of triumph, she felt only sadness.

"Apparently," Slade gritted, "I misjudged completely my prudish, inhibited little wife. I thought you could be trusted not to have the morals of an alley cat. And I was wrong. You're no better than the next cheating, two-timing, faithless wife."

Each word was like a slap across her face. In fact, she would have preferred the physical blows. "Look who is suddenly so self-righteous!" she cried. "The shoe hurts when it's on the other foot, doesn't it?"

"I don't know what you mean."

"Then ask Barbara Lange to explain it to you."

"Leave Barbara out of this," he said coldly. "Don't resort to your neurotic jealous streak to justify your sleeping around."

"I have not been sleeping around!" she said angrily. "I'm not going to stand here and listen to any more of your insults, Slade Huntington. I really can't blame you for being angry. It was not very smart of me to visit J.D. at his motel room, with the election race going on. I admit I made a mistake there. But I'm not going to listen to you calling me nasty names."

"What do you expect—" he began.

But she cut him short. "I'm not finished. I want to point out, Slade, that you forced me back into this marriage with blackmail. I have told you repeatedly that being your wife is a technicality that has no real meaning. You have no claim on me. You do not possess me. And, by the way, what were you and Barbara

Lange doing tonight during the time you accuse me of going to bed with J. D. Clayton? Hard at work on legal briefs?''

.''As a matter of fact,'' he said cuttingly, ''that is precisely what we were doing.''

''And I suppose you expect me to believe *that?*''

They glared at each other like antagonists facing each other on a dueling ground at dawn.

Veronica felt drained and empty. A weary sadness swept through her like a cold wind. Was this what it was like for love to die at last? Until tonight, in spite of how she tried to deny it, she must have clung to some remnants of the love she had once felt for Slade, or else how could he have still awakened passion in her?

But some words spoken could never be taken back. They cut too deeply, left scars that could not be erased. In tonight's bitter exchange, she and Slade had become strangers forever. She knew she would never again let him touch her. Never again would his lovemaking carry her to pinnacles of ecstasy.

They looked at each other across a chasm as deep and cold as a fissure in a glacier.

She knew that Slade would never believe she had not gone to J.D.'s motel room to have sex with him. And somehow what he believed no longer mattered to her.

Slade had turned away. Perhaps he, too, sensed that something had ended forever for them. He was pacing the hallway again, pounding one fist into the other palm. His voice had become cold, impersonal. ''This is going to cost us a lot of votes. And just when the polls showed we had an edge on Senator Malden. He's going to make political hay out of this. I only wish we knew which newspaper is going to print the story. Not that it would help a great deal, I suppose. . . .''

He was muttering to himself more than to Veronica.

Then he said, "Have to call Jake Foreman. He should know right away.

He moved to a phone, spun the dial.

Veronica stood nearby, feeling stiff and numb. No matter what this had done to her and Slade personally, she felt responsible for doing something foolhardy that could cost him the election.

He spoke rapidly into the telephone. When he hung up, he said, "Jake is coming right over."

Veronica nodded mutely. She dreaded the further humiliation of facing Jake Foreman. But she had no choice. No matter what Slade thought, she was not guilty of sexual immorality. But she was guilty of a thoughtless indiscretion that was going to put his political chances in desperate jeopardy.

Jake Foreman arrived, looking tense and agitated. His glittering black eyes pinned Veronica with a piercing scrutiny. He asked, "Slade, would you be so kind as to get me a glass of milk?"

While Slade was in the kitchen Foreman walked to the study, motioning for Veronica to come with him. He sank wearily into an easy chair. "Slade was pretty upset when he called. I'd like to hear your version of what happened. Please tell me everything exactly as it took place."

Veronica went over the night's humiliating events, from the time she phoned J.D. to the horrifying moment when the photographer snapped the flash picture. "I'm sure Slade told you I went to J.D.'s motel room to go to bed with him. That's absolutely not true. I was not having an affair with J.D."

The campaign manager looked at her somberly. "Well, it isn't going to make a whole lot of difference."

"It makes a whole lot of difference to me!" she retorted.

"I know, but if the photographer's timing was right he apparently got a shot of you and J. D. Clayton alone in a motel room, sitting on the bed, kissing. A scandal-sheet reporter will take it from there, and, rest assured the world will believe the worst. Have you been seen with J.D. very much lately?"

"Well," she said slowly, "we've spent some time together, during the first political meeting of Slade's campaign staff, then at the ranch during the barbecue rally. And, as you know, J.D. and I flew to Sanderson earlier today to hear Malden speak. On the way back we stopped at his private landing strip on his ranch and went for a horseback ride. Then he drove me into town."

Foreman nodded gloomily, rubbing the pit of his stomach. Slade brought the milk. The campaign manager chewed an ulcer tablet, washing it down with the milk. "Well, there's nothing we can do tonight. We'll just have to see who is going to carry this story. I don't know what we can do except try and weather the storm. We'll make denials, of course, but nobody will believe us. How much damage it will do . . ." He shrugged and waved his hands in a gesture of uncertainty.

Jake Foreman left. Veronica and Slade went to bed, he in his master bedroom, she back in the guest bedroom. She knew from now on that would be their sleeping arrangement. Slade would make no more attempts to win her back to his bed. She went to sleep with a mixture of relief and sadness, knowing now that what they had once shared was over at last, completely and forever.

A grim-faced Jake Foreman returned the next day at noon. He handed Veronica and Slade each a manila envelope. She opened the flap, drew out a glossy eight-by-ten photograph, and saw with a shock of cold horror that it was the enlarged picture taken the night before.

Waves of sickening humiliation flooded through her as the impact of the picture struck her. The scene took in the motel room, the drinks on the bureau. She and J.D. were seated on the bed. She was in his arms, and the picture had been snapped at the moment she had kissed him. Seeing the picture, anyone but herself and J.D. would view it as the sordid evidence of an illicit motel affair.

Slade's face was gray as he stared at the picture. A muscle in his jaw twitched. In a strained voice he asked, "What newspaper took the picture?"

Foreman said, "It wasn't a newspaper photographer. It's much worse than that. . . ."

Chapter Nine

*W*hat do you mean, 'worse than that'?" Slade demanded.

The campaign manager directed his grim, somber gaze toward Slade. "The photographs were delivered to my office by private messenger an hour ago. Shortly after that, I received a telephone call from a group working to reelect Senator Kirk Malden. The photographer who took the picture of Mrs. Huntington in J. D. Clayton's motel room last night was one of their men. They have the negative. They called to offer us a deal."

Slade's expression turned into black rage. Veronica felt a stab of cold fright. Slade exploded. "Deal? What kind of deal?"

Foreman replied, "They want you to announce your withdrawal from the race. If you refuse, they'll see that the story and photograph are delivered to every newspaper in the state."

Slade began pacing the room furiously. "That's a typical Malden trick, isn't it?"

"Of course it is." Jake Foreman nodded. "Though Malden is too clever to involve himself directly in this kind of blackmail. He's got one of his political organizations to do the dirty work. You can be certain, however, that he and his campaign manager know all about it and may even have thought it up. As I warned you from the start, they play dirty politics."

Veronica felt overwhelmed by the horror of this dreadful situation. A sick kind of fright engulfed her.

Slade asked, "But will newspapers print trash like this?"

"Some might not. But there are always the more sensational ones that would be delighted to release such a spicy item. Even if only one tabloid printed it, Malden's rumor machine would then take over and do the rest."

There was a moment's heavy silence. Then Slade asked, "What can we do to counterattack?"

"Not much." Foreman sighed. "We can hold a press conference and deny the whole thing, but, knowing human nature, I doubt if many people would believe us. They like to think the worst of a scandal involving a public figure—and Mrs. Huntington became a public figure when you entered this race, Slade. I'm afraid her name is going to be dragged through the mud. Unless you decide to surrender to their blackmail demands."

Slade sank into a chair, his shoulders slumped.

Veronica exclaimed, "I know the photograph looks bad and a stranger seeing it would think the worst. But I know I'm innocent. Can't I convince everyone of the truth . . . ?"

Her voice trailed off. With a feeling of despair, she could see in Foreman's and Slade's eyes that they did not believe her. How could she expect the voters of the state to believe her?

"What makes it even worse," Foreman went on, "is that a prominent person like J. D. Clayton is involved. The Claytons are well known all over the state, and hated by many because they have so much money and wield so much power. J.D. has a reputation of being something of a ladies' man. They'll make the most of

that, too. I can see the headlines now; J.D. Clayton
Caught in Love Nest with Slade Huntington's Wife."

A cold, sick feeling formed a lump in Veronica's
stomach. "Couldn't we sue the newspapers?" she suggested.

Foreman shrugged. "Well, we might do that just for
appearances, but it would be an exercise in futility,
right, Slade? You're an attorney."

Slade nodded heavily. "Yes, I'm sure the press would
be smart enough to word the story in a way that would
avoid a libel suit. And they'd fall back on freedom of
speech."

Veronica was trying to hold back tears. "I know I'm
innocent even if nobody will believe me. But I did a
bloody foolish thing, going to J.D.'s motel room last
night. If I'm in for a rough time, I suppose it serves me
right for being so stupid."

The campagin manager sighed. "The public can
become pretty vicious. The newspaper story would be
only the beginning. Malden's rumor-mongers would
take it from there, embellishing the story, adding new
dirty twists. Wherever Slade makes a public speech,
Malden would have hecklers in the crowd. Mrs. Huntington, you'd see your name in spray-paint graffiti on
fences and public walls. . . ."

Veronica felt her heart sink even farther into despair.

Slade asked, "What would this do to the campaign?"

Foreman winced, rubbing the pit of his stomach. "It
would be rough on us. The voters who are swayed
emotionally would become prejudiced against you,
Slade, because of the negative impact of a public
scandal involving your family life. I can't say how many
votes it would cost us. It could be a deciding factor,
especially in such a close race as this one has become."

Slade prowled the room restlessly, struggling with the situation. In spite of the gulf that now separated them, Veronica felt a stab of pity for him, mingled with guilt over the problem she had caused.

"Do you think I should announce that I'll withdraw from the race?" Slade asked his campaign manager.

Foreman's jaw knotted. "It's a heavy decision. But I'd deeply regret seeing you give in to this kind of underhanded attack. Now, more than ever, you can see the character of the man you're running against. Kirk Malden is a devil who wields a great deal of power in our state legislature. I think you should continue the fight. God is on our side. . . ."

Telling Aileen about the pending scandal was one of the most difficult tasks Veronica had ever faced. But she couldn't let her sister see the shameful photograph in a newspaper without being forewarned.

"I know the picture is incriminating," she told Aileen miserably over the phone. "No one will believe the truth, that it was a perfectly innocent good-night kiss. I swear I wasn't having an affair with J.D., Aileen. He has just been a good friend, a strong shoulder to lean on when the going got rough."

"Of course I believe you, little sister," Aileen said. "It's Slade I blame. He's brought you nothing but grief in your life. Why you went back to that man I'll never understand. He's gotten you involved in this political mess of his, and you're only going to suffer some more."

"I know how you feel about Slade," Veronica agreed, "and I can't blame you. But I really did a foolish thing, going to J.D.'s motel room. I should have known in this kind of political race, as personalized as Malden has made it, and with the newspapers prying into our separation and reconciliation, that every move I made would be watched."

"You couldn't know they'd pull something as under-handed as this!"

"Well, I know now." Veronica sighed. "I wanted you to be prepared when the scandal breaks. Looks like we've got a very unpleasant mess on our hands. I hope this won't cause any problems, indirectly, for *your* husband's political career."

"Of course not. Don't worry about Brian. You have enough problems of your own to contend with. Just remember, I love you with all my heart, baby sister. If there's anything we can do—anything at all—you just call at once."

"Thank you," Veronica whispered, tears trickling down her cheeks. "Just keep loving me. And it wouldn't hurt to say a few prayers for me. . . ."

Slade and Jake Foreman had left the house before noon to confer with the campaign committee over this crisis in Slade's political career. Shortly after one o'clock, there was a knock at the front door. Mrs. Salinas was in another part of the house. Veronica called to her that she would answer the knock.

When she opened the door, she was surprised to find J.D.'s young distant cousin, Nichole Clayton. "Hi," the attractive redhead greeted her casually.

"Well, hello, Nichole. W-won't you come in?"

"Guess you're surprised to see me," the Clayton girl murmured, sauntering into the hallway.

"Well, yes, I am."

Nichole looked surprisingly sober. Veronica realized it was the first time she had seen the young woman when she wasn't holding a drink in one hand. She looked cool and casual in sandals and an outfit of designer slacks and halter in a shade of emerald green that flattered her red hair and large brown eyes. Whenever Veronica saw her, she was struck by the girl's startling beauty.

"I'm a messenger," Nichole explained. "J.D. wants to have a talk with you, but he said you have to be careful because of the political business. He wants to know if you'll let me drive you to the airport. He's got a company helicopter waiting there to take you to a place that will be safe to meet him. He said to tell you it's pretty important that he see you."

Veronica hesitated. "Are you sure it's safe? I don't know if J.D. told you, but I've already caused all kinds of problems to Slade by being friends with J.D."

"I know all about what happened," Nichole said, looking at her in a peculiar way that Veronica couldn't interpret. "But it's okay. The copter will take you to a hideout of J.D.'s, a hunting lodge of his up in the hills. No one would ever know you're up there."

"Then I suppose it's all right," Veronica said reluctantly. "You say J.D. told you it was important?"

"That's what he said," she replied with a shrug. "I'm just the messenger."

"All right. Let me get my purse."

Nichole was driving a late-model Mustang. She whipped the sports car through traffic with a casual disregard for life and limb that had Veronica petrified. She uttered a prayer of thanksgiving when they arrived at the airport in one piece.

Minutes later, she was being whisked aloft in a helicopter that bore the Clayton Industries insignia, a giant red *C* in a circle of barbed wire.

The pilot was a taciturn individual who remained silent during most of the thirty-minute flight. Then he jabbed a finger downward. Veronica looked down on a ranch-style house nestled in a woody grove in the hills. This was a desolate region, miles from civilization.

They circled the area once, then came down to a landing on a flat surface a few hundred yards from the house. The giant blades above them slowed their slapping revolutions and came to a stop. Immediately a hush descended on them, broken only by the distant twitter of birds in the groves of trees near the house.

The pilot unbuckled his safety belt and reached behind the seat for a basket, which he carried with him when he stepped down from the helicopter. Veronica opened her door and joined the pilot on the ground. They crossed the clearing. At the same time, she spied J. D. Clayton leave the house and hurry up the lane to join them. He took the basket from the pilot. "Wait for Mrs. Huntington in the copter."

The pilot nodded and returned to the machine. J.D. took Veronica's arm, and they walked together down the pathway between trees and bushes.

"After you left last night, I decided to come up here and do some thinkin'," J.D. explained. "Not many people know about this place. I wanted to be alone for a while to see if I could come up with a solution to this mess we've created."

J.D. had led her to a grassy spot under huge oak trees. "I instructed Nichole to put together a picnic basket and then take you to the airport," he told her, spreading a cloth on the ground. "I thought we could have a bite to eat while we talked."

Veronica took a seat on the grass, watching J.D. spread out picnic meal of potato salad, pickles and olives, deviled eggs, cold sliced turkey, and fresh fruit. He poured glasses of wine and asked "Hungry?"

"I've been too upset to eat today, but it's so peaceful here, and that food does look delicious."

"I sure wanted to phone you," he said, "but I didn't know if it was the smart thing to do, considerin' what happened. Now, tell me what the situation is. Have you found out what newspaper took that picture?"

"It wasn't a newspaper," she said in a dead voice. "Kirk Malden's people contacted us today and delivered copies of the picture. They hired the photographer. They're using it to try and blackmail Slade into dropping out of the race."

Clayton was silent for several moments, shaking his head gravely. "That's worse than I thought. I was countin' on it being some eager-beaver reporter or a hungry free-lance photographer that we could buy off. I was prepared to tell Jake Foreman to offer the man any amount of money it would take to get the negative from him, and I'd supply the cash. It's been my experience that every man has his price. But," he added somberly, "I'm afraid Malden's price is winnin' the election."

"Yes," she said," and apparently he's ready to stoop to any level to be elected."

"So it seems," J.D. agreed. Then he asked, "What was Slade's answer?"

"Jake Foreman thinks he should stay in the race. Slade finally agreed."

Clayton absorbed that information with a look of concern. "Veronica, have you any idea what this would do to you?"

"Oh, I'm sure the picture is going to be smeared across the front pages of some sensational tabloids." She sighed. "Jake said there'll be nasty rumors circulating about me—"

"It's downright selfish of Slade to go on in the face of

this," J.D. said angrily. "He has no concern for what it will do to you!"

Veronica looked down at the grass, plucking a blade, her heart filled with warring emotions. "Slade has been selfish about a lot of things," she said slowly. "In this case, I suppose he'd consider dropping out of the race if I insisted, since I'll bear the brunt of the nasty publicity. But I don't see how I can bring myself to do that. Even though I'm innocent of any real wrongdoing, I am guilty of being foolishly indiscreet by going to your motel room, something that could cost Slade the election."

"So you're keepin' quiet because of feeling guilty about that?"

"I suppose you could say that." She sighed.

"I can't see you makin' a martyr out of yourself to keep Slade in the campaign. You shouldn't blame yourself that much for visiting my motel room last night. How could you know the photographer was followin' you?"

"Was it only last night?" she said wearily. "It seems like a lifetime has gone by in the past twenty-four hours."

"I'm afraid it's goin' to seem like more than that when this ugly story breaks. Do you realize fully what you're lettin' yourself in for?"

"Jake warned me," she replied. "I'll admit I'm frightened. I don't know if I'll have the courage to go through with it."

"Then go to Slade. Tell him it's askin' too much of you. Tell him to use his common sense and drop out of the race. He has a lucrative law practice to go back to. With this political mess out of the way, he could release you to live your own life. You'd be free to think about yourself—and us."

She gazed at him tearfully. "That's terribly tempting," she admitted. "And I'd really like nothing better. I didn't ask to get involved in this political stoush—that's a fight—in the first place. Slade forced me into it, as I told you. But—" again she sighed heavily—"I don't know if I have the right to make that kind of decision at this point. It's no longer just Slade and me. I don't know if I have the right to consider only my feelings. I—I'm terribly mixed up right now, J.D. Should I put myself first? How much do I owe Slade and his campaign? Will I have the courage to face this kind of public humiliation? I'm basically a shy, private person. To have my private life dragged into the public this way is horrifying to me. You see, all those questions are tearing at me until I'm a nervous wreck."

He squeezed her hand. "I'd like to take some of that burden off your shoulders. Do you want me to help you make some decisions?"

"I do and I don't," she confessed. "It would be so easy to let you tell me what to do. But I'm not sure that's right, either. It's a moral decision that I really need to make myself. And added to all the humiliation I'm going to face, how about you, J.D.? We haven't talked about you at all. You're going to be right in the middle of this scandal, too. Jake said the media will make a lot of your involvement because you and your family are so well known in the state. You have a lot of powerful enemies as well as friends. . . ."

He waved her concern for him aside with an impatient gesture. "Veronica, a man in this situation isn't the one who is the victim of scandal. I want to marry you, and I don't care if the whole world knows it. It's the woman the gossips pounce on and tear apart. Besides, the media couldn't say much about me they haven't already said."

"Well," she said, trying to force a smile, "perhaps we're all overly concerned. Maybe it won't be as bad as we think."

"I wish I could agree," he murmured sadly. "But I'm afraid it's goin' to be even worse than you fear."

They fell silent, holding hands. Veronica looked sadly at the untouched picnic. "It's too bad you went to all that trouble. I'm afraid food would stick in my throat."

"I understand. I'm not hungry, either. I'll put this stuff back in the basket and keep it in the refrigerator in the house. Maybe you can give me a rain check."

She raised her eyes to his. "J.D., last night Slade said some pretty dreadful things to me. I suppose I can't entirely blame him, but it was the end of whatever feeling I might have still had for him. I guess, in spite of everything, a part of me was stubbornly holding on to the past. Not anymore. Any residue of love I might still have for Slade is dead and gone now. I—I wanted you to know that it no longer has to come between you and me. I'm . . . not entirely sure yet how I feel about you. I don't think I'll be able to have any clear thoughts about my personal life until this miserable election is over, one way or the other. But then, perhaps, you and I . . ." Her voice trailed off, her feelings reaching a dead end at this point.

He smiled. "Well, you know I'll be around, waitin' for you."

He bent and kissed her. She trailed her fingertips over his face. His kiss became more intense. She felt his caress touch her body and seek the curves of her thigh. The heat of his mounting desire made itself known to her. But she gently disengaged herself from his embrace and pushed her dress down to cover herself. "I'm sorry I have to keep putting you off, J.D. But at this point I'm afraid I wouldn't be capable of making love with anybody. If you can be patient with me until after the election, when Slade is out of my life completely and we're legally divorced, perhaps I'll be able to react like a woman again."

Disappointment struggled with desire in his eyes. But, with a wry smile, he murmured, "Well, I've been patient this long.

"Then please be patient a bit longer and stand by me. In case things get rough the next few weeks. . . ."

"They're going to get rough . . . plenty rough. Unless Jake Foreman and Slade will be reasonable and give up. With a family scandal like this going against him, Slade couldn't win the race, anyway."

He gathered up the picnic lunch. "I'm goin' back to the city with you," he declared. "If Slade won't listen to reason, perhaps Jake will. I carry some weight with Foreman. If I can get him to agree with me, then perhaps he and I can persuade Slade it would be a mistake to go on with the campaign now, considerin' what it would do to you."

"You can talk to Jake and Slade if you wish," she said with a helpless feeling of being swept into a deadly current over which she had no control. "But I don't think anything is going to change their minds. They have the notion that this race has become some kind of crusade."

Chapter Ten

J.D.'s appeal did not alter Jake Foreman's o
Slade's resolve to continue the race despite the impend
ing scandal. Veronica braced herself for the ordea
ahead, knowing there was no way she could really mak
it any easier.

Their worst fears were realized. The story was car
ried in gossip columns and in tabloids, all of them
implying that Veronica was carrying on an extramarita
affair with J. D. Clayton. A gloomy air of crisis fell ove
Slade's campaign headquarters.

On the morning the scandal broke, Mrs. Salinas wa
kept busy running between the telephone and the from
door. *"Madre de dios!"* was an exclamation repeated
many times by the harassed housekeeper.

"We're taking no calls and letting no reporters int
the house," Slade ordered.

Mrs. Salinas's reply was to roll her eyes, mutter som
pungent phrases in Spanish, and retreat to the kitchen

Veronica shared a tense breakfast with Slade, the ai
between them as chilled as the orange juice Mrs
Salinas had served. Veronica had a cup of black coffe
and a half piece of toast. It was all she could get down

Then Slade said, "Well, we might as well run the
gantlet. Have to do it sooner or later. Let's get it ove
with. We'll talk to the reporters out front, then drive t

the campaign headquarters and see what news Jake has for us."

As soon as they stepped out the front door, they were surrounded by reporters who been waiting on the front lawn since early morning. Camera shutters clicked and mobile TV units zeroed in on them.

"Is it true you are divorcing your wife, Mr. Huntington?" was one of the first questions shouted at him as the reporters clamored for attention.

Slade held up his hands. "Ladies and gentlemen, please. If you'll hold it down for a moment, my wife has a statement to give you."

Veronica's stomach was twisted in a painful knot. With icy, trembling fingers, she fumbled with her purse and drew out a statement she had rewritten a dozen times last night. Tape recorders and microphones were thrust in her face. She cleared her throat and in a voice that sounded thin and strained read; "I find it impossible to remain silent while my husband's political opponents resort to lies and slander just so they can gain a few votes. Several nights ago, I went to the motel room of Mr. J. D. Clayton for a brief, friendly visit. As everyone knows, Mr. Clayton is actively supporting my husband's campaign. Mr. Clayton and I discussed the political race and some personal matters. As I was leaving, I gave Mr. Clayton a friendly good-night kiss. There was nothing improper about the visit. I am not intimately involved with Mr. Clayton as the gossips now have it. We are and have been good friends, nothing more than that."

Her statement ended, but it was immediately followed by a renewed clamor of voices. "The photograph that was published in several tabloids shows you on the bed with J. D. Clayton. Do you want to comment on that, Mrs. Huntington?"

Veronica's cheeks flamed. "I can only repeat it was a casual good-night kiss between friends. We were fully clothed."

"The picture shows bottles and glasses nearby in the room. Had you and Mr. Clayton been drinking?"

"We had one drink—"

"There are rumors that you have been intoxicated at several of your husband's political rallies. Do you have a drinking problem, Mrs. Huntington?"

"Certainly not!"

"There is a rumor that when you were separated from your husband you went back to Australia to have medical treatment in a sanatorium for alcoholism and a mental breakdown. . . ."

"That's a lie!" she gasped.

At that point Slade intervened, much to Veronica's relief. "The kind of slanderous rumors you have just quoted are examples of the ugly, mud-slinging gossip campaign being conducted by my opposition. Unable to reply to my challenges on the issues and refusing to meet me in an open debate, they have chosen to use personal attacks, gossip, and outright lies to win a few votes. Unfortunately, as we all know, political races often get personal and rough out here. But I want to add this to my wife's statement to put an end to some of this gossip-mongering: My wife and I are not separating or divorcing. She is backing me all the way in my bid for the senate seat. She is one of the hardest workers we have, helping with my speeches, heading our public-relations staff. There is no foundation to these back-door rumors about extramarital affairs, drinking problems, or separation."

With that, Slade's broad shoulders shoved a path through the reporters as he hustled Veronica to his car.

When they were safely out of the driveway, Veronica burst into tears.

Slade glanced at her with genuine concern. "Are you all right? Is there anything I can do?"

"No, I'm not all right, and you've already done too much, thank you!"

"I'm sorry. I wish I could have spared you this ordeal, Veronica, but—"

"But you think I had it coming, right?"

"I didn't say that."

"No, but I'm sure you are thinking it. You still don't believe I was not having an affair with J.D. that night at the motel, do you?"

Slade sighed. "I don't know what to think, Veronica."

She shrugged, directing her gaze to the scenes passing the car window. "It really doesn't matter what you think."

Her tears had ended, but her nerves remained raw and frayed.

A pall of gloom hung over Jake Foreman during the following days. He relayed reports from his field workers to Slade and Veronica. "Malden's people are having a heyday with this one," he said bitterly. "They're like a bunch of vultures. I'm sure they have been digging into every nook and cranny of your personal, business, and professional life, Slade. It must have been pretty frustrating for them up to now. You came from a poor but honest family. Your father, a farmer and lay preacher, worked hard and raised you and your brothers and sisters in a Christian home. The profile they put together on you, Slade, was simply that of an ambitious young man who pulled himself up by his bootstraps and became a successful lawyer. No crooked business dealings, no underworld involvement in your law firm. The one flaw they could find in your personal life was your marital problem: the two-year separation from your wife and subsequent reconciliation just as you started this political race. They've been hammering away at that on the theory that many voters in this state want their elected officials to be solid family people representing them. That photograph in the motel room was the ammunition they've been needing to add fire to the rumors."

Slade nodded soberly. "What next? Is there anything we can do?"

Foreman shook his head. "Just keep on the way we're going, hammering away at the issues. I've got my foot soldiers hard at work trying to talk down the rumors, but I don't know how effective they'll be. The problem is, Malden's bunch is not going to let up on this. I can lay odds that at your next public appearance they'll have hecklers and demonstrators in the crowd. That would be standard procedure for them."

Slade consulted his calendar. "I'm scheduled to address a labor group at one of their company picnics Friday night. I suppose we'll find out then."

Jake nodded. His glittering black eyes swung toward Veronica. "Please make sure you're with Slade, Mrs. Huntington. From now on, you need to keep a high profile beside Slade every time he makes a public appearance. It might be a bit unpleasant for you if Malden has hecklers in the crowd. But it's the most effective way we have of combatting this gossip."

"Very well," Veronica said reluctantly.

When they drove to the meeting on Friday night, Veronica was filled with a dark premonition. They pulled into the parking lot at the company picnic grounds. She saw, with a feeling of uneasiness, that they would be facing a large crowd. The parking area was a sea of cars. In the picnic area hundreds of families were milling around under the lights. How many of them, she wondered, with a sense of cold dread, were hecklers and demonstrators from Kirk Malden's camp?

They left Slade's car and walked to the picnic area. Veronica saw that a speaker's platform had been set up for Slade's address. To reach it, they would have to walk through the crowd to the far end of the area. How many here had seen the picture of her and J.D.?

When they started into the fringe of the crowd, Slade was spotted. People began crowding around them. Slade was smiling and shaking hands. Veronica stayed close by his side, wishing they could move quickly to the speaker's stand.

The first group who surrounded them seemed friendly enough, although Veronica was aware of curious stares directed toward her. Then, suddenly, something ugly began drifting into the milling group like a gathering dark stain. She heard a voice say loudly, "There she is, J. D. Clayton's girl friend!" Coarse laughter followed.

"Hey, Veronica, who did you sleep with last night!"

"When's your next date with J.D.?"

"What's the matter—wasn't Slade keeping you satisfied?"

"Tramp!"

Veronica's cheeks were a burning scarlet. Her heart fluttered like a wounded bird. She tried to cover her ears. Slade continued to move forward, a fixed smile like a grimace on his face. In a low voice he said to her, "Ignore them. They've been sent here to stir up trouble. Stay close to me."

It was not possible for her to ignore the swelling

number of voices. They grew louder. Their taunts became crude, vulgar. One group was waving placards. Veronica remembered Jake's warning that she would see her name in spray paint in public places. One of the placards bore a crude likeness of her kissing J.D. Other placards were directed toward Slade: Decent People Don't Want You. Keep an Eye on Your Wife—Let Senator Malden Represent Us.

Waves of mounting panic were building in Veronica. She felt like a trapped animal. A sea of leering, taunting faces seemed to surround her. Suddenly an overripe tomato came flying at her. It splattered the white jacket of her linen suit.

With a frightened sob, she began running. Dimly she heard Slade's voice shout her name, but she ignored him. She plunged into the crowd. Hysteria drove her. She fought her way through the wall of bodies. They melted away, giving her a path, then closed behind her, separating her from Slade. She didn't know where she was going, or care. She felt like a hunted animal driven by the instinct of self-preservation.

Suddenly a tall figure blocked her path. She was dimly aware of a pair of broad shoulders, a wide-brimmed western hat. Powerful fingers gripped her arm. She heard a voice saying her name.

It was J.D.

He took control, hustling her through the outer fringes of the crowd to the parking lot. The evening had turned into a nightmare of jumbled moments running together like blurred pictures. Vaguely she became aware that she was in his car, safe from the crowd. They had driven away from the parking lot. She covered her face and sobbed hysterically.

J.D. continued to drive while her flood of tears subsided and she regained control. She fumbled in her purse for some facial tissue. "Thank God you were there, J.D.," she whispered fervently.

"I was afraid somethin' like this was goin' to happen," he replied grimly.

"I don't know what would have become of me if you hadn't been there to rescue me," she said shakily, still near the ragged edge of collapse.

"I'm glad I decided to come." He reached for her hand and gave it a squeeze, which she returned with a flood of gratitude.

He continued. "I debated with myself about whether I should go. With this scandal breakin', I thought it wouldn't be smart to be seen around you or Slade. But at the same time I figured Malden was going to have his hecklers in the crowd, givin' you a bad time. Some of those people can be very nasty. I finally decided to be there tonight, but I stayed on the edge of the crowd, where I didn't think many folks would see me. I wanted to be there in case you got in serious trouble."

Veronica said slowly, "I think I had a taste tonight of what it was like for a woman to be publicly stoned for adultery. I expected to be tarred and feathered before it was over."

The insulated quietness of J. D. Clayton's big, luxurious car surrounded her with a feeling of safety, gradually easing the tension from her body. Soothing FM music played softly from four speakers. She slid close beside J.D., and his arm went around her, giving her the warmth of human comfort.

"Slade had no business exposing you to that kind of situation," J.D. said angrily.

She nodded. "I'm beginning to agree with you. Apparently he's willing to sacrifice anything, including me, in his fight against Malden."

"You don't have to stand for it," J.D. insisted. "Leave him, Veronica, before things get even worse."

"Where would I go?" She sighed. "Slade has made me a public figure. I'm a marked woman. I guess I could go back to Australia. Perhaps I never should have left there. . . ."

J.D. shook his head. "You don't have to go that far. You could go up to my place in the hills. Nobody, including Slade, could find you there. It would be a safe retreat. It's beautiful up there this time of year. Deer wander right into the yard. The hills are full of wild flowers. You could stay in seclusion there until Slade gets this political fever out of his system. When the race is over, you can get your divorce, and Slade Huntington will be out of your life for good."

"That does sound tempting, but I—I don't know . . ."

"You don't have to worry about me puttin' any pressure on you," he continued persuasively. "I know you want to be divorced before you become involved with someone else. I can respect that. I'll send a lady up there to keep house so you won't be alone. You need some peace and quiet for a while."

She nodded. That was certainly true. She had been through an ordeal ever since the day Slade walked into her office and back into her life. Her nerves were near the breaking point.

"Let me think about it, J.D. It sounds like heaven. . . ."

"I'm staying in town. If you decide to go up there, you can reach me at my motel room or the Petroleum Club in the evening, or at the Clayton Industries business office here in town during the day."

They rode around for several hours. The security and

comfort of the rich, powerful car gave her a feeling of calmness. The rhythm of motion was soothing. But she knew she couldn't spend the night in J.D.'s car, and reluctantly she told him he'd better take her home.

When they pulled into the driveway, she saw that Slade's car was parked there. The feeling of turmoil returned to her emotions.

"Don't forget," J.D. said when he opened her door. "Call me if you want me to take you up to the house in the hills."

She gave his hand a parting squeeze.

When she walked into the house, Slade appeared in the doorway of the study. His face was dark with anger. Their eyes clashed like the cold steel of dueling rapiers.

Slade said, "I didn't want to believe that picture of you and J. D. Clayton in his motel room. I wanted to believe that you were telling the truth—that you were not having an affair with him. Tonight you made the truth clear enough by running into the arms of your lover in front of hundreds of people. Where have you been the past two hours?" he asked bitterly. "Back in J.D.'s motel room again?"

Veronica's face whitened. "I did not run into the arms of my lover. I ran away from a mob that was humiliating me, making me a public spectacle! I didn't see you making any move to protect me."

"How could I? I told you to stay close to me. Instead, you darted off into the crowd, away from me, straight to J. D. Clayton."

"I didn't even know he was there. Thank the Lord, he was!"

"I no longer believe anything you tell me about your relationship with J.D.," Slade said coldly. "Don't you realize what you did tonight? If you had done what I said, stayed right beside me, we would have been up on the speaker's platform in another two minutes. We could have turned this whole thing around. The people who were there—not Malden's hecklers, but the real crowd—would have seen you as a brave woman who had been insulted by a mob, your dress stained by the tomato they threw at you. They would have seen a wife standing loyally at her husband's side. The security people would have thrown the hecklers out of the picnic grounds. Public sentiment and sympathy would have swung to you and to our side. It could have put an end to the rumors about you and J.D. Instead, you have reinforced them. Now everyone is going to believe you are sleeping with J. D. Clayton."

"And I suppose 'everyone' includes you!"

"Yes," he retorted coldly, "that includes me."

"Fine! If you and the rest of the world want to believe I'm J.D.'s mistress, I don't care," she cried in tears. "Slade, tonight I realized more than ever that you care absolutely nothing about anything except getting elected. You have some kind of notion that you're on a crusade for truth and justice, and you're perfectly willing to sacrifice me to get there!"

"You're twisting things around a bit, aren't you? Yes, I do want to get elected, and when one is involved in this kind of race, he has to give it his all. As for it being a crusade for truth and justice, I suppose it is, in a way. You've seen at first hand how morally corrupt Kirk Malden can be. But as for your so-called sacrifice, need I point out that you've brought this ugly situation on by becoming involved with J. D. Clayton?"

"No, I didn't bring it on myself," she retorted. "I didn't ask to become involved in your political race. You forced me into this position by blackmailing me—

threatening to ruin my sister's marriage. I went along with it up to this point, but now I want out. It so happens I am not a brave woman. I was utterly terrified out there tonight. I felt like Hester in Hawthorne's novel, going around in public with the scarlet letter *A* for adulteress printed all over me. I can't take any more of it! I have no interest in this political race. I want to go someplace where people will leave me alone. I want out, Slade. I want to leave."

"So you can spend all of your time with J.D., I suppose," Slade said bitterly.

"I'm not going to debate that with you anymore," she said wearily. "You've made up your mind that I'm having an affair with J.D., so I'd be wasting my breath to deny it. The point is, I've become a liability to you. Let me leave, Slade. I'll only make matters worse for your campaign. I want out of this whole mess."

His face had a gray, haggard look. She was suddenly struck by how weary he was. The strain of the campaign was taking a heavy toll on him. If their relationship had not deteriorated so sadly, she would have felt a rush of sympathy for him. But she felt nothing except an empty void.

"Go, on. Go!" he muttered with an angry wave of his hand. "Go to your lover!"

"You won't go to Aileen's husband as you once threatened? You won't tell him about Aileen's past?"

"Of course not." He sighed. "I wouldn't have done that in any case. I just used that as a bluff to get you to come back."

"A bluff!" she gasped. A wave of renewed fury shook her. "And I was a bloody drongo—a fool—to fall for it. I subjected myself to all this grief and humiliation because of a lousy bluff!"

Tears streaming down her cheeks, she ran upstairs. In her room, she flung clothes in a suitcase. Then she called J.D.'s motel room. When he answered, she said, "J.D., I'd like to take you up on your invitation, if it's still open. I want to go to your place in the hills where nobody can find me!"

Chapter Eleven

J.D.'s hill-country hideaway was indeed beautiful. In this remote, quiet place, close to nature, Veronica found a peace she hadn't known in weeks. She felt like a patient recovering from a debilitating illness. For the first few days she pampered herself, sleeping late, eating leisurely meals, wandering outside under the great trees when she felt like it. She watched deer and squirrels from her window, smiled as long-legged jackrabbits frisked playfully across the yard. She went for long walks over areas of rocky boulders where wild flowers nestled in splashes of vivid colors. The sky overhead was a brilliant blue. The sun was warm and relaxing.

True to his promise, J.D. did not intrude on her solitude or put any pressure on her about their relationship. He did send up a housekeeper, Miriam Long. She was the wife of a ranch hand on one of the Clayton properties. Her children were grown, and she was pleased for the opportunity to keep busy and earn some extra money. She was a cheerful, outgoing woman who loved to cook. She served meals in the robust tradition of ranching folk: golden fried chicken, thick steaks, mashed potatoes, corn on the cob, fresh vegetables and fruits, homemade ice cream.

"I'll have to go on a six months' diet when I leave here," Veronica told her.

"Won't hurt you to put on a little flesh," Miriam said, giving Veronica's figure a critical glance. "You're skinny as a rail. Need some sunshine, too. You're too pale."

It was true, Veronica thought, examining her reflection in a mirror. She had lost weight the past weeks. The strain she had been under showed in her face. Circles formed dark smudges under her eyes.

Every other day Miriam Long drove a Jeep down a bumpy mountain road to a small community where she bought supplies. Among the items she brought back were newspapers. Veronica had vowed to isolate herself from the outside world completely, but curiosity overcame her resolve. She couldn't fight the compulsion to pick up the newspapers and read what was happening in the political race.

Several of the papers that were backing Kirk Malden carried items in gossip columns and in their editorials about Slade's family problems. "Where is Slade Huntington's missing wife?" they asked. They hinted that either Veronica had run off with J. D. Clayton or she had been secluded in a private sanatorium where she was undergoing treatment for a nervous breakdown. There were even cartoons. One depicted Veronica on a horse with J. D. Clayton, who was wearing an exaggerated Stetson hat. They were galloping off into the sunset, leaving a helpless Slade watching them while Kirk Malden slipped unnoticed back into the state senate building.

Veronica felt humiliated and outraged. She had been made into a public spectacle, an object of ridicule and scorn. How she hated Slade for dragging her into this political quagmire, turning her life upside down! She could never be comfortable in public again. This scandal would destroy her ambition to start a successful public-relations firm. She was going to be left with two choices: marry J.D. or go back to Australia for good.

One morning she was in the yard under the trees, tossing out crumbs for the birds, when she heard a car coming up the road. The housekeeper had left early to pick up supplies. Veronica assumed she was returning, and she didn't look up until the car was in the yard. When she did turn around, she saw with surprise that it was not Miriam Long's Jeep but a small sports car.

She saw a familiar mop of red hair as the driver, Nichole Clayton, stepped out. Then her gaze swung to the passenger and she felt a stunned shock.

It was Slade!

The two walked toward her. She felt her body go rigid. "What are you doing here?" she gasped angrily.

Slade stood before her. He looked grave. His eyes were filled with a strange expression.

Veronica turned to Nichole. "Why did you bring him here? J.D. promised I'd have privacy. He's going to be very angry with you."

Nichole shrugged and looked at Slade. He said, "Calm down, Veronica. I have something shocking to tell you. I think you'd better hear me out."

Veronica was on the verge of an angry outburst, but the deadly serious note in Slade's voice stopped the words on her lips. She became aware of a chilling tension.

Slade nodded toward the house. "Can we talk there?"

"Yes."

"Are you alone?"

Veronica nodded. "The housekeeper is in town." She was beginning to feel strangely frightened. What had brought Slade here?

They walked to the house. The main room had the

atmosphere of a lodge: a beamed ceiling, roughly paneled cedar walls, western furniture. Slade turned again to face Veronica. "You'd better sit down."

Veronica took a seat on the couch.

Nichole was prowling restlessly around the room. "Do you have anything to drink here?"

Veronica pointed to a cabinet that held liquor supplies. "Slade," she said angrily, "if you're pulling another of your underhanded tricks . . ."

He drew up a chair, sitting before her. "Believe me, Veronica, it's nothing like that. I don't know exactly where to begin." His brown, gold-flecked eyes were gazing directly at her with a strange, burning intensity. "When I get through with what I have to tell you, I think you're going to agree you and I owe each other a lot of apologies. Probably I owe you more, because you've been the innocent victim."

"I—I don't understand—"

"Please. Hear us out. Nichole came to me late last night with a shocking bit of information. I think it might be better for her to tell you first what she told me. Nichole?"

The lovely red-haired girl had mixed herself a drink. She plopped into an easy chair, swinging a leg casually over the arm. She sipped her drink, giving Veronica a smoldering look. "I went to Slade because I've gotten fed up with the way J.D. has mistreated me and because I'm fed up with the whole Clayton family. They're nothing but a bunch of double-dealing rattlesnakes. J.D. has used me for years." Tears suddenly filled her eyes. Veronica saw a flash of deep hurt, an emotion Nichole had covered before with her defensive act of drinking and wildness. "I was in love with J.D. since I was a little girl, and he's known it. He took

dvantage of me when he wanted me because I was too
oung and too much in love with him to know any
etter. Then he'd turn around and flaunt his girl friends
n my face. J.D.'s big on macho, in case you hadn't
oticed. He likes to make conquests. You're number
ne on his hit list now, in case you weren't aware of it."

Veronica felt a rushing emotional response, a mix-
ure of sympathy and resentment. She started to speak,
ut Nichole interrupted.

"I know what you're thinkin', that I'm jealous be-
ause of the attention J.D. has been showing you. Sure
'm jealous, the way I have been with all his other
omen. But I'm tired of it and I'm not taking it
nymore. Besides, it's a whole lot more to it than
hat's between J.D. and me. I'm up to here with the
hole Clayton family." She drew a line across her
hroat. "I feel like throwing up when I hear the Clayton
ame. Old Elijah Clayton rooked my daddy out of his
art of a family inheritance of ranchland that would
ave given us a good living. It left my daddy dirt-poor
nd brokenhearted. That's why he drank himself to
eath at an early age, and my mom died of a broken
eart."

Tears now trickled down Nichole's cheeks. "My
rother and I had no place to go, so Elijah took us in,
retendin' to be so generous and all. Probably it was a
op to his conscience. My brother accepted the charity,
ut I've resented it all my life."

Nichole suddenly swung her leg from the arm of the
hair. She put her drink down and leaned forward, her
yes blazing. "Veronica, the Claytons will do anything
or money and power. For years they have just about
ontrolled the state legislature. If you think they're
acking Slade because they want to get him elected,

you've been fooled just the way Slade and Jake Fore
man and all the rest have been fooled. Elijah and J.D
have tricked all of you!"

Veronica stared at the girl with unbelieving confu
sion. "I—I don't understand. They've put a lot o
money into Slade's campaign."

"They've *promised* a lot," Nichole said cuttingly
"That doesn't mean anything. It's all a big doubl
cross. Kirk Malden is their man. They want him electe
so they can get the dam built at the Three Oaks Canyo
site. Would you like to know who really owns all tha
land up there?"

Veronica looked from Nichole to Slade, trying t
comprehend this shocking new development.

Slade explained. "You've heard Jake Foreman an
me talking about the New Land Horizons Developmen
Company that owns most of the property around th
Three Oaks Canyon site. We were never able to get
clear picture of who really owns that corporation. It'
part of a larger conglomerate. In legal terms, w
weren't able to pierce the corporate veil. But last nigh
Nichole brought us papers she'd found in Elijah Clay
ton's desk that cleared up the mystery. There's n
longer any doubt—the Claytons are the owners of tha
corporation and the land at Three Oaks Canyon."

Veronica shook her head, feeling dazed. "But i
that's true," she gasped, "why would they back you
Slade?"

"That's an example of double-crossing, devious poli
tics," he explained. "You see, open backing of Kirk
Malden by the Claytons would not have helped hi
campaign. They have a lot of enemies who would hav
claimed, rightly, that the Claytons stand to gain a lot by
having the laws relaxed on gambling and prostitutio
and having the dam located at Three Oaks Canyon. By

pretending to be on my side, they took the stand that they were backing reform and what was best for the people of the state."

"It was pure hogwash," Nichole chimed in angrily. "The truth is, all of them were runnin' scared from the beginning that Slade was goin' to win this race. I know, because I was in the same room with Kirk Malden and the Claytons when they plotted it all out. They decided they could do more harm to Slade's campaign by working behind the scenes with him, gaining his confidence to try and find a vulnerable spot and make him lose the race. That was where you came into the picture, Veronica. They decided the only weak spot in Slade's private life was the trouble he and his wife had been havin', the way the two of you had been separated, and then you gettin' back with Slade right when he started his campaign. A scandal involving Slade's wife with another man in the heat of the campaign was bound to cost Slade a bunch of votes—maybe just enough to swing the election."

A deathly silence followed Nichole's bombshell. Veronica was aware of the pulse throbbing in her temple. She heard the song of a bird outside, but now it had a strangely discordant sound. Her face had grown warm, as if from a fever. Her stomach had knotted in a painful cramp.

"I—I just can't believe that," she gasped. "I can't believe J.D. would be party to anything like that."

"I know," Nichole said, her gaze softening with sympathy. "J.D. is a charmer, all right. He can be very convincing and sincere. At first I didn't much care. Living with the Claytons all these years has deadened my conscience, I guess. I just drove the fast cars Daddy Elijah bought me and drank a lot and tried not to think too much or face my own feelings. But I started liking you, Veronica. I could see you were a decent, nice person. It just made me sick, what they planned to do to you—draggin' your name through the mud. . . ."

"Do you mean," Veronica whispered, blood draining from her face, "that photographer taking our picture in the motel room had been planted by J.D.?"

"Think about it, Veronica," Slade insisted gently. "Why do you suppose the photographer could get into the room so easily? Wouldn't J.D. have kept his door locked if he was entertaining another man's wife in his room—especially with the election involved? J.D. had a photographer on call. He'd been waiting for just the right opportunity. It came the night you went to his room."

The events of that dreadful night raced through Veronica's mind. With chilling facts, they backed up what Slade and Nichole were telling her. She remembered how J.D. had made an excuse for not having transportation that night and asked if she could come to his room. And she remembered him asking how long it would take her to get there—thus letting him know if he had time to call his photographer. The fact that he'd left his door unlocked was the most convincing evidence.

She pressed her trembling fingers against her face. Tears of rage and humiliation were welling up in her eyes. "If all this is true," she whispered, "I must be the most gullible fool who ever lived."

"It's true, all right," Nichole assured her. "That last night at the company picnic, when Malden's hecklers gave you such a bad time and threw the rotten tomato at you—it was all planned, including J.D. being handy. They hoped you'd panic and try to get away from the hecklers. Then J.D. was to step in, grab you, and hustle you out of the crowd, right in front of everyone's eyes,

hus adding fuel to the gossip. It worked beautifully,
ust the way they planned."

Silence followed Nichole's words. Veronica had the
sick feeling that she was very near to losing her
breakfast.

Then Slade spoke up in a voice that was more
humble than she had ever heard. "I've done you an
injustice, Veronica. I said some pretty awful things to
you. I sure can't blame you for despising me. But I have
to apologize, whether you'll have it in your heart to
accept my apology or not."

Veronica rose, feeling dazed, and began pacing the
room. "I don't know if the two of you are telling me the
truth or not. This whole thing has me so confused I
don't know who to believe anymore. But if it is the
truth, it sheds a completely different light on the
situation. Up to now I frankly didn't give a hoot who
won the election. If you're telling me the truth, I'd give
my right arm to pay back J. D. Clayton and see that
scoundrel Kirk Malden never holds public office in this
state again!"

"Well," said Slade, "we're on our way to confront
Elijah and J. D. Clayton right now. Why don't you
come with us? Perhaps you'll hear the truth from their
lips!"

The confrontation took place in the living room of
the big white Clayton ranch house. Veronica remembered the two times she had been here before. The first
time had been on the day of the barbecue and political
rally when she'd had too much to drink and fallen
asleep on the couch here. The second time was the day
J.D. and she had gone horseback riding.

She remembered those times of near intimacy with
J.D. with a sense of burning rage. She had trusted him

completely. He had been her faithful friend. I Nichole's accusations were true, how could Veronic. ever trust anyone again?

Elijah Clayton had an expression of superiority and sneering cruelty as Slade hurled his accusations.

The powerfully built, white-haired rancher rake Nichole with a searing glance. "Well, little girl, suspect you better have your bottom blistered. Yo sure have shown your ingratitude for all the thing we've done for you."

Nichole returned his glance with a look of contemp and hatred. "What I've done," she said, "is get bac my self-respect, and at the same time I hope I've paid you back a little bit for what you did to my daddy, yo corrupt old man!"

Elijah Clayton took a menacing step toward Nichole She stood her ground, raising her chin defiantly. "Yes you're corrupt," she cried. "You're an evil, ruthless devil, rotten to the core."

"Well, I suspect I'm just going to have to deal with you after these folks leave," the elder Clayton said, his face dark with anger, his eyes deadly.

Nichole shook her head. "You're not going to put one dirty hand on me. I'm leaving too. This family has been turning me into an alcoholic failure. If I live under your roof another day, I'm either going to finish mysel off in a car wreck or wind up in a hospital with d.t.'s!"

Veronica faced J.D., who was lounging against the bar, a look of amused indifference on his handsome face. "It's all true, then," she choked. "You only pretended to back Slade. And you pretended to be my friend. You did have that picture of us taken in the motel room! From the start you were just using me to hurt Slade's campaign."

"Not entirely," J.D. said, his gaze raking her body.

"You're a very attractive woman, Veronica. And you were a challenge. Most women are eager to have an affair with me. I made up my mind I was going to have you eventually. I thought maybe after the election, when I had you convinced I wanted to marry you, you'd finally give in. . . ."

Veronica trembled from head to foot. "Now I think I know," she gasped, "how people feel when they want to commit murder. It's a good thing I don't have a gun handy."

J.D. only laughed.

Slade told Elijah, "I'm going to expose this whole rotten, double-crossing scheme of yours—"

But the white-haired patriarch of the Clayton family only sneered. "It won't do you a bit of good, boy. You're done for politically. Look at the polls. Senator Malden has gotten a big lead on you. Very few people will believe you if you try and tell them your wife's scandalous affair with J.D. didn't actually happen. Human nature bein' what it is, folks prefer to think the worst; it's more fun. Furthermore, now I'm withdrawing all financial support from your campaign, which I'd planned all along to do at this point. Without that, your campaign is goin' to collapse like a punctured balloon. Other backers will desert you, too, when I give the word. You're goin' to be skinned at the polls, boy. All you'll wind up with is a bunch of debts you won't be able to pay off. You'll be sadder and wiser, son. You'll have learned that it's Elijah Clayton who really runs his state. . . ."

Chapter Twelve

*V*eronica, Slade, and Nichole returned to the city in Nichole's sports car. She drove them to Slade's home. "I'm going to be staying with a friend," Nichole told them. She scribbled an address and phone number on a scrap of paper. "If there's anything I can do to help you fight the Claytons and Kirk Malden, please call me. I really want to help."

"Thank you, Nichole," Slade said, pocketing the address. "You've been a tremendous help already. I'm sure we will be calling on you. I have to get together with Jake Foreman and thresh this whole thing out to see where we stand now."

Veronica squeezed the red-haired girl's hand. Their eyes met in a glance of mutual understanding. Veronica felt a new warmth of affection for Nichole. The look they exchanged told her they were going to become close friends.

Slade carried Veronica's suitcase into the house. They had not spoken during the trip back from the Clayton ranch, and now that they were alone together, Veronica became self-conscious.

Slade broke the awkward silence. "I told you back at J.D.'s hunting lodge that I owed you an apology, Veronica. I want to tell you again that I am sorry for the things I said to you and the accusations I made about you and J.D.. I think you can understand why I said those things."

Veronica gazed at the broad-shouldered, silver-haired giant before her. She had the curious sensation that she was gazing at the image of two men, one superimposed upon the other. The sharper image was that of a stranger. Behind it was a more faded image of someone she had known in another time and place.

To the stranger she said, "I . . . accept your apology, Slade. We both have been victims of the Clayton charm and the Clayton double cross. I don't know how I could have been so gullible, and I suppose you feel the same."

He took a step toward her, but she backed away from the stranger, at the same time steeling herself against the other Slade, the one in the poignant memories.

"This hasn't changed anything personal between us, Slade. If there was anything left at all between us, the past weeks have killed it. So many angry words have been exchanged, so much bitterness on both sides, that I see nothing left for us. We've become strangers, and let's leave it at that." She didn't add that his relationship with Barbara Lange had ended their marriage even before that. The events of the past weeks had only made the gulf wider.

She turned away, hugging her arms, moving restlessly. "Now I have a little speech to make, and please don't say anything until I have finished." She turned to face him. Her cheeks were flushed. The pupils of her eyes expanded. Emotions boiled inside her. "Slade, all personal feelings aside, it's clear to me now that you are the good guy in this political race. Whatever else I feel about you—or don't feel—I can see that you are honest and you're trying to do what's right for the people of

this state. If I had any doubts about that before, I don
anymore. You are clearly on the side of what is best.
once told you I didn't give a tinker's damn who won th
race. Well, I've had a complete change of heart—
conversion, if you want to call it that. I want to see Kir
Malden defeated. I want to see the Claytons knocke
off their high horses. And I stand ready and willing t
do everything I can to help bring that about!"

Slade gazed at her with a look of mixed reactions
"Thank you, Veronica. It means a lot to hear you sa
that. I'm afraid, though, we're fighting a losing battl
now. The polls have showed a recent drastic fall in m
popularity. Now the Claytons are going to withdra
their financial backing. Our budget won't be able t
afford the media blitz that is so important during th
final days of a campaign. Frankly, this race has taken
lot out of me. I'm tired of fighting. . . ."

She had never before seen him look so utterly wear
or heard such a note of defeat in his voice. Was it goin
to be up to her to be the strong one now? "You can'
just give up!" she exclaimed, her eyes flashing. "
refuse to believe the race is lost."

Slade phoned Jake Foreman, who arranged to mee
with them that afternoon. He was enraged when h
arrived and Slade revealed the duplicity of the Clay
tons.

"What a blind fool I was to trust them!" the cam
paign manager exclaimed, slamming one fist into th
other palm. "I should have known the Claytons don'
do anything unless there is a profit in it for them."

"We were all taken in by them—me most of all,'
Veronica admitted with a wave of shame. "But cryin
over spilt milk is not going to help us. What can we d
now?"

Foreman slumped in a chair, rubbing the pit of his stomach. He had the same look of defeat as Slade. "Without the Clayton financial backing in our war chest we're in serious financial trouble. Old Elijah wasn't making an empty threat when he said one word from him and we'd lose other financial backers, too. I'm beginning to see clearly that old devil has this state in his vest pocket. Kirk Malden isn't the real villain. He's only a pawn of the Claytons. Probably the reason we were never able to trace organized-crime links to Malden was that it was the Claytons who have those connections. The payoffs to Malden came through the Claytons."

Veronica said, "Well, how about this information we have that it's the Claytons who really own the Three Oaks Canyon dam site land and would profit most by having the reservoir located there? Can't we use that in the campaign against them?"

"Yes," Jake agreed. "That will certainly be to our advantage. But, you see, Slade's personal popularity has been badly eroded. Many voters are convinced that his wife was having an affair with J. D. Clayton. That kind of sordid family situation has put Slade in a bad light with many people in this state."

"Then I'll make some speeches myself!" Veronica cried. "I'll tell them the truth—how J.D. engineered the scandal, how he took advantage of an innocent friendship to make me look like a cheating wife—"

Foreman scowled. "Yes, but at the same time J.D. will be going around the state bragging about his conquest. Their rumor and gossip machine will be working overtime. It will just be your word against his. In a situation like that, who do you think most people will believe—the man or the woman?"

Veronica stormed. "I can't believe an important political race could be decided on the issue of who a candidate's wife is sleeping with!"

"Then wake up to reality," the campaign manager said sadly. "You're right, it shouldn't; but the fact is personal, emotional issues can be important. When Adlai Stevenson campaigned against Eisenhower some held the fact that Stevenson was divorced against him. Of course, our biggest problem will be finances. A candidate's biggest media expenses are in the final days of the race. We plan the campaign to rise to a climax just before election day. That's when we need to saturate the district with TV and radio spots and large newspaper ads. How can we afford that now, without the backing of the Claytons and their friends?"

When the meeting ended, Veronica was left with the clear impression that both Jake Foreman and Slade were convinced that the race was lost. She thought Slade was seriously considering dropping out.

That night he barely touched his evening meal. Later, he sat in his study, staring blankly at a local TV news analyst who predicted Kirk Malden would win the senate race by a wide margin. Then Slade walked heavily up the stairs to his room.

Veronica roamed through the silent downstairs rooms, in the grip of strange emotions she couldn't understand. Slade's depressed mood of defeat had weakened her defenses in a way his magnetic self-assurance had not. She felt a dangerous wave of sympathy for him, realizing at the same time with a stab of guilt that she was partly to blame for his predicament. She owed Slade something to make up for that.

Slade appeared down and out. That awakened in her one of a woman's strongest needs—to bring comfort and strength. She felt needed, something that was hard for a woman to fight against.

Her instinct told her that it was up to her to give Slade's morale a boost. She had to encourage him to continue the fight. Now she was the determined one.

Under the spell of this strange mood, she slowly mounted the stairs going to her room. It had nothing to do with any feeling for Slade, she told herself; the past was dead. They had a fight on their hands. This time they were united against a common enemy.

Veronica lay awake much of the night, planning her strategy.

The following day, she contacted Nichole Clayton and invited her to have lunch. When they met, Nichole was dressed in a pale green skirt, blouse, and jacket. She was sober and subdued. Veronica was conscious of a change in the red-haired girl. She appeared determined to make a fresh start.

They each had a sandwich and salad in a quiet restaurant. Over lunch, Veronica explained her plans to Nichole. "Slade and Jake are pessimistic, but I'm not giving up. I want to know how much I can count on you for help."

Nichole's large brown eyes flashed. "I'll do whatever you want. It's time the people in this state know the truth about my relatives."

"Good. You can make the difference in whether or not Slade wins."

"I want him to win," Nichole affirmed. "Slade is a fine man, Veronica. I admire him a lot. He'd do a lot for the state."

Over coffee, Nichole asked, "How did you meet him?"

"Slade? Oh, we were in college together." She

laughed softly as she recalled their meeting. "I was so impressed the first time I saw him that I rode my bicycle straight into a tree."

Nichole smiled. "Love at first sight?"

"Something like that, I suppose. Slade cuts quite an imposing figure with those broad shoulders and that premature silver hair, and those brown eyes of his with the strange gold flecks. He was an all-American football player in college, you know."

Nichole nodded. "He looks athletic." She was looking at Veronica thoughtfully. "You must have loved him very much then."

Veronica looked down at her coffee cup, her eyes clouded with memories. "Yes," she murmured. "I'm sure I did. There was something quite gallant about Slade. I respected and admired him. He seemed capable of accomplishing anything. I felt protected with him. I suppose I thought of him as a modern Sir Lancelot, a brave, strong knight stepping out of the pages of a King Arthur legend." She laughed self-consciously. "I was quite young and rather naive about men, I suppose. Although I was twenty when we met, Slade was my first love . . ."

She caught herself in midsentence and apologized with a blush. "Forgive me for blabbing on like that, Nichole. I usually don't carry on about my personal feelings like that."

"I didn't think you did," Nichole replied. "I thought of you as being kinda reserved—pretty much a private person. Maybe you don't mind talkin' to me because I've told you all about my personal life, the way I've been living off the charity of the Claytons, and turning into a first-rate lush. Sometimes," she said slowly, "it helps to have a friend you can tell your private feelings to. I—I'd like to think we're becoming friends like that. . . ."

Impulsively Veronica touched the girl's hand. "I'd like to feel the same, Nichole. Perhaps we're both going through a crisis in our lives. That makes it easier for us to talk to each other."

Nichole gave her a long, thoughtful look. "If I sound too nosy, please just tell me to shut up. But I can tell, the way you talk about Slade, that you must have loved him very much. What happened to break the two of you up?"

Veronica's eyes clouded. "The old, old story, Nichole. Another woman. Slade's law partner, Barbara Lange."

"Yes, I've seen her with Slade." Nichole nodded. "She's sexy and glamorous, but not nearly as nice a person as you. What on earth could Slade have seen in her?"

"Well, they're in the same profession. They worked on law cases together. That last year, Slade was with her more than with me. I was finishing my degree. Slade was wrapped up in his career. I began to suspect they were becoming involved. Friends tried to warn me. I suppose I just didn't want to believe it. Then, one morning, I got a tip from an anonymous caller. Slade was out of town with Barbara on an important criminal trial. I drove to the motel where he'd spent the night. He and Barbara were at the courthouse, but when I walked into his room, the evidence was plain enough. She'd spent the night with him. . . ."

Veronica's voice trembled. She blinked back tears. "I went home, packed, and caught the first plane to Australia. I never intended to see Slade again. He forced me to come back with him during this political

race. I—I can't tell you why. It's a family matter
involving my sister. But I had no choice. When the
election is over, I plan to be out of Slade's life
permanently."

Nichole's eyes had filled with sympathy. "Gee, you
have had a rough time of it. Makes my troubles pretty
small. I guess I've just been spoiled and self-centered."

Veronica felt a wave of embarrassment. It wasn't like
her to talk so openly about her personal life to anyone
but Aileen. But she felt a rapport with Nichole that
broke down her usual barriers of reserve.

She finished her coffee, then smiled. "Enough of this
crying-in-our-beer girl talk. We've got a big job ahead
of us. The first thing I plan for us to do is have a talk
with Jim Baxwell, publisher of the *Morning Sun*. His
newspaper has been Slade's strongest supporter. I want
him to hear firsthand what you told us about Elijah
Clayton."

In the newspaper publisher's office, Veronica told
the story of the Clayton conspiracy. She explained their
plot to involve her in an apparent scandal with J.D. She
told Baxwell about the Clayton control of the New
Land Horizons Development Company that owned the
property around the Three Oaks Canyon reservoir site.

"That's one hell of a story!" Baxwell exclaimed with
astonishment. "Do you have any kind of proof of the
Clayton interest in New Land Horizons?"

"We certainly do. Nichole made photocopies of
papers she found in Elijah's desk that prove it beyond
any doubt."

Nichole took the photocopies from her purse and
handed them to the newspaperman. He scanned them
nodding as he muttered sharp exclamations. "We'll run
the story," he assured Veronica. "You know we've

been behind Slade from the beginning. As you probably also know, Malden controls most of the other newspapers in the state. Beside them, our circulation is small. But we'll do what we can."

"This story isn't the only reason I've come to talk to you," Veronica said. "The Claytons are pulling out of their financial backing of Slade. That leaves his campaign desperately short of funds. I'd like to see if we could put together a five-hundred-dollar-a-plate fundraising dinner in a hurry. Do you think we could find two hundred business and civic-minded people who would back Slade that amount?"

"In this senatorial district?"

"No, I'm thinking beyond that. I'm thinking statewide. Senator Malden through his seniority is the senate party whip. He heads a lot of powerful committees. This election goes beyond just who is going to represent this district. Issues are at stake that affect the entire state. I'd like to think there are at least two hundred people in the state who aren't controlled by the Clayton family willing to invest five hundred dollars in ridding us of their power. A hundred thousand dollars isn't a lot of money in a political campaign, but it would go a long way to buying the media coverage we need in those important last days."

Baxwell nodded thoughtfully. "I believe I could put a list together for you of two hundred people. Maybe even a few more, after we run this story."

She smiled. "I plan to contact every one of them personally."

Veronica felt herself driven by inner demons. She became a dynamo of energy, working day and night. The fund-raising dinner surprised Jake Foreman and Slade by being an outstanding success. Slade gave a rousing speech that was interrupted repeatedly with applause. Nichole spoke to the audience, telling of her firsthand knowledge of the inner workings of the Clayton power structure.

Afterward, Jake Foreman was both jubilant and cautious. "We have the funds to continue, if we count every penny. But we still have a lot of hurdles. Those people who came to the dinner and contributed five hundred dollars each have been committed to Slade from the beginning. We still have to reach those undecideds and the indifferents."

Veronica was meeting with Jake Foreman in his campaign headquarters office the day after the successful fund-raising dinner. He was sitting back in a swivel chair, feet crossed on his desk, collar open, sipping a glass of milk.

"You're the political wizard," Veronica pointed out. "How about pulling some vote-getting rabbits out of your hat?"

"Well," he mused. "I was thinking about a stunt Barry Goldwater used in his successful senatorial race in 1958. In a campaign, timing is all-important. It's like a baseball game. The eighth and ninth innings are when you have to hit your winning runs. Now, you take bumper stickers. They attract a lot of interest when they first appear. But after a while people become so used to seeing them on cars that they don't pay any attention to them anymore. Malden has put his bumper stickers out far too early in this campaign. I've been holding off to the last week. Back in the 1958 campaign I was talking about, Goldwater's people used window strips that are pasted inside the back window instead of on the bumper. They're smaller and cheaper, and we can send them out by direct mail. Goldwater's people used the stickers shortly before the election. They appeared suddenly. Everyone noticed them. It gave the impression that the driver of every other car in Arizona was backing Goldwater."

"That's neat," Veronica agreed. "And Slade's name makes a perfect alliteration. 'Slade for Senate.' That's all we'd need on the stickers."

"Exactly. Name recognition. That's a big part of it. More than one indifferent has walked into a voting both on election day and pulled a lever just because the name was so familiar to him."

Veronica said, "Y'know, I was thinking of something we studied in an advertising promotional course I took in college. They talked about the success of the Burma-Shave signs back in the 1930s. They were a series of five or six small signs along the road painted in bright colors. Each sign carried the phrase of a jingle that the people in cars would read as they drove past. I could have some like that done up quickly with a silk-screen process. The jingles can be silly, catchy bits of nonsense. Something like 'Slade's the man to lead our state. He's honest, faithful, true, and great.' And a final sign; 'Vote for Slade Huntington.' The jingle could be broken up so just two or three words appear on each successive sign. You're almost compelled, when you notice the first one, to keep reading to see how the jingle will end."

"A super idea!" Foreman exclaimed enthusiastically. "More name recognition. I can have our foot soldiers find locations for them along major highways and farm-to-market roads leading into all the major towns in this senatorial district. If we work fast, we can get them in place a week before election, which would be good timing."

Veronica's hard work and enthusiasm lifted Slade from his defeated slump. He got a second wind. Once again he was the fiery orator, swaying audiences with his magnetic charisma.

Meanwhile, Veronica and Nichole went on a swing through the district on their own. They spoke to civic and women's groups. Veronica told how J.D. had engineered the scandal involving her. Nichole told of her firsthand knowledge of the Clayton dynasty, how their power had reached into all areas of the business and political life of the state, and how Kirk Malden was no more than a puppet who jumped the way the Claytons pulled the strings.

Tension mounted in the Huntington camp as election day approached. "How do you assess our chances now?" Veronica asked Jake Foreman a few days before the election.

"According to the polls, it's a dead heat," he replied. "Y'know, a candidate's standing never is static. He's always either getting ahead or falling back. Slade has been steadily closing the gap since we broke the story about the Claytons and you pulled off that successful fund-raising dinner. But Malden had gotten a big lead. The sixty-four-dollar question is, can we get ahead these last few days, or will Malden pull some last-minute dirty-rumor trick that will win him the election?"

Veronica had planned a strong media appeal for the final two days. They had carefully budgeted their funds, buying as much television and radio time and newspaper space as possible, as well as using direct mail. She was proud of what they had done, but her heart sank when she saw the extent of Kirk Malden's last-minute advertising. He virtually dominated the television screen. It seemed that every station she turned to on the radio was giving a Kirk Malden commerical. And full-page newspaper ads sprang out at her when she turned the pages.

Even the weather was against them. They had hoped for a large voter turnout to combat Malden's entrenched constituency, who would go to the polls in a hurricane. But it began raining the night before and poured steadily all election day. Jake Foreman walked around, rubbing his stomach, muttering to himself, and staring gloomily out of windows.

An election-night party was planned for Slade's campaign headquarters to hear the returns. That night, Veronica wore a simple black jersey dress. Her accessories were a single-strand pearl necklace and pearl earrings. She wore a raincoat and carried an umbrella out to Slade's car.

They were silent on the drive to the campaign headquarters. The car radio was turned to a local station that had started giving the first returns. Early precincts were giving Kirk Malden a huge lead.

"That doesn't mean much," Slade muttered. "We knew he'd take those."

When they pulled into the parking lot, Slade switched off the engine and turned to Veronica. "Well," he said a bit unsteadily, "this is the big night. We're going to know in a few hours if our hard work has paid off or if it was all an exercise in futility."

"Yes. I said a prayer before we left the house."

He nodded. "I've done some praying, too."

There was a moment of silence. Then Slade said, "Veronica, no matter how this thing turns out tonight, there is something I have to tell you before we are swept apart by the party going on inside. These past weeks you have been a tremendous inspiration to me. I could not have gone on without you. I want you to know that."

She turned away. "Slade, please . . ."

"No, I have some things to say, and I'm going to say them. When tonight is over, I am no longer going to try and force this marriage on you. We can proceed with the divorce as you wish. You'll be free. I'll make no more demands on you."

She gazed through the window at the rain trickling down the glass and realized that the drops were matched by silent tears trickling down her cheeks. "That's what I want," she whispered, "And I'm sure it's what you and Barbara want."

Before he could say anything else, she jumped out of the car and ran through the rain into the campaign headquarters. The election-night party was already under way. The room was mobbed. Streamers across the walls bore Slade's name painted in red. Balloons floated to the ceiling. Veronica saw Barbara Lange, looking her usual poised, seductive self in a low-cut cocktail dress that had a black beaded bodice designed to hug her luscious curves. She spied Slade when he walked in and was immediately at his side. Angrily Veronica turned her attention elsewhere. She chatted with all the people she had come to know during the campaign. Everyone was talking loudly. There was a mood of near hysteria in the air.

As the evening wore on, the returns became more frequent. Groans ran through the crowd when the early returns showed Kirk Malden in the lead. The groans turned to shouts of elation when Slade began to close the gap.

At ten-thirty a local TV commentator came on the screen. "We are now able to project a winner in the enatorial race. It is clear that Slade Huntington has lefeated the incumbent Kirk Malden."

A deafening shout screamed through the room. A and hired for the occasion blared triumphantly. treamers flew, confetti rained down, balloons popped. Men shouted and women sobbed. Hands were wrung. Friends were kissed.

Veronica's reaction was one of numb shock. She hought that later she would feel the triumph. Now she was dazed.

Jake Foreman appeared before her in the crowd. His black eyes were glittering like marbles, his sallow face wreathed in smiles. He was holding a glass of Scotch mixed with milk. He laughed. "My ulcer feels better lready." Veronica hugged him. "We did it!" he cried. Then he shook his head. "No, Mrs. Huntington, you did it. You got us going again when we had all given up."

"Don't you think," she said, beginning to feel a bit hysterical herself, "that after all this time you could call me by my first name?"

He shook his head. "I think a senator's wife should be respected by addressing her formally. However, you may kiss me if you wish."

She did that.

Then she felt a strong hand on her arm. She looked up at Slade. "They want a speech. You should be with me."

Then she was on a speaker's platform at one end of the room. Slade made a brief, emotional speech of thanks to the people in the room who had worked so hard. It was the first time Veronica had ever seen him hed tears in public. She liked him showing that human ide of himself.

When the speech was over, she tried to escape into

the crowd again, but Slade's grip on her arm would
release her. He led her into one of the back roo
where they could be alone.

Slade said, "I started to tell you some things ou
the car, but you ran away before I could finish."

"Slade, I—"

"No," he said firmly. "You keep running away fr
me. But this time I'm going to finish what I wante(
say. Out in the car, I was going to tell you someth
you must know. You thought I forced you back into
marriage because of my political ambitions. I didn't
to talk you out of that notion, because it didn't seen
me you would believe me. Whether you'll believe
now or not, I don't know, but I'm going to tell :
anyway. When I learned you were back in the State
wanted desperately for us to have another try at
marriage. So I concocted that blackmail scher
threatening to tell Brian about Aileen's past, to get :
to come back to me. Of course I never would have h
Aileen. I had the notion that if I could force you
come back to me, be my wife again, I could win :
into staying. For a while I thought it was going to wo
the way you responded to our lovemaking. I knew :
couldn't have done that if you didn't still feel someth
for me. Then the mess about J.D. came between us.
you said, we said things to each other that are hard
forget. I think that for a while I no longer cared w
became of our marriage. But my love and admirat
for you were rekindled by the courage and the fight
spirit you showed in the last week of this campaig
guess it reminded me of all the fine things about yo
loved so much from the start—"

"Love!" she whispered bitterly, starting to cry aga
"Slade, how can you talk to me about love after mak
Barbara Lange your mistress?"

"You should be convinced it's you I love," he said, his eyes filled with emotion. "You noticed I did not get a divorce from you and marry Barbara while you were in Australia."

"That—that doesn't prove anything, only that she likes her independence. It doesn't take away that night you spent with her, when I saw the bed you slept in together—"

She caught herself abruptly.

He stared at her with a strange intensity. "This is the first time you've been able to make yourself talk about that, isn't it?"

She refused to look at him.

His strong arms grasped her arms, forced her to turn toward him. "It was your stubborn pride, wasn't it?"

She raised her chin, her eyes blazing. "What was the use talking about it? You knew better than I what was going on between you and Barbara Lange. It was too painful and shameful to discuss. Too sordid. . . ."

"So you just ran off to Australia."

"That seemed the sensible thing to do. I'm not the kind of wife who can adopt a martyred silence while her husband is sleeping with another woman. If that's stubborn pride, then so be it!"

He continued to hold her, forcing her to look at him. A curious smile tugged at a corner of his lips. "I should spank you," he murmured. "Do you realize I never would have found out what was really eating you if it hadn't been for Nichole?"

She felt confused. "What has Nichole got to do with it?"

"A whole lot. We probably would have gotten a divorce after tonight, gone our separate ways, and I never would have known the real reason. Fortunately, little Nichole knew and came to talk with me about it

one day. She has probably turned out to be one of t
best friends we have. She saved my political caree
And she's given me the chance to straighten out a tra
mistake."

Veronica remembered the lunch she had had wi
Nichole when she talked about finding the evidence
Slade's affair with Barbara Lange in the motel room.
talked with Nichole in confidence," Veronica sa
angrily. "She had no business going to you—"

"She had every business," Slade corrected. "Nicho
thinks you're still in love with me. In spite of everythi
that's happened, she could be right. Anyway, s
wanted to see if she could get us back together. Sl
jumped all over me for betraying you and taking
with Barbara Lange. I had a heck of a time convinci
her I never had an affair with Barbara."

"You'd never convince me!" Veronica gasped.

"No, I know I wouldn't. But I think somebody el
can. You wait here," he ordered.

Slade left the room. He returned in a few minute
bringing with him a pale, sullen Barbara Lange. "I h
a long chat with Barbara early this evening over in
corner, he said, "and now she has something to te
you."

Veronica stared at Barbara. She felt even more nun
than before. Her mind became dazed, barely able
comprehend what Barbara was telling her.

"I fell in love with Slade when I went to work in h
law firm," Barbara said, slowly and with obvio
reluctance. "I wanted Slade—I told you that. I thoug
I could give him a lot more than you did. We were
the same profession, we talked the same language. Bu
although I threw myself at Slade, he showed no intere
in me that way. He admired me as a lawyer, liked me

a friend. No more than that. I decided if you were out of his life, I might stand a chance . . ."

She hesitated, chewing her bottom lip.

"Go on," Slade prompted. "Remember, I have offered to break your pretty neck if you don't tell the truth. I probably should do it anyway for all the grief you've caused us."

The threat in Slade's voice was no bluff. Barbara paled, then swallowed hard and continued. "That motel room that you saw, where it looked like I'd spent the night with Slade . . . It was all a setup. I did it," she confessed. "We were both staying at the motel while that trial was going on, but we had different rooms. Early that morning, a pipe broke in my room. Slade and I had to be at the courthouse by nine o'clock. Slade was on his way out to breakfast. I asked if I could use his room while the mess in my room was cleaned up. He told me to go ahead, make myself at home. He was having breakfast in the coffee shop, then was going straight to the courthouse.

"I took my suitcase to his room," she continued, avoiding Veronica's eyes. "After I changed, I realized what a compromising scene I could arrange. I tossed some lingerie and a dress on the bed and smeared lipstick on a pillow. I knew the maid service would change linens later in the day before Slade got back to the motel. Meanwhile, though, I put in the call to you, Veronica. I disguised my voice. I didn't know if the scheme would work, but I was willing to try anything to break you and Slade up. Actually, it worked far better than I'd dreamed. I thought you'd confront Slade with what you found. He'd try to explain what happened, that I'd just used the room to change, but it would start some doubts in your mind, and maybe I could plant

more in time. It turned out that wasn't necessary. Yo
just left Slade on the spot and ran off to Australia. I w
overjoyed. I had Slade all to myself. I thought surely
catch him on the rebound. But no luck. No matter ho
hard I've tried, Slade just isn't interested in me—"

Barbara's voice broke. She gave Slade a tearf
brokenhearted look. "I've loved you with all my bein
No one could ever love you more than I did. I w
willing to lie . . . to do anything to get you—"

Suddenly she tore loose from his grasp and r
sobbing from the room.

She left behind a stunned silence. Veronica w
vaguely aware of the sounds of the party going on in th
other room. She felt her own heart beating. But h
thought processes seemed frozen. She put her hand
her forehead with a dazed gesture.

"Now do you believe me?" Slade demanded. "The
has never been anything personal between Barbara an
me. I love you, Veronica. All I want is for us to pat
things up and get back together."

Veronica shook her head. She felt groggy, ha
stunned. "I—I can't quite grasp all this. Please give n
a little while to sort it all out, will you?"

"Do you want to go home?"

"Yes. I don't want to go back to the party."

They escaped through a back door. On the driv
home, Veronica huddled on her side of the car, repea
ing to herself Barbara's astounding revelation. If it wa
true, the bitterness, the jealousy, the anger, she'd fe
toward Slade for the past two years had been entire
groundless. She'd done him and their marriage a
injustice.

Then she thought about Slade's words. "I love you,
he'd said. "All I want is for us to patch things up an
get back together."

A glimmer of joy was forming in a world of darkness that had existed in her heart for two long years. It was not yet a full light. It would take some nurturing, but it was beginning to grow warmer and brighter. She wondered if eventually it would suffuse her entire being as it once had.

When they were home, Slade said, "I'm not going to rush you to make a decision, Veronica. I know how all this has driven us apart. It takes time to put something back together when it's been shattered. Just remember that I love you very, very much."

He bent and kissed her. Then he went up the stairs to his room.

Veronica used the guest room to change. She took a leisurely bath, soaking in a scented bubble bath. The warm suds caressed her body with slippery, soothing fingers. A languorous mood stole through her. She allowed her imagination to roam into romantic fantasies, recalling the times of passion she had shared with Slade. She remembered that first night Slade had brought her here and their soap-slick bodies had embraced in the shower. The blood began coursing through her body with strong surges, awakening a deep heat within her.

Her heart seemed to be singing a song. *Slade loves me . . . Slade loves me . . .*

As she listened to it she began to believe it, to accept it, to know it was a reality. All that had happened in the past two years had been a bad dream she could forget. Slade's love was the reality.

She dried on a rough towel, rubbing every inch of her body until it was a glowing pink. Then she powdered herself all over with rose-scented bath talc, giving her body a soft, smooth feeling of silk. She walked naked into the bedroom. There, she spent a while

painting her toenails and fingernails a bright carmin
She stretched out on her bed, letting her nails dry. SI
was very conscious of every curve of her body, ve
much aware of being a woman. When she thoug
about Slade, her breasts throbbed, her bare fle
tingled.

When her nails were dry, she selected a filmy blac
nightgown from her wardrobe. The garment settle
around her like a dark mist through which her bod
gleamed in pale ivory contrast. She brushed her ha
into a bronze-highlighted cloud. Then she gazed wid
eyed at her reflection in the mirror, and whispere
Slade's name, somehow again reassuring herself of tl
reality of tonight.

She touched herself with a hint of perfume, SI
stepped into gold high-heeled slippers, then walke
down the hall to Slade's room. She tapped lightly at h
door.

Slade's voice told her to come in. He was in a set
blood-red pajamas, lying on the bed. He laid aside
book he had been reading, looking at her with
questioning gaze. His brown eyes burned into he
intensely.

His shock of silver hair against the red of his pajama
sent a shiver racing down Veronica's spine. He looke
more masculine and at the same time more vulnerab
than she had ever seen him before, even in the earl
days of their marriage. Dark hairs on his chest curle
out from the opening of his pajama top. Veronica
gaze settled there, and for a moment Slade's masculin
ty was symbolized in the strength of his body and th
ruggedness of his build. What a brutally good-lookin
man he was! There was so much more depth to hir
than the flashing handsomeness that had swayed jurie

and catapulted him to the ranks of most eligible man-about-town during Veronica's absence.

Slade Huntington possessed something about him that had held Veronica's heart through the rocky last days of their marriage, something that only sure evidence of his infidelity could have shattered. How much Veronica would have lost if she had surrendered this man to the arms of another woman. This man . . . the only man who had ever won her heart, the only man she could ever truly love. How she longed to have his arms around her, to feel the warmth and hardness of his body against her again, to recapture the lost love they had almost let die. A throbbing in her temples spread throughout her body. It whispered a rhythmic message: "I want him . . . I want him . . . I want him . . ."

"Can't sleep?" she asked, lingering in the doorway.

"No. Thought I'd read for a while." His gaze trailed from her face down her body, bringing a blush of warmth to her flesh. An unasked question was in his eyes.

She moved toward him and sat on the edge of his bed.

Slade asked, "Have you made a decision about us?"

She gazed steadily into his eyes. She slipped the gown from her shoulders. It fell around her waist. Huskily she asked, "Does that answer your question?"

She bent forward, cradling his head. He buried his face against her quivering breasts. She sucked her breath in softly as his lips drew fire.

Then she slowly unbuttoned his pajama top, her carmine-tipped fingers lingering over each button. She kissed him gently. "Just relax," she murmured. "As the saying goes, this one is on me."

"For old times' sake?" he whispered huskily.

"Something like that."

Her kisses trailed to his shoulders, to his old footba
scar. Her tongue played with the nipples of his broa
chest. She heard his breathing deepen.

She raised her head, giving him a teasing look. "
could stop now," she threatened.

"You wouldn't!" he groaned.

She cocked her head to one side. "Well . . ."

Then her head bent over him again. Her kisse
roamed over his body as her fingers toyed with th
drawstring of his pajamas, giving a teasing tug, then a
last untying it.

The room fell silent except for their breathing. Slad
groaned softly.

At last she was locked securely in Slade's embrace
and her heart sang in rhythm to their lovemaking. *It
true . . . it's true . . . we're together again. . . .*

Later, when she rested in his arms, her head agains
his chest, she murmured drowsily, "Senator, I love yo
very much. . . ."

If you enjoyed this book...

...you will enjoy a Special Edition Book Club membership even more.

It will bring you each new title, as soon as it is published every month, delivered right to your door.

15-Day Free Trial Offer

We will send you 6 new Silhouette Special Editions to keep for 15 days absolutely free! If you decide not to keep them, send them back to us, you pay nothing. But if you enjoy them as much as we think you will, keep them and pay the invoice enclosed with your trial shipment. You will then automatically become a member of the Special Edition Book Club and receive 6 more romances every month. There is no minimum number of books to buy and you can cancel at any time.

--- **FREE CHARTER MEMBERSHIP COUPON** ---

 Silhouette Special Editions, Dept. SESE-1C
120 Brighton Road, Clifton, NJ 07012

Please send me 6 Silhouette Special Editions to keep for 15 days, absolutely free. I understand I am not obligated to join the Silhouette Special Editions Book Club unless I decide to keep them.

Name _____

Address _____

City _____

State _____ Zip _____

This offer expires September 30, 1982

Silhouette Special Edition

Coming Next Month

December's Wine by Linda Shaw

Padgett Williams' laughing eyes dared Leigh Vincent to give herself in love. She felt alive again, as his tender touch stirred feelings from the very depths of her soul.

Northern Lights by Jacqueline Musgrave

Beneath the brilliance of the Northern Lights, Rod and Jan shared a love warm enough to set the cold Alaskan nights aflame. He taught her the meaning of trust, the beauty of a lover's touch, and the secret of the heart.

A Flight Of Swallows by Joanna Scott

Karin couldn't believe that Lucas McKay was out for revenge—not when she matched him touch for touch, promise for promise, and soared with him to the land of paradise, the edge of ecstasy.

and a new novel from
Linda Shaw in future months

Silhouette Special Edition

Coming Next Month

All That Glitters by Linda Howard

Jessica had once been involved in a marriage rocked by scandal, but in Nikolas Constantinos' arms she found a peace she thought she'd never know. His lips told her of delights that were to follow, and his hands led her down a path of desire and surrender.

Love's Golden Shadow by Maggi Charles

Guy Medfield's waning sight left him feeling bitter and alone—until Tracy's healing touch taught him to live again and to read the promise of their future in every heartbeat and caress.

Gamble Of Desire by Diana Dixon

Unhappy with her singing career, Kendra traveled with Paul to Martinique. In this land of shadowed forests and scorching sands Paul carried her on wings of passion and happiness that come only from true love.

Look for more Special Editions from **Janet Dailey** and **Brooke Hastings**, and a new novel from **Linda Shaw** in future months.

Silhouette Special Edition

April Special Editions
Available Now

Bitter Victory by Patti Beckman

After years of separation, Slade's appearance still ignited the burning desire and hatred that had driven Veronica to leave her husband. Could their love mend their differences?

Eye Of The Hurricane by Sarah Keene

There were two sides to Miranda: the practical miss, and the daring, wild dreamer. And in Jake she found a passion that would weld the two together.

Dangerous Magic by Stephanie James

Elissa fought her way up the corporate ladder and into Wade's arms. Her sultry innocence intrigued him, and his desire for her was overwhelming.

Mayan Moon by Eleni Carr

Beneath the Mexican moon, Antonio Ferrara, a man of fierce Mayan pride, took Rhea on a journey that encompassed the ages.

So Many Tomorrows by Nancy John

Having been mistaken in her first marriage, Shelley wasn't thinking of love—until Jason taught her the meaning of life, and of a love that would last forever.

A Woman's Place by Lucy Hamilton

Anna's residency under Dr. Lew Coleman was difficult—especially when she saw the answer to all her hidden desires and dreams in his compelling gaze.

Dear reader:

Please take a few moments to fill out this questionnaire. It will help us give you more of the Special Editions you'd like best.

Mail to: **Karen Solem**
Silhouette Books
1230 Ave. of the Americas, New York, N.Y. 10020

1) How did you obtain **BITTER VICTORY?**

( ) **Bookstore**　　　　　　**10-1** ( ) **Newsstand**　　　　　　**-6**
( ) **Supermarket**　　　　　　**-2** ( ) **Airport**　　　　　　　**-7**
( ) **Variety/discount store**　**-3** ( ) **Book Club**　　　　　**-8**
( ) **Department store**　　　**-4** ( ) **From a friend**　　　**-9**
( ) **Drug store**　　　　　　**-5** ( ) **Other:** _____
　　　　　　　　　　　　　　　　　　(write in)　　　**-0**

2) How many Silhouette Special Editions have you read including this one? (circle one number) **11- 1 2 3 4 5 6 7 8 9 10 11 12**

3) Overall how would you rate this book?
( ) **Excellent 12-1** ( ) **Very good -2**
( ) **Good -3** ( ) **Fair -4** ( ) **Poor -5**

4) Which elements did you like best about this book?
( ) **Heroine 13-1** ( ) **Hero -2** ( ) **Setting -3** ( ) **Story line -4**
( ) **Love scenes -5** ( ) **Ending -6** ( ) **Other Characters -7**

5) Do you prefer love scenes that are
( ) **Less explicit than**　　( ) **More explicit than**
　in this book 14-1　　　　**in this book　-2**
　　　　( ) **About as explicit as in this book　-3**

6) What influenced you most in deciding to buy this book?
( ) **Cover 15-1** ( ) **Title -2** ( ) **Back cover copy -3**
( ) **Recommendations -4** ( ) **You buy all Silhouette Books -5**

7) How likely would you be to purchase other Silhouette Special Editions in the future?
( ) **Extremely likely**　　**16-1** ( ) **Not very likely**　　**-3**
( ) **Somewhat likely**　　**-2** ( ) **Not at all likely**　　**-4**

8) Have you been reading . . .
( ) **Only Silhouette Romances**　　　　**17-1**
( ) **Mostly Silhouette Romances**　　　**-2**
( ) **Mostly one other romance**_____
　　　　　　　　　　　(write one in)　　　**-3**
( ) **No one series of romance in particular**　**-4**

9) Please check the box next to your age group.
( ) **Under 18**　**18-1** ( ) **25-34**　　　**-3** ( ) **50-54**　　**-5**
( ) **18-24**　　**-2** ( ) **35-49**　　**-4** ( ) **55+**　　　**-6**

10) Would you be interested in receiving a romance newsletter? If so please fill in your name and address.

Name _____

Address _____

City _____ State _____ Zip _____

　　　　　　　　19 ___ 20 ___ 21 ___ 22 ___ 23 ___